Praise for the Melanie Hogan Mystery Series

Shear Madness

"Great story – Took a twist at the end that I hadn't anticipated! Rhonda writes in a way that helps the reader visualize the scene – makes it a very fun read and even more suspenseful. I'm ready for the next one in the series!"

Shear Madness

"It was an excellent read, caught your attention at the beginning and held it to the end. Likable characters that are well developed. Rhonda Blackhurst has a way of writing that is very visual."

Shear Madness

"Loved this cozy mystery and can't wait for the next one in the series. Melanie is a charming character, the dialogue is witty and funny, and the mystery has a twist I didn't guess."

Shear Deception

"Wonderfully written, kept me in suspense!"

Shear Deception

"Once again Rhonda has written an excellent mystery. Her characters come alive, you feel you know them personally. She gets you interested from the first page and keeps you to the last page. A very good read."

Shear Deception

"Melanie Hogan's story continues in this next book in the series - and Blackhurst does not disappoint. All the lovable characters are back, and one that's not so lovable-a surprising foe to Melanie's sweet character."

Shear Murder

"Very enjoyable cozy mystery. The dialogue draws the reader into the story and helps to develop the characters and story development. I was drawn in from the beginning. The main character attended a reunion gathering of old friends when the unthinkable happens. Great who-done-it with likable characters and a surprising ending. Highly recommended."

Shear Madness

A Melanie Hogan Mystery
Book 1

Rhonda Blackhurst

Books may be purchased in quantity and/or special
sales by contacting the publisher, Lighthouse Press at
303-523-6815

Published by: Lighthouse Press, Colorado
Cover design by: Isabel Maria Figueiredo Robalo dos
Santos

Library of Congress Control Number: 2015943508

ISBN-13: 978-1-7359393-1-5

Second Edition
Printed in the United States of America

www.rhondablackhurst.com

Also by Rhonda Blackhurst

- ➤ The Inheritance

The Melanie Hogan Cozy Mystery Series
- ➤ Shear Madness
- ➤ Shear Deception
- ➤ Shear Malice
- ➤ Shear Murder
- ➤ Shear Holiday Mayhem
- ➤ Shear Camping Caper
- ➤ Shear Fear
- ➤ Shear Misfortune

The Whispering Pines Mysteries
- ➤ Finding Abby
- ➤ Abby's Redemption

To Ben and Alex, my precious sons, who have become amazing men. No mother on earth could possibly be prouder of her children. You are my sunshine and my joy.

"Mothers hold their children's hands for a short while, but their hearts forever." - Unknown

And to my grandmother. My memories of you contributed to the creation of Nana. You may be gone from this earth, but you will live forever in my heart.

To everything there is a season, a time for every purpose under heaven:
A time to be born, and a time to die;
A time to plant, and a time to pluck what is planted;
A time to kill, and a time to heal;
A time to break down, and a time to build up;
A time to weep, and a time to laugh;
A time to mourn, and a time to dance;
A time to cast away stones, and a time to gather stones;
A time to embrace, and a time to refrain from embracing;
A time to gain, and a time to lose;
A time to keep, and a time to throw away;
A time to tear, and a time to sew;
A time to keep silence, and a time to speak;
A time to love, and a time to hate;
A time of war, and a time of peace.

Ecclesiastes 3:1–8 (NKJV)

1

"Ordinary" had always held a certain appeal to me, much like blood sucking does to a vampire. And yet there can be too much ordinary. I couldn't say as much for the vampire since I had no experience in that department.

The old, wooden, reclining desk chair creaked as I sat back and looked about the office I shared with my best friend, Claire. I stretched my arms and clasped my hands behind my head, holding the weight of my head from falling back. Despite my original burning desire to be a private investigator since the age of ten, due in part to watching too many episodes of *Murder She Wrote*, I loved being a cosmetologist. I loved my clients—most of them anyway—and the work. The freedom of having my own salon didn't hurt, either.

Claire and I took on this adventure of buying our own business after working together for six years in a salon both of us came to despise after it changed ownership. We dreamed of how we would run it if it were ours until we finally put an end to the dream and made it a reality. We knew without a doubt we would be compatible, despite numerous warnings from well-wishing naysayers that one should never go into business with a friend. *It may be the beginning of a business, but it will be the end of the friendship,* they'd warned. Claire and I never bought into that hogwash. If anything, it made us more determined than ever to make it work. And work it did. Like a well-oiled machine.

Therein lies the problem. My entire life was like a well-oiled machine running so smoothly that sometimes I forgot it was running at all. Everything about me was so—predictable. I began to feel one of my pursuits to try to spice things up a bit take its viselike hold. I looked on my desk at the metal-plated name plaque with my engraved name looking back at me as if proving a point. *Melanie Hogan.* Even my name was blasé.

My thoughts traveled miles away from where I was, gathering momentum the further they got, until Claire rounded the corner into the office, pulling me back. My gaze followed her as she plopped her five-foot-six frame into the chair on the opposite side of the desk.

"Uh-oh," she groaned and rolled her eyes.

"Uh-oh what?" I asked, trying to muster enthusiasm.

"I know that look."

"What look?" I narrowed my eyes, challenging her

to continue.

"That one that says you're bored." She eyed me for a moment. "It always makes me nervous when you get like this."

"I have no idea what you're talking about." My eyes never wavered from hers.

"Don't even try that one with me. You do so know what I'm talking about. You, Miss Stable Mabel, who can't even go to the bathroom off schedule. But when you decide enough is enough, you go overboard. You don't just dip a toe in the water, you jump in over your head." She shook her head and chuckled, crossing her arms in front of her. "What do you wanna do with the salon now?"

Claire and I complemented each other well as business partners. Where I was rather plain, she was flamboyant, a little eccentric, a dreamer, and a tad flighty—okay, a *lot* flighty—and I was more grounded, serious, and levelheaded. And perhaps a little sarcastic. Okay, in all fairness, Claire would say I was a *lot* sarcastic.

"What makes you think I want to do something to the salon?" I asked as I realized she was still waiting for my answer. I sat upright and leaned slightly forward, one elbow on the desk, my chin resting in my hand, the other hand absently playing with a pencil.

"Stop tapping that darn pencil. You're driving me crazy."

I tapped a little more insistently and smiled at her. "Nice to have you with me in Crazyville. It's a ton of fun here."

She reached over and snatched the pencil from me.

"I've been thinking—"

"I knew it!" She said it more to herself than to me and rolled her eyes again.

I pulled a face at her. "I've been thinking," I began again, making her listen to it twice, and then paused nice and long. "What can we do to drum up some excitement around here? Maybe we can bring in some live entertainment or something."

"Where would we put them?"

She stared at me with her big brown eyes that looked hopelessly innocent. She must have had it easy as a kid because a mother could never stay mad very long at those doe eyes. All she would have had to do was bat those inch-long coal-black lashes I would have died to have.

"I could have Sydney's dance team perform," she offered.

I involuntarily tittered. "While that would be cute as heck, it's not exactly what I was thinking." Claire's daughter, Sydney, was the cutest kid I'd ever seen and every bit as spunky as any kid I'd ever known, not to mention just a little bit spoiled. By me as much as anyone. I loved that girl as if she were my own, and since I'd never been able to have kids, I had a whole lot of love to give to Sydney. And believe me, she got it. "Anyway," I said, walking around to hug her, "I've gotta run. You can still close up, right?"

"Yup." She grinned at me, that slight gap between her front teeth looking cute as can be. "I have a color coming in late anyway."

"Call if you need me to come back here when you close. I don't want you closing by yourself if it's too late."

"I'll be fine." She waved me out the door. "Now scoot, or Rose will never forgive me for making you late."

"She'll always forgive you. Now forgiving me, on the other hand…" I laughed, grabbed my shoulder bag, blew Claire a kiss over my shoulder—which she dramatically ducked to miss—and left.

My grandmother had raised me from the age of four when Violet, my biological mother, decided she no longer wanted to be a full-time mother but rather a full-time aspiring actress who never really aspired to anything. But the last I heard, she was still trying, so I had to give her that. No one could ever call her a quitter except when it came to parenting. But in the end, it was for the best. My grandmother was the best parent and role model a girl could ever have.

As soon as I stepped outside, the heat, intensified by the asphalt beneath me, nearly took my breath away. August in Minnesota could get hot, but when it was coupled with a level of humidity that made me feel like I was drowning, it was downright suffocating. And yet there was nowhere else I'd rather be. Unless it was on the white sands of a beach in Mexico sipping a cold glass of Long Island Iced Tea with a little umbrella. And I knew that was never happening anytime soon. If ever.

I unlocked my car and let the door stand open for a few moments, allowing the air to circulate. Even though it was sweltering, at least it allowed for a little air movement in the stifling heat baking inside with the black interior. This was one of those summers I cursed my decision to have a black car. Nonetheless, I loved my little Nissan 370Z. It was everything I wasn't and wished I were. It was a present to myself after my then-husband left me because he wanted kids. He let me know in no uncertain terms that since I couldn't reproduce, then he couldn't commit, a fact proved when he was a father less than eight months after leaving me and engaged before the ink was even dry on our divorce papers. Jerk.

I could feel bitterness creep up on me as I thought about Cain. Seriously? With a name like Cain, I should have known right off the bat that he was bad news. My grandmother told me as long as I stayed bitter and angry, I was giving him power, and I needed to take that power back by forgiving him. But that being said, she hadn't forgiven him yet either.

I finally braved the heat and slid into the driver's seat, turning the key in the ignition before closing my door so the air conditioning could begin its job. Even though my linen pants stuck to the back of my legs as I sat on the black leather seat, I was grateful I didn't have on my typical blue jeans that I wore ninety percent of the time. Who didn't love blue jeans? Except for Claire. They went with everything and were the most practical thing ever because these days they could stretch, allowing me to bend in every which way as I worked around the salon.

The car's air conditioning struggled in its fight against the heat, and by the time I got to my grandmother's, it finally reached a comfortable temperature. I sat for just a moment longer before stepping back out into the heat.

I looked up to see dark ominous clouds beginning

to gather off in the distance. If the weather app on my smartphone was right, it wouldn't be long before they gathered momentum and rolled in with a storm or two. I'd developed my grandmother's respectable fear of storms. My grandfather used to stand at the window and watch for the next strike of lightning to cut through the sky. A couple of times, I attempted to watch with him, but he'd shoo me downstairs as soon as he realized I was standing beside him. I'm not sure what made me go—the fact that he told me to or the adrenaline pumping through my veins, hurtling me downstairs quicker than my young legs could carry me.

Just before I reached the door to the house, the sky lit up off in the distance. I listened for the accompanying thunder, but it didn't come. That meant it would be a while before it reached us. The trick, my grandfather used to tell me, was to count the seconds between the flash of lightning and the thunder, because that would tell you how close it was.

My grandmother met me at the door with a hug as usual.

"Hi, Nana," I said, my voice muffled against her shoulder. She wasn't a big lady, but it didn't take much to dwarf my five-foot-two, hundred-and-ten-pound frame. She finally pulled back, wrapped her arm around my shoulders, and led me into the house. "It sure feels nice and cool in here. And what's that fabulous smell? Are you baking brownies?" My mood suddenly took on new life. It was a wonder what the smell of her brownies could do to me.

"With walnuts. Just like you like them."

I looked at her with renewed love. "How come you're so good to me?"

"You make it easy."

I met her eyes with mine.

"Well, usually," she added with that smile of hers. "How was work today? Anything exciting happen?"

"Nah. Same stuff. Different day." I plunked down on a stool by the counter.

She turned to look at me over her shoulder as she pulled open the oven door. "It could be worse, dontcha know."

"Yeah, I know. I'm fortunate to have a job that I love and to work with someone I adore. Not to mention who keeps me entertained."

She pulled the piping hot pan of brownies from the oven and placed them on a cooling rack and then crossed to the refrigerator and pulled out a pitcher of fresh lemonade, casting me a glance over her shoulder. "What's the problem, then?"

"I don't really know," I mumbled. "Just feeling

kind of blah. Probably just the heat." I reached to touch the still-steaming brownies, hoping to get one while they were gooey and fresh, but Nana swatted my hand away. "Not even a taste?"

"Stop pouting. Not until after dinner or it will — "

"Ruin your appetite," I finished for her and narrowed my eyes. "I can't help it if you put them right under my nose. That's cruel."

Nana chuckled. "Sit with me and tell me about your day while dinner is getting done." She looked at the big, old country clock on the wall behind me. "Fifteen more minutes until I take it out of the oven."

"It'd be done already if you'd put it outside. It's hotter than Hades out there."

She handed me a cold glass of lemonade, and I followed her to the little table tucked in the corner between two windows, one on either side. This table had heard many years' worth of mine and Nana's conversations; usually, me pouring my heart out to her as she sat and listened like she had nothing else in the world to do and like I was the only thing that mattered at that moment. Even if that moment turned into hours. I loved this old kitchen.

"Nana," I said, hearing the wistfulness in my voice, "I love that this kitchen has been decorated the same for the past twenty years. It's like coming home every time I come in here."

I looked around the small nook which used to be a butler's pantry years ago, or so I was told. In the middle of the kitchen sat the old walnut pedestal table with a bench that ran along one side, walnut chairs on the other. I glanced at the wall that held a chalkboard, my name and phone number scrawled in Nana's handwriting in white chalk.

"Coming here is comfortable and safe all rolled into one." I looked at her and saw her watching me, her cornflower-blue eyes so gentle and sparkling with life. "Mrs. Johnson came in today." Velma Johnson is the neighborhood gossip who knows everything about everyone. "I think she just comes in to see what she can find out from me. She was supposed to get her hair done but said something came up and she needed to reschedule for tomorrow. Like it's that easy to work her into my schedule at the last minute. And who gets their hair done like that anymore these days anyway? In those tight little pin curls."

"Well, obviously Velma does." She chuckled quietly. "Were you able to work her in for tomorrow?"

"Yeah, I squeezed her in tomorrow morning."

"That was very kind of you. But I'm not surprised."

"One of these days, I'm going to think of something really good to tell her and see how long it takes to make the rounds. I bet it wouldn't even take a full day. It's like that old game of telephone that I used to play as a kid. Remember that game? By the time it got halfway around the circle, the truth had changed so much it was impossible to tell what it started out to be." I took a sip of my lemonade and puckered at the tartness.

"She's a nice lady, dear." I could tell she was trying her best to be kind. Problem was she didn't have to try very hard. It just came naturally to her. I felt a wave of gratitude that it was she who raised me and a simultaneous wave of fear that I had more of Violet coursing through my veins than Nana.

I continued relaying the mostly uneventful events of my day at the salon and ended with telling her about an invitation Claire received to be part of a panel of widowed military spouses on a television special.

"She must feel good about that."

"One would think. But she doesn't know if she's going to do it yet or not." I took another drink of the tart lemonade. "She said she needs to think about it."

"Goodness gracious! What's there to think about?"

My heart warmed hearing her well-used phrase.

"You look as confused as I still am. Claire's not acting like herself about this. She's usually so spontaneous and—well—out there. Maybe I'm rubbing off on her."

"Well, I've never known Claire to process anything for too long."

"She doesn't have a choice in the matter. The show is taping next Sunday."

"Well, I'd say she better decide quick then. And I know she will." She glanced at the big clock again. "Dinnertime."

"I thought it'd never get here. I'm starving!"

"Good. We need to put—"

"Some meat on your bones, Melanie," I finished for her in my best Rose Donnelly voice. We stood up, and she swatted my behind with the dishtowel embroidered with purple and pink lilacs that was draped over her shoulder only a moment ago. The smell of spice wafted through the air as she opened the oven door. "What are we having?"

"What is your favorite?"

"Besides pizza and lasagna? Meatloaf," I said, despite knowing full well she already knew the answer.

"Well, then, I believe you just answered your own question."

"I can smell it. I was just making sure."

She stepped aside to reveal the most delicious sight since the last time I'd seen her meatloaf. She'd wanted to teach me how to make it, but I'd always made an excuse for why I couldn't. Too busy, no time, too hot, too cold, and on and on. Truth was it was just more special when it came from her oven.

"And sweet potatoes?" I asked hopefully, feeling like I was ten years old again.

Her smile told me all I needed to know. Not only were there sweet potatoes, but they would be loaded with cinnamon butter and sugar. My ever-spoiled self was ever so grateful.

Throughout dinner we talked about the salon, about Claire and Jack, and even about Cain. It wasn't often she asked me about him, but I guess she figured tonight was the night. And as was the case every other time, I didn't have an answer because I hadn't seen or heard from him. And I believe that was exactly the answer she hoped for whenever she asked. In fact, it was probably exactly why she asked. She was a sneaky one, my grandmother.

After all but licking my plate clean, I scooped up the dishes as Nana sat back in her chair enjoying the last of her iced tea. When I finished, we refilled our glasses with sweet tea and settled in on the three-season porch, each taking our usual place in the old wooden rockers that have held our behinds on so many evenings while we enjoyed the gardens she took such pride in. Next to her kitchen table, this was where we spent most of our time together.

We rocked quietly save for the familiar creaking of the rocking chairs, both of us enjoying the slightly cooling temperatures. I took in all of the colors and textures that surrounded us and noticed again, as I marveled at every time, the way her gardens and walkways were all curved. She didn't like squared gardens but rather circles and curves. She said it's more inviting and comforting. I couldn't say I understood what she meant, but I smiled when she said it. Even the slate pavers that formed the walkways between her gardens didn't have sharp corners or straight lines.

I marveled at how gorgeous her flowers always looked. She knew exactly which ones were native to Minnesota as well as which could adapt to the hot, humid summers and cold, snowy winters. The colors were breathtaking. The bright-orange day or wood lilies, the purples of the coneflower and the purple milkweed, the yellows from the heart-leaved alexanders and the yellow pimpernel. My gaze lingered on my favorite, the vibrant blue of the Asiatic dayflower.

"A dime for your thoughts," Nana said quietly.

I smiled at her version of the phrase. "What's Violet's favorite flower?"

Her gaze traveled to the array of flowers. "She's never been much of a flower person, but she liked the Asiatic dayflower."

A bittersweet feeling mixed with fear swept through me. "Do you ever worry that I'm too much like her?"

"I'm going to answer that the same as I do every other time you've asked me. No, I don't worry about that."

I thought I saw a shadow pass through those usually sparkling soft blue eyes. "But that's my favorite flower too."

"As it is a million other people, Melanie." Her voice was quiet, steady.

"I suppose." I wanted to believe that, but I wasn't entirely convinced.

"Don't go borrowing trouble, dear."

A comfortable silence fell between us again. We drank in the beauty as the sun, which was just moments ago a fiery ball of orange, changed to a soft orange glow off on the horizon as it finished setting. When neither of us could stand the sting of the mosquitoes that had invaded our space, we picked up and went back in the house, where I left her to head back to my little log house on the lake.

Right after Cain left me, my grandmother pushed for me to move back in with her. But as much as I loved her and knew she just wanted to take care of me, I enjoyed having my own space to retreat to. And at nearly forty years old, I needed to take care of myself. Over the past few years, she finally realized it was a losing battle and one in which she wasn't gaining any ground, so she stopped asking.

As soon as I pulled up in front of my house, I felt my phone buzz, alerting me to an incoming text message. I glanced at the screen and saw Claire's message illuminated on the screen. *Made up my mind about the television show. Will talk tomorrow.* My grandmother knew her as well as I did.

2

I got to the salon early the next morning, so I had time to make coffee, drink a couple of cups in silence, and do some bookwork. It appeared Claire had the same idea because it wasn't even fifteen minutes after I sat down that I heard her key in the lock and the tinkling of the bell as she opened the door.

"I'm in here," I called.

"Figured as much. Saw your car out front," she said as she rounded the corner into the office and smiled. "Wow! Two days in a row you're not wearing jeans. What gives? Should I be worried?"

"You should be impressed. That means it's two days in a row I've decided to venture outside of my comfort zone and live dangerously."

"Oh, Mel," she said, sounding overly sympathetic. "You really do need some adventure, huh? And I thought it was just a passing thing when you were talking about it yesterday."

I smiled and watched as she dropped her shoulder bag onto the floor. She poured herself a cup of coffee and sat down in the chair across from me. "How do you do that?"

"What? Sit down?"

I made a face at her, and she laughed. "How do you look so fresh and alive every single morning no matter what time it is?"

"I wake up and shower. Try it sometime." She giggled.

I rolled my eyes at her and said drily, "Okay, you're just a laugh a minute here." Claire could pull off wearing anything so perfectly. Today she had a bright floral scarf tied around her hair, a matching sleeveless blouse, and a short but bouncy skirt showcasing her endless legs. "I hope you have Spanx on under that skirt," I teased.

"Of course I do. Wanna see?" She laughed that silvery sound that was endearing from her but would be irritating coming from anyone else.

"Spare me. By the way, my grandmother was right."

"About what?"

"She said you wouldn't have to think about the TV show too long before deciding. I just don't know why you hesitated to begin with."

"The color client I had after you left yesterday, Sophie Walker, was invited too. We're going to ride together."

"Not wanting to go alone can't be what made you

hesitate. You've never been afraid to go anywhere by yourself."

"It's complicated."

"Tyler would be proud of you, ya know."

"Wanna go with us?"

"I'd rather watch my little girl."

"You mean *my* little girl?"

"Same thing. When you're not around, I pretend she's mine. Don't take that from me." I loved the chance to spoil Sydney like crazy and then send her home to her mom. I got to be the good guy all the time, and it satisfied me immensely. I felt a pang of self-pity and wondered if my inability to conceive was a message from God that I wasn't mother material. That I was just like Violet.

"Better get a move on. I have a busy day." She bounced up from the chair, tugged on the bottom of her skirt a bit, and left me sitting alone again. "I see Velma's coming in first thing this morning, so I'll get the coffee going out here," she called from the salon area.

We kept a Keurig in the office for just Claire and me, the other two stylists, and the nail tech, and we brewed a pot of coffee in the working area for our clientele.

Ten minutes later I heard the bell tinkling above

the door again and went out to greet Velma Johnson, who already seated herself in the chair at my station and was attempting to put the cape on herself. Either she was in a hurry, which suited me just fine, or she was eager to get started because she had some bit of gossip to spew.

I watched as she struggled to fasten the cape around her thick, doughy neck before I made my way over to help her. "Velma, your job is to sit back and relax. My job is to make that possible for you to do." I took the cape from her hands and finished fastening the ends. "What are we doing today? Same thing?" I looked at her through the mirror we both faced.

"Of course." She looked at me as if I'd lost my mind. "What else'd I have done? Why, my hair could probably curl itself by now, it's been so many years." She leaned forward in her chair as if getting closer to my reflection in the mirror would help me hear her better. She lowered her voice to a harsh whisper. "So, know what I heard?"

The bell jingled, announcing someone else had come through the door. *Saved by the bell. Literally.* I placed my hand on her shoulder and interrupted her continuing story. "Excuse me, Velma. I'll be right back."

"Well, do hurry, dear. I'm on a timeline, dontcha

know," she huffed.

And I worked you in at the last minute, so you're welcome. I turned toward the front desk to see Daniel Craig's identical twin brother. I felt my cheeks flush.

"Can I help you?"

"Is there a possibility of getting a haircut?" *Okay, Daniel Craig minus the accent.*

I looked at his well-trimmed hair, wondering what he wanted cut. It looked perfect already. "Uh...sure," I looked down at the appointment book. "My coworker can get you in. Claire?" I called over my shoulder.

"If Claire is the tall, dark gal, I saw her walking toward the grocery store."

I looked at his brilliant white teeth as he smiled. Huh—I hadn't even heard her leave. "We have two other stylists that will be in shortly — "

"What about you?"

"Melanie," Velma's voice complained behind me. "Whatever is the holdup? I'm in a hurry, and I was just telling you about something important."

I looked at the gentleman, my eyes extending an apology. "I can if you wouldn't mind waiting. It's going to be about twenty minutes or so." I pinched the fabric of my blouse away from my chest a bit. *Whew! It was getting hot in here!*

"Twenty minutes it is." He smiled that dazzling smile again, the one that made it feel like the room was spinning as my knees turned to jelly. He looked around briefly before spotting the waiting area nook over by a set of product shelves.

"I'd suggest sitting outside at the little bistro table on the patio out front, but even with the umbrella, I'm sure it's too warm."

"Melanie," Velma complained loudly. "For heaven's sake! I need to be out of here by Christmas, dontcha know."

"You better go," he whispered, clearly amused. "I'll be fine right over here."

I watched him briefly as he retreated to one of the chairs in the waiting nook before I hurried back over to Velma, who leaned forward again as soon as I reached her chair as if nothing had happened.

"So, as I was saying, know what I heard?" she asked.

"What did you hear, Velma?" I glanced over to the gentleman, hoping he wasn't listening to Velma for fear I would be guilty of being a gossip by association.

Her voice dropped back to a harsh whisper. "I heard Tillie's son-in-law is having an affair." She hissed the last word, as if that would make it juicier gossip. "Can you believe it? I've never seen that boy,

24

but I sure don't like him. What kinda man does that?"

"Did Tillie tell you that?"

"No. Tillie's neighbor said she saw him wit' a girl much younger than him." Her nose wrinkled in disgust, the corners of her mouth turning downward.

"Is that so?" I struggled to keep my focus on Velma and her dirty little gossip. What Tillie's son-in-law did was none of my business. Except Velma was making it my business.

"Yes!" I could see the excitement escalate in her eyes as she continued. For being disgusted with Tillie's son-in-law, she sure was taking a liking to the story she was telling. "So anyway," she continued, by now nearly breathless, "the neighbor said there was something fishy about it. She said there's no way they're just friends."

I listened as Velma told me the rest of the town gossip she'd heard since the last time she was in here, which was four whole days ago. And in those four days, she'd heard more than the rest of the town put together could have ever been privy to.

As soon as I got her under the dryer with a fresh cup of coffee, I called my gentleman client over to my chair. The other two stylists, Maria and Connie, had both attempted to take him back to their chairs, both likely thinking it was their lucky day, but he let them know he was waiting for me. *No, ladies, it's* my *lucky day.*

It wasn't often that I was so taken with a man that came into the salon, but this one had my curiosity piqued, to say the least. He clearly wasn't from around here. He was dressed far too suavely in his blue striped seersucker sport coat, white spread-collar dress shirt, blue khaki pants, and white buck shoes. Even his belt matched. Everything about him screamed "city boy," including his Ray-Ban sunglasses, which were perched upon his head until a moment ago. He was in sharp contrast to the north woods look we were used to around here.

I saw my phone light up with an incoming text and tore my eyes away from Mr. Stud only long enough to see it was Claire saying she was going to be a few more minutes. Like maybe thirty.

"Is there a problem?"

The sound of his voice was yet another indicator he was a foreigner to these parts. Most people thought we Minnesotans had an accent like we were all straight from the movie *Fargo.* I believed that we spoke normally, and the rest of the world had an accent.

"No," I smiled, feeling my upper lip quiver ever so slightly. "I'm sorry for the disruption. William, right?"

"That's right."

"What are we going to do today? With your hair," I added, feeling my cheeks flush. *Geez, could I be any more juvenile?*

"Just a trim."

I began combing through his hair, noticing its fine texture. "Why don't we go back to the shampoo bowls."

I began walking back to the shampoo area, feeling his presence behind me and Maria's and Connie's eyes watching us. I even caught Velma watching him. Closely.

Leaning over him at the shampoo bowl, I tried to avoid his eyes, if only so he couldn't see mine and discover the childish girl crush I was experiencing. I hurried through the process just to get him back to my station where it was a little less intimate. By now, Maria and Connie were each tending to a client in their chairs, so we weren't the center of their attention anymore. Thank goodness.

"It looks like you've just recently had your hair cut," I said, making small talk.

"Not too long ago."

"How frequently do you get it trimmed?"

"Every six weeks or so."

Velma began calling my name, I suspect for no other reason than to be sure I hadn't forgotten about her. Which, to be honest, I had. I assured her I would be back to get her by the time the hairdryer shut off and after her hair cooled enough for me to comb it out and back comb and spray the heck out of it like she prefers me to. A tornadic wind could come and not move a hair on her head by the time she told me to stop spraying. And if I stopped before she said to, she would grab the can herself and spray until I was certain my lungs were lacquer-coated.

True to my word, no sooner was William out the door (after leaving me an impressive tip), and I was at Velma's side.

"That man looks very familiar," she said almost to herself.

Who didn't look familiar to Velma? She made it her business to know everyone. "Maybe you've seen someone that looks like him on TV."

"Maybe it *was* him I saw on TV. He's certainly handsome enough to be on one of those soap operas."

"Velma," I said, hiding a smile, "I didn't know you watch those things."

"I don't," she said too quickly. "I have friends who do."

"Of course." *The old "I have a friend" excuse.*

As Velma was hurrying out the door, Claire was rushing in.

"Man, is it hot out there!" she exclaimed.

"It was in here, too," Connie added, laughing. "You shoulda saw the guy Melanie just had."

Claire looked at me, her eyebrows raised. "Yeah? Tell me."

"He was okay," I said as I turned away from her so she couldn't see my face flush.

Claire laughed that cute, silvery sound.

3

On Sunday Sydney and I settled in to watch Claire on the television show she nearly backed out on at the last minute. I hadn't seen her that nervous in a long time. If ever.

Sydney sat on the edge of the sofa cushion right beside me, clearly impressed with her mom. She looked at Claire as if she'd made the big break to stardom and had become a movie star overnight. We sat there munching on popcorn sprinkled with ranch seasoning and M&M's, our favorite combination.

Whenever Claire spoke, Syd looked at her with such obvious admiration, a seven-year-old thinking her mom was nothing less than God Himself. A pang of envy sliced through me. I had never looked at Violet as anything other than the one who deserted me. The one who didn't want me. The one who thought finding herself in the world was more important than the child she gave birth to. And yet I was the one who still clung onto hope, like a toddler clinging to her blanket at naptime, that one day her mother would come back and finally want to be a mother again.

The music signaling the show was wrapping up

began to play and Claire, adorned in her signature headscarf taming her wild curls—this one a purple and turquoise paisley print, matching her sundress that showed off her perfectly sculpted shoulders—stood tall. Tall as in the tallest on the show besides the host. The show segued into a commercial loudly announcing that a particular brand of dog food would magically turn one's dog into an overnight sensation and award winner. I always wondered how many people actually bought into that line. Apparently a lot, since it was the number-one-selling dog food. Or at least that was what they said on the commercial, and I obviously bought into that. Unusual for a skeptic such as myself.

Syd and I gave each other a high-five and nearly spilled the remaining popcorn—which wasn't much. For a skinny seven-year-old, she sure could pack in the food.

"What d'ya say we go get you something good to eat?" I asked her.

"McDonald's?" she asked, excited.

"I said good, not fried and greasy."

"McDonald's *is* good. If you don't want fried and greasy, then get a thalad." Her cute slight lisp on words beginning with an *s* got me every time.

"Still not good," I mumbled more to myself. "But

McDonald's it is. Grab your flip-flops and let's get a move on." I swatted her backside as she jumped and squealed, running to get her shoes. "Your mom is going to kill me for taking you there, ya know."

"Well, my mom's not here, is she?" she answered in her smart tone that she was getting too good at.

"Well, all the same, I'm not asking you to lie, but you don't need to go telling her I took you to eat junk food either."

"You're such a dork." She giggled.

"Yes, I guess I am," I answered, giving her a slight shove out the door.

***

After McDonald's we swung by my grandmother's house. She was outside in the garden kneeling by a patch of white daisies. When she saw my car pull up, she slowly got up on one knee and pushed herself upright with one hand. She bent backward slightly, stretching her back, and removed her gardening gloves, swiping her brow with one hand.

"Nana!" I scolded as I crossed over to hug her, Sydney in tow. "What on earth are you doing out in this heat?"

"What does it look like?" She smiled and folded me into a sweaty hug.

"You know it's not good for you to be out here in this heat," I continued to scold.

"Neither is you treating me like I'm Sydney's age." She continued to smile and now folded Sydney into a hug, at which the child giggled.

"Ewww!" Syd squealed and wriggled free. "You're all wet." At which time I giggled. Served the little smarty-pants right.

"What are you two up to today?"

"Aunt Melanie just took me to McDonald's."

My grandmother looked at me, her eyes twinkling with amusement.

"Tattletale." I glared playfully at Sydney, who giggled and ran into the house.

"Glass of cold lemonade, dear?"

"Don't mind if I do."

I followed her up the cobblestone path to the house and through the door, where a wave of cool air greeted me. She poured three tall glasses of fresh-squeezed lemonade, and Sydney and I followed her out to the back porch where the slatted overhang sheltered us from the scorching sun. Nana and I sat on the porch swing and Sydney wiggled in between us, pushing the swing with the tips of her toes. It wasn't long before she spotted Nana's calico cat, Callie, peeking out between the tall decorative grasses before darting across yet another perfectly placed cobblestone path where a chipmunk had scurried just a moment before. I prayed the chipmunk was faster than the cat and was relieved when I saw Syd come up the path carrying the fat cat minus the chipmunk.

"You really need to stop feeding that cat so much, Nana. It's almost bigger than Syd."

Nana smiled. "She's fine."

"Syd or the cat?"

We watched as the cat struggled against the tight grip Syd had on her and finally wriggled free from her grasp, running fast, Syd close behind. "Callie, get back here this very instant!" Syd demanded.

"She's such a bossy little thing."

"That's a seven-year-old for you." Nana laughed softly. She watched Syd, tenderness sparkling in those old bright-blue eyes, the fragile skin crinkling at the corners. I looked at her silver-white hair in a loose single braid, something she'd favored for years. Her hand smoothed a few loose, wiry tendrils that had escaped.

"I wasn't that way at seven."

"Says you." She chuckled. "Her mama sure looked good on TV. She did a fine job."

"Claire always looks good. Syd thinks her mommy is a movie star."

I'm guessing she knows where my thoughts went just then, because she said quietly, "She loved you the only way she knew how."

"Stop sticking up for her." My eyes looked out over the flower beds, not seeing any of them.

Nana stayed quiet as we swayed back and forth, the swing creaking a comfortable, familiar sound. She finally said, so quietly I hardly heard her, "You never stop hoping the best for your children."

Her eyes held just a moment of sadness before she perked up again. One thing about her, she never allowed self-pity to take root and dig its claws into her. Her quiet yet fierce faith kept her afloat with joy that I often envied. "You had a gentleman caller today."

"Here?"

"Of course here. I don't answer the phone at your house."

My curiosity rose like mercury in a thermometer. "Who was it?"

"I don't know. He said he's an old friend from high school."

"It wasn't Cain, was it?" I was suddenly wary.

"No, it was not." Her voice took on a glint of

anger, which was a rare occurrence. "I would know the voice of that scoundrel anywhere."

"A friend from high school..." I said to myself, my mind spinning as I ran through my senior class. "What did he say?"

"He asked if you were here, I told him you don't live here, and then he asked where you live because he wants to surprise you."

"You didn't tell him, right?"

"Of course not. I was born at night, but not last night, dontcha know."

I laughed at her favorite phrase. "Didn't think you would. He didn't give you a name, though, huh?"

"Nope. Sounded about your age though. It wasn't the voice of anyone I remember from your high school days, but I imagine even if it was someone I'd met, his voice wouldn't sound the same as it did back then. Asked for your phone number, but I told him I couldn't give that out."

I leaned over and gave her a peck on the cheek. "You're the best, Nana. If he really wants to get a hold of me, it wouldn't be hard to search my name and see where I work. He can reach me there."

We fell into perfect rhythm on the swing and watched with quiet amusement as Sydney finally caught Callie again, the poor cat looking defeated. She carried him up to the swing, but when she loosened her grip the slightest bit to wedge her way between me and Nana again, the cat grabbed the opportunity to run like a wildcat. Syd sighed loudly with frustration.

"Come on, cat wrangler." I stood and draped my arm loosely around her shoulders. "Let's head on out. Your mama will be home soon."

"I don't wanna go," she complained.

"Too bad," I argued back. "We don't always get what we want." She shot me a look, and I laughed loudly, tugging at her ponytail. "I'm feelin' the love, my girl." She jerked free and walked ahead of us to the car, where she climbed in the back seat, arms crossed. I hugged Nana and pecked her cheek. "No more gardening in the heat of the afternoon, please?"

"I'll do my best," she said.

But I knew she was only placating me and would be back at it as soon as we pulled out of the drive. "I'm sure you will."

***

When we pulled into my driveway, I saw Claire's little Honda parked in front of my house. I had my house keyed the same as the salon, even though the one-key-fits-all thing bothered my grandmother and Claire to no end. They didn't think it was safe. I told them both that since I was nearly forty, they needed to trust that I knew what I was doing. They may have had a valid point, but I didn't want them to know I thought so. Some may have called it stubborn. Including me. But it was what it was. I admitted my stubbornness was a work in progress.

Sydney was completely over her pouting fit from having to leave my grandmother's — not without a little bribing on my part with some ice cream when we arrived at my house. But when she saw her mom's car, she hightailed it out of my car and into the house, the ice cream a distant memory.

As soon as I walked through the front door, I saw Claire through the large bay window at the back of my house, sitting in one of the Adirondack chairs on the deck that overlooks the lake. Sydney was already on her lap, arms wrapped around her mom's neck.

"Geez! You'd think I beat the poor girl while you were gone. I swear I didn't. Honest!"

Claire giggled as Sydney took off and ran in to collect on her promise from me, getting her favorite ice cream from the freezer, mint chocolate chip. I watched through the screen door as she got the ice cream scoop from the drawer and struggled with the rock-hard ice cream. I excused myself from Claire, even though she was a million miles away while she watched a sailboat glide across the lake, the orange glow of the setting sun behind it.

I slid the ice cream back into the freezer as Sydney took her bowl in front of the television. I knew it wasn't something Claire allowed at home, so I took advantage of allowing her that special treat at my house.

I sank into the chair next to Claire. "Whatcha thinking, my friend?"

Claire rested her head against the back of the chair. "The whole experience today makes me miss Tyler all over again." Her brown eyes were moist with memories. "I always miss him, but sometimes it's just so much that it hurts. Know what I mean?"

"Yeah, I do. When Cain left, I thought I would die. It still hurts a lot sometimes, but I'm all the stronger for it."

"I know this might not be right, but sometimes I wonder if it hurts as bad with Cain. I mean, he's still alive."

"He may be alive, but he left me with a lot of painful memories that I have to live with. Tyler left you with a lot of good ones."

"I'm sorry, Mel." She rested her head back again,

staring off over the lake.

And I knew she was. Claire couldn't hurt an ant without feeling bad. "Don't be. I know what you meant."

We stayed quiet for a few moments. Other than the birds chirping, which wasn't as loud as usual, the sound of the television coming through the screen door was the only sound in the area. I loved living in the country, away from everyone. After being immersed in people all day, it was my private little retreat to be alone and regroup.

"I just love these chairs." Claire ran her hand lightly over the old, worn wood of one of the arms, the white chipped paint showing more gray wood than white. "Don't repaint them."

"Talked me out of it." I smiled as I studied the beauty of the water before me and the tranquility of it all surrounding me. "So how are you doing? Today was a big day for you." My voice was little more than a whisper for fear of contaminating the purity of the moment.

"Sad. Melancholy. It's all kind of bittersweet, ya know?" I waited for her to continue, the sailboat only a fraction further than it was a few moments ago. "Other than the live audience, just knowing that so many viewers were watching out there—it's like…"

she trailed off, trying to find the right words.

"Letting a lot of strangers into your personal life?"

"Exactly! It's almost like Tyler died all over again. And yet I'm so proud of him, Mel."

"As he would be proud of you." I knew that without so much as a solitary doubt. He had worshiped the ground she walked on. It was almost sickening, in a sweet sort of way.

We watched the sailboat until it glided toward a slight bend in the lakeshore, and the branches of a big oak tree blocked it from our view.

"It's so peaceful out here, Melanie. How do you tear yourself away every day to come to work?"

"Speaking of work, has anyone called there for me when I wasn't around?"

"Not that I can remember. Why?" She turned her focus on me. I turned briefly to look at her before once again looking over the water.

"Some guy called my grandmother asking for me. Said he went to high school with me."

"Ooh." Claire giggled a light, sweet sound, but one that was more tired than joyous. "Melanie has a secret admirer."

"Better that than a stalker." Had I known then, no truer words were ever spoken.

4

The following Wednesday, after I got Velma situated under the hairdryer, I escaped to the office to get some bookwork done and to make a telephone call or two. I hadn't even been in there five minutes when I heard the bell above the salon door tinkling the arrival of a customer. The salon was buzzing with activity. Maria and Connie both had clients in their chairs, and the part-time nail tech, Gina, was in today too. It was a happy little place, with the sound of hairdryers and chatter and the air ripe with the smells of hair color, hair spray, and acrylic nails. Claire had left only five minutes ago to run some errands and take Sydney to lunch before Syd left for a few weeks to stay with her grandparents. In fact, she would spend two weeks with Claire's folks and another two with Tyler's.

"Melanie!" Connie's loud voice boomed over the chaos.

I got up to see what she wanted. "Good Lord, Connie." I laughed. "I'm not at the end of the shopping complex, you—" My voice caught in my throat as I spotted an exceptionally handsome William standing at the desk. Today's flavor was snow-white linen slacks and a linen short-sleeved shirt the color of cornflower-blue icing. I felt my cheeks flush — pink sherbet to his blue icing. We could make a scrumptious cupcake or ice cream cone, the two of us.

"Hello," I said, my stomach somersaulting.

"Good morning." His voice reminded me of sanded wood. Smooth, perfected. "Would it be presumptuous to ask you if you're free to have lunch with me?"

"Today?" I asked, instantly wanting to kick myself.

"That's what I had in mind, yes."

I glanced at Velma Johnson, who should be done under the dryer in only ten minutes. I saw her staring at him. He continued to look at me, waiting for my answer. I looked down at the appointment book, sure my chest was heaving with my pounding heart. "It wouldn't be presumptuous, but I can't. Today," I quickly added. "I have a client under the dryer and another coming in just a few minutes." I couldn't decide if I was disappointed or relieved. The last thing I needed was to get caught up in a relationship. And while I realized one lunch hardly qualified as a relationship, they all start somewhere. "Rain check?"

"Or I could come back later."

What a persistent man. Someone who's used to getting his way. And now I couldn't decide if I was flattered or put off.

"Melanie," Velma's voice called out. "Goodness, girl, I'm melting under here."

"I'm sorry," I said as I backed up toward Velma's voice. "We'll have to make it another time."

As I lifted the dryer off of Velma's hair, I saw William leaving something on my station before he gave a slight wave and headed out the door. I hurried Velma back to my station so I could see what he left me and saw a phone number, written in near-perfect handwriting, with "Call me" written below. I snatched up the slip of paper, grabbed Velma's half-empty cup of coffee, and told her I would be right back with a refill. I slid the slip of paper into the pocket of my smock, a move I hoped would get past Velma, but it wouldn't at all surprise me if it hadn't. When a mother tells her children she can see everything they do because she has eyes in the back of her head, I was convinced that saying originated with Velma. She saw all. She heard all. She knew all.

I handed her the cup of coffee, hoping she would focus on the contents rather than asking me questions. And to my surprise, she did. Would wonders never cease? The wonder continued for another ten whole minutes, when she became oddly quiet. I looked at her in the mirror. "Velma? Are you okay?" Her breathing was rapid, but she seemed to stare at something, seeing nothing. "Velma?" Her breathing slowed.

"I feel so—dizzy—headache." Her voice was thready and quiet. "Something—dear, maybe you should call—"

Suddenly she began seizing, her body jerking in every which direction, reminding me of a horror movie I'd watched a long time ago. I ripped the cape off and bent over in front of her, my hands on her shoulders so she wouldn't fall out of her chair.

"Velma! Look at me, please! Call 911!" I yelled to no one in particular. "Velma, what's happening?" Fear gripped me as I watched her transform before my eyes. And then nothing. She went completely limp. "Maria! Connie!" I yelled again, trying to sound as normal as possible, failing miserably. "911!" I snapped. Both continued to stand there, staring at Velma, their eyes wide, mouths hanging open. "Now!" I ordered, at which they both jumped for the phone.

Velma's coffee cup had fallen onto the floor, spilling the last bit of her coffee into little droplets that seemed to splatter over the entire area. "Gina, please call Claire," I ordered.

"I don't have her number."

My head snapped to look at her. "How can you not have her number? You've been working here for—here, use my phone." I tossed it to her, and she caught it just before it fell on the floor. My heart was pounding so hard I half expected that I would need to be carried away in the ambulance right beside Velma. I continued talking to her and felt her wrist for a pulse. Nothing.

Above the sound of the blood pulsing in my head, I heard the siren from an ambulance in the distance, quickly approaching. I placed two fingers against Velma's carotid artery, still feeling nothing. *What in the world happened?*

I turned to see Connie run out of the salon to greet the paramedics. A squad car pulled up to the curb right outside the front door, an officer getting out from each side.

Before I knew what was happening, the paramedics had Velma out of the chair. One got the gurney ready while the other attempted to resuscitate her. When he stopped and leaned back on his heels, I knew it was too late. The words, "She's gone, call the coroner" from one paramedic to the other seemed but a blur as I was still trying to make sense out of it all.

5

When it was clear Velma was gone, and there was no bringing her back, the paramedics packed up and left.

"She belongs to the coroner now," one of them stated, making it sound like she was a mere possession. A car that an ex-spouse got in a settlement. Or the last piece of cake won in a contest.

The two officers spoke with each of us as they waited for the coroner to arrive. One of them — Officer Straus, according to his name badge — steered me over to the side, one hand on his duty belt, the other on the radio hooked on his shoulder. He half listened to the radio chatter and half talked to me.

"Ma'am — "

"Melanie." My voice sounded far away, my mind still scrambling to make sense of what happened.

"Melanie, how well did you know the deceased?"

The deceased. A chill cut through me. "I've known Velma for over five years now." Despite the heat, I wrapped my arms around myself.

"Joe!" The other officer called to him. "Come 'ere a second."

"Excuse me." He walked over to the other officer

as he examined Velma from under a lifted corner of a sheet the paramedic left covering her. I walked over, wanting to see what they were looking at. Maria and Connie stayed huddled with their clients in the waiting area talking in whispers, watching from a distance as if what Velma had was contagious and getting too close may cause the same predicament. I noticed Gina standing by herself by the reception desk. From what I could tell, she looked like she wasn't thinking anything at all. Perhaps she was simply trying to pretend this wasn't happening. Seemed likely that it would be her way of coping. I would have to be sure to check in with her after all was said and done here.

"Whatcha lookin' at?" Officer Straus squatted down beside his partner to get a look under the sheet. I walked around to stand behind them, tuning in to their hushed voices as they talked between themselves. And to me. They just didn't know it.

"Lookit her skin."

"A little too red."

"Yup."

"What d'ya make of it? Don't look natural to me."

"Nope."

They both inspected what I was looking at now as well. Velma's face looked unnaturally pink, almost red. I looked at her fingers, the same odd color.

"Odd," said Officer Straus, reading my mind.

"We should prob'ly keep our options open. Maybe not a natural death."

"What do you mean by that?" I startled at my own voice. "By 'not natural'?"

Officer Straus stood and talked to me as he continued to look at Velma. "What I mean is we might need to look at unnatural causes of death."

"Such as?" I was certain I wouldn't like one little bit where he was headed with this.

"We just need to keep an open mind is all." He reached for a pen from his pocket. "You said you'd known the vic," —he looked at his notepad—"Mrs. Johnson, for five years or more?"

The vic? What does he think this is, CSI? I halfway wondered if Ted Danson would make an appearance. "Yes."

"You been doin' her hair since then?"

"Yes."

"Any family you know of?"

"She has a daughter and a son, but—" After five years of listening to Velma tell me about the neighborhood gossip, I realized I knew little about *her* life.

"Live around here? Her son and daughter."

I felt my cheeks flush with either shame or embarrassment. Either was uncomfortable right now. "I don't know." I felt him look at me for a second too long. "Don't judge me."

"Do you know if she had any health problems?"

"Not that I'm aware of. I mean, she complained about typical aches and pains, but who doesn't? Especially when people get older."

"Any heart problems you know of?"

"No. But that doesn't mean she didn't have any."

I felt Claire's presence beside me, and her arm circled my shoulders. "You okay?"

"As okay as I can be under the circumstances." I was grateful for her presence.

"Gina told me what happened."

"Who are you?" Officer Straus asked, a question sounding more like a testosterone-loaded accusation.

"Claire."

I found an odd comfort to see Claire was a good six inches taller than he was. I tried to decide why I found comfort in that but gave up as quickly as I started. "She's my business partner."

"Did you know the deceased?"

"Velma?"

Even amid the severity of the situation, I almost laughed out loud at her naivety. "No, the other dead woman."

Claire scowled at my tasteless humor, especially when we heard both officers chuckle. "No, I didn't know *Velma* very well." She looked directly at me. "Only from what I've heard."

"And what would that be?" asked the other officer, whose name badge I read as he now stood up. Corporal Matthews. Both perked up with renewed interest.

"Not much. Just that—" Claire stopped, hesitant to proceed.

"Just that what?"

"Well, just what the other girls have said."

"Which is?"

She had their full, undivided attention.

I jumped in to save Claire from herself. "Velma is—*was*—the neighborhood gossip."

"That so," said the Corporal.

"So she mighta had an enemy or two?"

I swear he looked directly at me. "I'm not so sure I like your inference, Corporal." My eyes narrowed at him.

The four of us looked toward the door as the bell announced the coroner's arrival. Claire and I stood back while they loaded Velma onto the gurney and talked among themselves, me wishing I was like

Stretch Armstrong and could stretch my ears to where they talked. I would die to hear what they said. Well, not die, per se. I wasn't ready to see Velma again quite so soon. I heard the words "suspicious" and "toxicology" and filled in the blank space between them. Claire tried to say something, but I shushed her without having to say a word.

The coroner was finally gone, and I went in the back to get some towels to clean up the spilled coffee. Officer Straus and Corporal Matthews talked with Maria and Connie and their clients, who were still waiting for their haircuts to be finished. I looked around for Gina and spotted her outside talking with Buford Woods of all people. Buford was a past client who I wouldn't accept appointments from anymore because he kept asking me out and wouldn't take no for an answer. I wasn't sure how he knew Gina unless he'd been in when I'd been gone. I'd have to remember to ask Claire.

I had just gotten down on all fours to clean up the floor when Corporal Matthews's boots, black and spit-shined, appeared six inches from my face. I heard his voice above me.

"Ma'am—"

"Melanie," I corrected him. Again. I pushed off my hands, sat up, and leaned back on my heels, towel in hand. "Did you come over to help?"

He reached down to give me his card. "Call me if you think of anything else."

I took his card and stood up. Despite my wearing three-inch heels, he was still a good foot taller than I was. That's the one thing I got from my grandmother and not Violet—my height. Or lack thereof. "Thank you."

"I'll be in touch."

"So what happens from here?"

"Autopsy should be done within the next day or two, tops."

"And we'll know for sure what she died from?" I reached up to wipe my forehead with my forearm, towel still in hand. I froze. It was faint but definite.

"Melanie, what is it?" Claire asked. I realized she and Corporal Matthews were both watching me.

"What's that smell?"

"I don't smell anything," she said.

"Yes, it's—it's almost like—almond." As I looked at Corporal Matthews, my eyes felt like they were going to pop right out of my head as I realized what caused Mrs. Johnson's death. The question was who. And why. And I was going to find out.

6

Claire and I were hanging out in the office after the events of the day had passed. Connie, Maria, and Gina were long gone, and we were both grateful to have some time to ourselves where we could hypothesize about the possibilities surrounding Velma's death.

I kicked my shoes off, sat back in the chair, and stretched my legs up onto the desk, crossing my legs at my ankles. Claire pulled two chairs together on the opposite side of the desk and stretched out, her legs hanging off the end of the second chair. Neither of us wanted to be in the salon area right now, but neither of us wanted to go home either. Each time Sydney left to visit her grandparents, the first few evenings were the hardest for Claire. I didn't want to go home alone to relive the events of the day. And frankly, we were both too wired to think about anything except who would have a reason to want Velma dead. There was enough nervous energy between the two of us to ignite an electrical fire.

"I couldn't help but look at the girls today and wonder which of them killed Mrs. Johnson," I said for what seemed like the thousandth time.

"I can't believe one of them would do that, and you don't believe it either."

"Well, if it wasn't one of them, and it certainly wasn't me, and you weren't here, who else could have done it?"

"All three had clients at the time, right?"

"Maria and Connie did. And honestly? I can't remember if Gina did or not." I traced back through the day, trying to remember. "I think she did."

"It had to be one of them. But how and when?"

"And why?"

"She was fine until she drank her coffee."

"Who made the coffee?"

My stomach rolled over. "I did."

"Oh." One eyebrow shot up and she bit her lower lip.

"Oh?" I encouraged her to add to that sentiment, but she didn't take the bait. I decided I was likely more than a little on edge. "Sorry." I tipped my head back and leaned it on the back of the chair, staring up at the ceiling, my eyes burning from exhaustion. "Okay, so we know if she was, indeed, killed, it had to be someone that was in the salon."

"I vote for not jumping to conclusions over something we don't know for sure until they do the autopsy. And even then we still won't have a definitive answer until the toxicology results are in. Corporal Matthews said that could take two weeks. At the least."

"Claire, I'm *certain* she didn't die of natural causes. She has never had a heart problem—"

"That you know of."

"As much as she talks—or talked, rather—one would think she would have mentioned it if she did."

"She didn't exactly talk about herself. She talked about everyone else."

"Good point." I entertained my own thoughts for a moment, feeling rather like a circus was going on in my mind. I finally forced myself to stop, lifted my head that felt like a thousand pounds, and logged on to the computer.

"What are you doing?"

"I'll tell you in just a sec." As I typed, I felt Claire's eyes burning a hole through the back of the computer screen. "I just love Google."

I scrolled down the list that my search yielded and opened a few windows, not uttering a word.

"It's been a lot longer than a sec. Tell me what you're doing."

"Velma died of cyanide poisoning. I'm sure of it." I turned the monitor so she could see. "Look at this. Every symptom she experienced is on these lists."

"A computer-educated doctor is dangerous." But she was reading with more than just slight interest. "You're right!" she finally exclaimed.

"Ignorance is what's dangerous, Claire. Knowing what killed her is what gives us a chance." I waited until she finished reading and turned the monitor back toward me. I powered off. "I'm too worked up to go home to bed, but we can't do anything at this hour. Feel like going out for a cup of tea?"

"Not really. How about we go to your house? I don't wanna go home anyway with Syd gone."

"Deal."

We both stayed completely still until I finally forced myself up and out of the chair, my legs feeling weak as I realized I hadn't eaten all day. I was running on pure adrenaline.

I followed Claire, shutting off the office lights. When we walked into the salon area, I felt goosebumps on my arms as I visualized Velma lying there, lifeless. I shook my head to clear the image.

"Mr. Gorgeous came in today," I said. "He wanted me to go to lunch."

"I take it you didn't go."

"Nope. Velma kind of took care of that one. When she was still alive."

Claire's jaw dropped. "Geez, Mel! That's a terrible

thing to say!"

I realized how it must have sounded. "I didn't mean it like that. It's just that when he tried to talk to me, she kept interrupting to get my attention. And I think her staring at him chased him away."

"Well, she's not—wasn't—too old to appreciate a good-looking man."

"He left me his phone number and a note to call him."

"Are you going to?"

"Part of me wants to, part of me doesn't." Claire locked the door behind us and double-checked it while I lowered the umbrella over the little bistro table we had on the patio in the front of the salon.

"Let me guess. The part of you that doesn't is the part of you that's afraid of a little challenge."

"Not so."

"Prove me wrong."

"Like you're one to talk. You have tons of wannabe dates, and you turn every single one of them down."

"That's different." Her voice got quiet as she turned to look at me, the lights in the parking lot illuminating her eyes, open pools of memories.

"No, Claire, it's not." I tried to be gentle. "Tyler's been gone for four years. He wouldn't want you to be alone forever."

"Four years is hardly forever." I could hear defensiveness creep into her tone. *Time to change the subject.* There were more pressing matters at hand anyway.

"I'll give it a couple of days and see if he calls me first. Jack is coming tomorrow sometime anyway. His last shipment really sold well." Jack Dancy is a clothing and jewelry designer who uses our salon as one of his venues to house his displays. His creations are one of a kind, and everyone who's anyone in the industry admired the quality of his work. The three of us had become exceptionally close over the past few years. Next to Claire and my grandmother, Jack knows me better than anyone ever has. Even Cain. And yet he still likes me. The wonder of it.

"Is Bryce coming with him this time?"

"Doubt it." Bryce is Jack's significant other of seven years, and the two couldn't possibly be more different from one another. "Maybe the three of us could do dinner."

We were standing by our cars, a siren wailing in the distance, getting closer as the lights splashed patriotic red, white, and blue against the night sky as a police car screamed by on the highway in front of the salon. Claire and I stopped talking until the obnoxious, deafening noise became a dull scream before we continued carrying on a conversation we could just as well have when we got to my house. I'm not sure what we were hesitating for, but it almost felt wrong to leave. And yet there was nothing more we could do at the salon tonight anyway. Staying there wouldn't get the autopsy done any faster or make the day's events change.

"So dinner tomorrow night with Jack at my house? I promise I won't cook."

"Yeah, cause that would be a deal-breaker," she teased and mistook my silence for something it wasn't. "I'm kidding. You're cooking is getting better."

"Liar." I attempted to smile.

"I'll stop and pick up pizza and wine after work."

"I'll call Jack and let him know." We opened our car doors, but neither of us made any indication that we were getting in. I stood there with one foot planted on the ground and the other on the bottom edge of my car. I leaned against the frame, my arms resting on the roof. "Hey, I didn't even ask you, how did Sydney do when you dropped her off?"

"It helped that my parents met me halfway at a McDonald's. Which, by the way, a little birdie told me you took her there when she was with you last time."

She tried to sound accusatory, but she wasn't very good at faking it. I could see the slightest smile in the dim glow of the streetlights.

"Tattletale," I muttered under my breath and got in my car, closing the door to the sound of Claire laughing.

The first thing I did was roll back the sunroof, letting in the fresh night air. I turned on the radio and surfed through the stations, nothing striking me as exactly what I wanted to listen to. I took a moment to flip through my CDs, something Claire teased me about, saying CDs were so old school. I like them and told her old school wasn't such a bad thing to be. It encouraged consistency.

I found *The Best of James Taylor* and slid it in the slot. Yes, that one would be perfect right now. I stayed still, my car idling, waiting until "Something in the Way She Moves" began pulsing through the speakers before I moved, backing out of my parking space and narrowly missing a little dark-green BMW parked at an awkward angle behind me. Until then, I hadn't even noticed it. I turned out of the parking lot we shared with several other businesses and onto the highway. A couple of miles later, I glanced in the rearview mirror and changed lanes so I could turn off on my exit that was coming up. I looked a second time a beat later. Other than Claire's car, something the first time I looked had caught my attention, but I couldn't place what it was.

When I heard the ringtone on my cell phone play the tune I had programmed for my grandmother's calls, I forgot all about my curiosity from a moment earlier. I knew I would get an earful if she knew I answered while driving, so I let it go to voicemail and would call her back when I got home.

I veered off on the Highway 3 exit just as James Taylor was singing "You've Got a Friend" and noticed another dark-green BMW fly by on the highway I had just exited. Two in one day. What were the chances? I made it into a game to see if there would be three by the time I got home.

Once on the side road that eventually led to my driveway, I rolled down my side windows and let the night air ripple through my hair. This was pure freedom—a country road on a Minnesota summer evening. I thought about Velma again and felt a pang of guilt. She could never experience this again. But Nana would tell me she would now have something much better than any of us could ever imagine.

Only a mile and a half away from my perfect little lakeside log heaven, I stuck my arm out the window, feeling the air flow through my outstretched fingers. I looked down the dirt road on my left, the one that runs parallel to the big cornfield that Cain and I had snuck some corn from one time. My head swiveled back to the left as I passed. *Was that three?* Nah...my tired mind was playing tricks on me. But it was nothing that a tall glass of sweet tea and Claire's company, sitting on my deck facing the lake, wouldn't soothe. Yes, life was good.

7

As usual, I arrived at the salon before Claire the next morning and parked in my typical spot. The same BMW from the previous evening was still parked at its crazy angle. *An employee from one of the other businesses?* Whoever it was must have stayed the night. I scanned the lot for another vehicle that looked as though it had been there overnight. Perhaps there was a love affair going on within the business complex. I hoped to spot a second vehicle, mildly disappointed when I didn't see one.

I opened the umbrella over the outside bistro table, picked up the newspaper from the sidewalk in front of the door, and turned my key in the lock. My vision automatically traveled to where Velma had lain lifeless less than twenty-four hours before.

I walked around the short wall behind the reception desk to my station and looked around for something—anything—I might have missed the day before. Something that would help make sense of what happened. Seeing nothing, I went back to the reception desk and looked at the appointment book. Two friends of Velma's were scheduled to come in today, Tillie and Ruth. Both of them had likely heard by now and would want to know what happened. I had every intention to find out what I could from them as well. I thought of it as helping each other. Except I would be selective in how much I said because of my instructions from Corporal Matthews before he left. I locked the door before I went into the office. Not even five minutes later I heard a key in the lock, the door opening, and the bell jingling.

"Hey!" Claire called. I looked at my watch, startled to realize thirty minutes had gone by, not the mere five I had initially thought. "Whatcha doin'?" She rounded the corner into the office, her eyes wide. She looked like she'd already drunk a pot of coffee.

"Getting an order ready. We have an Aveda shipment coming in today, but I need to order some Paul Mitchell and a few hair coloring supplies. Anything else you can think of? Like a case of bourbon?"

"Gross." Her nose wrinkled, and she stuck out her tongue. "Nope, I don't need anything. What time is Jack coming today? Are we still on for dinner?"

"Haven't talked to him since you left last night, so I'm assuming he's still coming around three. And, yes, we're still on for dinner, even if he doesn't know it yet. And since he has said the same thing as you in the past—"

"Which is what?" She dropped into the chair opposite me.

"That my cooking stinks."

"I so did not say that."

I looked at her, my head cocked to the side.

"Well, not exactly in that way." Her glance darted away from me, and she bit her lower lip. She looked back at me, the moment of shame forgotten. "Hey, whose car is out there? We're the only ones other than the grocery store on the complete opposite end of the complex that gets here this early. And we're not even open yet. For business, I mean."

"It's been here since we left last night. Apparently the person doesn't have a life. Or they have one they didn't want to leave last night."

Claire laughed, got up, and grabbed a clean smock off the coat rack. She headed for the dryer to fold a load of towels she threw in before we left last evening.

"Have you heard anything more about Velma?" she called, her voice muted from leaning over and pulling the towels out of the dryer.

"No. I don't suspect we will until tomorrow. Or late this afternoon at the earliest."

"I wonder how Maria, Connie, and Gina are doing. Poor girls were pretty shaken up."

"You thought Gina was shaken up?" I hadn't

gotten that impression at all, and I found it curious.

"How could she not have been?"

"Hey, Claire?" I sat back in the chair, holding each end of a pencil with my forefingers, my elbows resting on the armrests.

She turned and looked at me. "Yeah?"

"Has Buford been in when I haven't been here?"

Her forehead wrinkled, and she looked toward the ceiling as she pondered my question, her gaze coming back to me. "No, not that I know of. Why?"

"I'm just wondering how he and Gina know each other."

"What makes you think they do?"

"I saw them talking outside yesterday while I was talking to Corporal Matthews."

"Doesn't mean they know each other. Maybe he was just happening by."

"Happening by?" I set the pencil down and shook my head. "We're on the end of the complex, and he's not a client here anymore."

"Thank goodness for that. The guy gives me the creeps."

"Yeah," I said, almost to myself as my mind replayed the sight of the two of them talking yesterday. "Do you know if Gina's coming in today?"

She went back to folding towels. "Who knows? I

can never keep track of her schedule."

"I guess as long as she pays her rent on time, it doesn't really matter. I just wanted to be sure she's okay after yesterday."

She folded the last towel and put them in the cabinet above the dryer. "Going to get a cranberry muffin from the bakery before my first client gets here. Want one?"

"You know it."

I smiled at her as she slipped out of her smock that she'd just minutes ago put on and headed out the door, calling over her shoulder, "I'm gonna leave the door unlocked cause Tillie will be in any minute."

Not two minutes after Claire left, Tillie was walking up to the door. I noticed somewhere between the time Claire arrived and now, the green BMW had left the parking lot.

"Morning, Tillie." When I greeted her with a hug, she stiffened. I stepped back and looked at her. "Everything okay?" I shook my head and then smoothed my hair back with my hand. What a dumb question to ask at a time like this. Things were anything but okay. By her gaping mouth and arched eyebrows, I could tell she thought the same thing. "I'm so sorry; of course it's not."

"I was going to cancel, but now I especially need

my hair done since I'll have a funeral to go to and all."

"How are you holding up?" I put my arm around her and led her to my chair. "Coffee?"

"Heavens no, dear! Isn't that what made Velma — well — isn't that what did Velma in?" Her voice dropped to a hushed whisper as if the coffee pot would hear and retaliate.

"They're not sure what Velma died from," I lied. Well, giving myself some credit, it wasn't completely a lie. They didn't come right out and say what she died from, even though I knew what they would find. "As far as I know, they haven't done the autopsy yet."

"Well, I heard — "

"Tillie, *who* did you hear this from?" I interrupted, wanting to know the source of the information she was about to make me privy to.

She looked at me as we faced each other in the mirror. "People."

"Which people?"

"I don't see how that matters." Her voice sounded tight. Strained.

I put the cape around her, fastening the Velcro ends together.

"Be sure it's not too tight, now."

Yes, because this is the first time I've done this. I brushed off a sliver of irritation. "Tillie, do you know if Velma had any health issues?"

"No, she was as healthy as a horse." Her eyes were wide as she looked back at me.

"No heart problems? On any medications?"

"No and no. Like I said, I heard it was probably the coffee."

"Well, I'm not sure who you heard that from, because the police don't even know that." I was getting pretty good at this lying—er, altering the truth—stuff. And after listening to Tillie, it was easy to deduce that Velma wasn't the only one involved in the town business. "Do you know if Velma had any enemies?"

Tillie leaned forward slightly, reminding me of Velma the last time she was trying to tell me a secret. "She said she ran into someone she thought she knew. She said it wasn't good and wanted to tell me about it but not over the phone." Tears suddenly sprang up and threatened to spill over, but she sniffed them away. "We were supposed to meet for dessert and coffee after her hair appointment yesterday. But the last cup of coffee she had was here. With *you*."

Did I detect a little resentment there? I was sure of it.

"Did she give you any hint at all what it might have been about?" I asked.

"No. And now I'll never know."

The tears again. I couldn't help but feel sorry for her.

I let it rest for the time being and talk about other more pleasant things, like the weather, which she seemed almost bored with today. I breathed a giant sigh of relief when I finally moved her under the dryer, and she settled in with a magazine—and a bottle of water she brought herself instead of the usual coffee. When doing her comb-out, I'd have to make my questions a little more subtle. But I had to get answers somehow.

"I see the lucky party left," Claire said as she breezed in the door.

"No, you're back."

"The overnight guest," she elbowed me and laughed as she handed me the bag with my muffin. "Besides, why would you say I'm lucky? Other than having Syd, I mean."

"Cause you get to work with me." I dodged the stream of water she sprayed in my direction and began sweeping the floor. I reached to lean the broom against the wall and caught a reflection in the bright glint of sunlight as it bounced off one of a mirror, nearly blinding me. I refocused my eyes to see what caught my attention but saw nothing. "When is it supposed to cool off already?" I complained. "It's so hot it's messing with my head."

Maria came through the door, and it was apparent she hadn't slept well last night. Her thick, dark hair was thrown up in a quick ponytail, making the white-blond streak nearly invisible. And this was one of the few times I'd seen her without her septum ring in. When she removed her sunglasses, her puffy, red eyes were impossible to miss. Without so much as a hello, she disappeared into the back room. I followed her.

"Maria?"

Despite keeping my voice down, she gasped and jumped a mile.

"I'm sorry. I didn't mean to startle you. Are you okay?"

She turned to look at me as if I'd lost my mind, her face contorted in disbelief. "Not exactly."

Guess I was a slow learner. That was the same mistake twice within a matter of an hour. "Why don't you take the day off?" I suggested. "The rest of us can fit your clients in if you want. Or we can reschedule if you'd prefer that."

"No. I'm already here, so I might as well just stay."

"Let me know if there's anything I can do." I put my hand on her shoulder, a gesture I intended as extending comfort. I felt her stiffen. "Okay, then..." I began leaving and turned when I reached the door. "Maria?"

"Yeah?"

"Have you spoken to Connie or Gina?"

"Connie, yeah. She came over to my house last night."

"Is she holding up okay?" I quickly remembered my past sins and decided not to make it three strikes. "I mean as well as can be expected?"

"Yeah."

I began leaving again and couldn't resist one more question. Or two. "What about Gina? Have you talked to her?"

"No. Haven't seen her."

"Do remember seeing Buford Woods in the salon lately when I haven't been in here?"

"Maybe." She studied her reflection in the mirror, no doubt looking at her pale complexion that almost looked translucent. "Yeah, I think he was in once or twice talking to Gina. Why?"

"No reason. I was just surprised to see him yesterday. I wasn't aware they knew each other."

"Oh."

I hung around for another second in case she felt the urge to share any more information, not surprised when she didn't. "Okay, then. I'll see you out there in a few."

The rest of the day sped by at lightning speed. Ruth called and canceled at the last minute, which was just as well because Maria ended up leaving early. The rest of us fit in her clients for the day into our already tight schedules. But I had to admit I was disappointed when she canceled. I was hoping to get any information I could. Maybe a house call was in order. In the name of checking on her well-being, of course. I felt guilty for thinking such a thing but not enough to stop me from doing it.

At one o'clock, I gave Connie money to get us all sandwiches from the deli, but I wasn't able to string two minutes together to wolf it down. Instead, it found its way into the trash can four hours later when I still hadn't had time to eat it. We were all so busy, none of us noticed Jack was two and a half hours late until he breezed through the doorway at five-thirty.

My stomach loudly complained as if seeing him triggered the reminder of pizza and the fact that I hadn't eaten all day.

"Weren't you supposed to be here about three?"

"She asks me two and a half hours later." He pursed his lips. "I see you were so worried you tried to call." He dramatically looked at his phone. "Oh! I guess you didn't."

I laughed. Man! It was so good to see him. He lifted my spirits as if a cool breeze had just swept through the salon. "What'd you bring us?"

"Oh, honey, you will be so impressed." He waved his hand.

"I'm always impressed with your stuff."

"Careful now. Bryce will get jealous."

"Let him. Maybe next time he'll come with." I winked at Jack. His fine Asian features were more prominent than the white, of which he's half. His thick, black hair, moussed and slicked back like a greaser's from a 50s movie, looked like John Travolta reborn. "What's with the do?"

"Like it?" He grinned and winked back at me through the thin lenses of his black, thick-framed glasses.

"It'll do."

"What's with those dang bangs in your eyes, girl? The honey highlights are gorgeous, but those bangs?" He looked at Claire. "Do something with her bangs, dear."

Claire grinned, exposing that endearing small gap between her front teeth.

"I like my bangs just the way they are, thank you very much. That way I can hide what I'm looking at."

"Yes, honey, but you're hiding those gorgeous

green cat eyes."

I felt like a child being reprimanded and complimented at the same time. I looked around the salon. "Hey, what happened to Connie? Did she leave?"

"If you could see, you would have seen her leave."

Claire let out a belly laugh. "Yeah. She wanted to get home."

Jack squeezed my shoulders, and I contemplated whether I should tell him about yesterday's events or wait. After a split second, waiting seemed the best idea. Claire must have agreed because she didn't say a word.

He began unpacking the bags he brought, revealing the finest workmanship I'd seen yet. Claire stood over my shoulder, looking on. Even though I was wearing my usual high heels, she still towered over me. She whistled, scaring me to death.

"Holy moly, Jack! Those are some gorgeous pieces!"

"Sugar, you haven't seen anything yet." He smiled a broad smile that showed his perfectly white teeth as he enjoyed the admiration from both Claire and me. We both continued admiring his work until it was nearly seven o'clock, and we all three decided it was time to head for my house.

I scanned the parking lot on our way out and noticed the same dark-green BMW on the opposite side of the parking lot this time, close to the grocery store, and I smiled to myself. It was enjoyable living out my lack of a love life by imagining another's. An image of William flashed through my mind, and my heart skipped a beat. I looked toward the BMW again, and this time I was sure I saw movement. I quickly averted my gaze, feeling almost guilty for catching something that could be very personal and intimate. However, the odds that I saw anything in the car from that far away was a hundred to one at best.

I took a slight detour through the parking lot on my way out, mentally capturing the BMW's license plate number, and eased out onto the highway, both Jack and Claire in tow.

Once again, as I exited off the highway, I rolled my windows down and drank in the fresh evening air as it permeated the car. Cruising down the last leg of my drive home, I turned my head as I passed the old dirt road that ran alongside the cornfield, the same one that just the evening before partially hid the car that had been grabbing my attention as of late. It was empty. And somewhat lonely looking. Precisely what I would *not* be, since I would spend the evening with my two dearest friends. Claire was stopping off to get wine, Jack the pizza, and then let the party begin. I couldn't wait to tell Jack about Velma.

8

Jack and Claire arrived simultaneously, one pulling in the drive followed on the bumper by the other. I went out to greet them, the screen door slamming shut behind me. I smirked as I heard my grandmother's voice in my head scolding me for letting the door slam. The minute Claire stepped out of her car, she pulled off her signature headscarf, her wild curls springing free. Jack rolled up the sleeves on his cotton shirt and stretched, lifting his arms as high as he could. The country lake air had that effect on nearly everyone that came to my house. Relaxing, exhilarating freedom.

Claire poked him in the stomach with a finger, handed him the pizza box, and grasped a bottle of wine in each hand, red in one, white in the other.

"We could sit outside, but I'm afraid the mosquitoes would carry us away."

"I can do without those pesky little things," Jack said, lips pursed. He wasn't much of an outdoors kind of guy, but he loved to sit on my deck when the bugs weren't too bad. This last hot spell brought the mosquitoes out in full force, and the little buggers weren't scared of any repellent I'd tried.

I retrieved the plates and forks while Claire reached for the stemware.

"Hot diggity! This smells amazing!" Jack was staring over the pizza box.

"Hot—"

"Diggity?" Claire finished before we both doubled over in laughter.

"Ladies, I won't hesitate to take this pizza elsewhere," he threatened in his don't-mess-with-me tone, begging one of us to give him a reason.

"You wouldn't dare," I challenged him.

"Yeah? Why not?"

"Because you value your life, and taking food from Claire and me is suicide."

"Good point."

We each carried our plate and wine into my living room, and as habits die hard, we each took the same chair we usually did when we're all together at my house: Jack in the chair with the aqua cushions and wooden arms, a chair that he, and he alone, used, and Claire and me on opposite ends of the sofa, each leaning on a throw pillow. I got back up to open the windows and leaned a box fan against one of the screens to draw in the fresh evening lake air. I left the curtains open on the large bay window that overlooked the patio and faced the lake. It would be a shame to block the view of the moon rising as it shone on the water's glassy surface.

"I'm not much of a country guy, but I sure like it out here." Jack sat back and inhaled slowly and deliberately.

"You just like my company," I teased.

"And your humility." The ball was in play, and we played it so well, something we enjoyed every time we were together.

We raised our wine glasses, his red and mine white, smiled at each other, and took a drink.

"I'm here too, ya know," Claire pouted in a way that only Claire could get away with. "It's not nice to leave out the black girl."

"Oh, don't even pull that card on me, girlfriend." Jack looked directly at her. "Or I'll play the gay guy card."

"And I'll play the harp."

Claire looked at me, one perfectly shaped eyebrow raised, and Jack looked at me over the top of his glasses. It was as if time was suspended until all of us were laughing and none of us could stop. Or at least Claire and I couldn't. Jack apparently had more self-control. But when Claire was laughing so hard she snorted, it started all over again. Until I spilled my wine. Thankfully, on the hardwood floor.

I jumped up to get a towel from the kitchen and looked out the window directly in front of me. Dusk had given way to darkness, and I saw my reflection in the glass pane from the light of the room against the darkness outside. Jack was right. My bangs were getting long. I'd have to take scissors to them tomorrow.

I startled at a sudden movement off to one side of the front yard, just out of reach of the yard light that shone from a tall, wooden pole. I turned and looked into the living room to see if perhaps Jack or Claire had shifted and caused the movement I saw, but not only were they in the same spots they had been, they were in the same positions.

"Hey!" Claire called. "Are you coming with the towel or what?"

"Yeah, I'll be right there." I took one last glance out the window, paused for just a moment, and realized I was being ridiculous. Velma's death had me a little more freaked out than I even suspected. It was probably a raccoon or a dog from somewhere in the neighborhood. Cabins and summer homes in the area were buzzing with activity this time of year. It was a rare night that I didn't smell bonfire smoke from a neighboring campground and hear laughter and kids screaming in the distance.

Jack's eyebrows were knit together and his lips in a thin line as he was earnestly listening to something Claire was saying. "Stop talking about me behind my back." But Jack's eyes told me he wasn't in a teasing mood right now.

"What's this I heard about Velma yesterday?"

"I was going to tell you." I sounded defensive even to my own ears.

"When, next year?"

"Oh my gosh! Can you be any more dramatic? It just happened yesterday."

"So I take it you haven't heard anything more today?"

"No. I'm hoping we hear something tomorrow. I'm positive I know what they're going to find, though."

"Which is?"

"Obviously it wouldn't disappoint me if they say she died from natural causes, but I know that's not the case."

"So what do you think it is?"

"I think—I *know* someone poisoned her, Jack. When I was wiping up her coffee that spilled, I smelled the faintest scent of almond. And it wasn't flavored coffee." I saw how he was looking at me, and the defensiveness crept back in. "Okay, that's the same look the police gave me when I mentioned it. I know it sounds like I watch too much TV, but you guys both know me, and you know I don't watch hardly any TV at all. Anymore, anyway. Just wait— you'll see I'm right."

"But what does that say about the people who were in the salon? That would mean there's a murderer right under your nose. Who was all there?"

"Connie, Maria, and Gina, and they each had a client."

"Well, it's no secret Connie's client wasn't a friend of Velma's," Claire added.

"Only because Velma was telling the entire town about Sue Ann's daughter."

"Who's Sue Ann?"

"Connie's client," I said.

"Did she dislike her enough to kill her?" Jack asked. "Not liking someone and wanting them dead are miles apart."

"What about Maria's client?" Claire asked me. "She's new and has never been in the salon before."

"I think Maria knows her from somewhere, though. They didn't appear to be meeting for the first time."

We were all quiet for a moment while we tried to come up with possible suspects if the autopsy results would be what I assumed they would be.

"Gina was acting strange. But then again Gina *is* kind of strange."

"I wouldn't say she's strange." Claire came to her defense. "Just very private."

"That's one way of putting it." Claire's interpretation of Gina amused me. "Hey, Claire, did you know Gina and Buford—oh yeah!" I exclaimed, suddenly remembering. "Buford was there, too. Talking to Gina. According to Maria, he's been in a couple of times to see her."

Claire's forehead crinkled, her brow furrowed. "I've never seen him since you've told him you wouldn't cut his hair anymore."

"If he's smart, he'll stay far away," Jack's protective voice warned. "I'm staying tonight, and I'm staying until you hear something."

"You don't need to stay, Jack. Really. I can call you when I find something out."

"Or I can just stay."

"Or you can just stay," I agreed, knowing he wouldn't budge on this.

My phone rang. I picked it up, looked at the caller ID, and grinned at my protective friends before picking up the phone.

"Hi, William."

"Hello, there. I'm stuck in bumper-to-bumper traffic and thought talking with you might make the wait more bearable."

"Here in town?"

"Just a few miles out."

"Jack, Claire, and I heard sirens when we left the salon. I wonder if there was an accident somewhere?"

"Appears so."

I listened as he told me about the meeting he was coming from, eventually hanging up to see Claire and Jack each texting.

"You guys know these things are just electronic leashes, right?" I held up my cell phone.

"You're the one who started the chain reaction," Jack said, setting his phone down, followed by Claire.

9

The watcher darted behind a grove of trees and shrubs on the edge of the expanse of the large yard. Had she spotted him? He thought she'd looked right at him. He worked his way around the wooded lot next to hers until he safely reached the grass and trees in the back of the house that sloped down toward the lake. He had a better view here anyway. Leaving the curtains wide open like she did was an invitation that he wasn't going to waste. It was a prime opportunity. And the open windows were just the cherry on top. Once or twice he dared to get close enough to make out what they said as they talked loud enough to hear each other over the fan propped in the window.

Quite the odd group of friends they were, as opposite as the moon was from the sun. One so petite and blond but huge on attitude. He could tell just from watching her. The other tall, dark, and always smiling. So happy, that one. He'd take care of that for her. And the man...where did he fit in? He didn't appear to be with either of them. He took in the muscular, athletic, and solid build and found it in sharp contrast to how he sat so prim and proper. A chuckle escaped him, wondering if he had figured that one out. Every girl's best friend? Regardless, with that build, he might be an unwanted problem to eliminate.

He watched his target closely, studying, monitoring every move, every sound he could catch. He turned his attention again to the other two. The more he knew, memorized, the easier his job would be. He hoped she understood and appreciated that all this was for her. He could feel her presence with him everywhere he went, the memories of the last day they'd spent together etched into his mind like it was yesterday rather than the six years it had been. He was doing this because he loved her and always would.

When the short one walked over to the window, scanning the yard, he quickly dove onto his belly, low as he could go. Had he made a sound without realizing it? She couldn't have heard anything above the hum of the fan. Could she? He was still too far off. He watched as she turned her head to the others in the room, said something he couldn't hear, and went back to sit on the couch with the tall, dark beauty. How he'd love to run his fingers through that wild hair.

He felt the dampness from the evening dew soak

through his shirt, and he cringed, wishing he had worn something more suitable for the job. But he never would have guessed he'd find himself out in the middle of nowhere. He half expected to discover he was actually on the set of *Cabin in the Woods*, and he would become the hunted instead of the hunter. And what was with all these mosquitoes the size of birds? He was getting eaten alive out here.

He got on his knees and pulled the damp shirt away from his skin. He detested that feeling of dampness against his skin. It reminded him of high-school gym class, getting sweaty and doing whatever he could to mask the odor when he went back to class. The last thing he would have thought to do was take a shower in those germ-infested showers that everyone else used. And where everything was out there for everyone to see. Not him. No way.

He watched through a tiny pair of binoculars he thought to bring with him. The small one picked up her cell phone, looked at it, and grinned, apparently pleased with the caller. She stayed on the phone for about five minutes before she hung up and turned her attention back to the others in the room.

The trio engaged in a serious discussion. The small one's back was facing him. He could tell by the other two that she was talking again, and they were listening as though weighing every word. The dark one said something, and the other two laughed. He watched through the lenses and saw her eyebrows raise. He could almost hear her say, "what?" Her mouth, lips beautiful and perfectly shaped, now pouted as she sat back and pulled the throw pillow close. Now it was the man who was talking. They were working through something that looked more serious than fun. For three friends spending an evening together, he would have thought it would have been a little more lighthearted. What could they be discussing so heavily? And then it occurred to him like a bolt of lightning had just struck. Ah, yes. He smiled to himself. How could he have missed it? Of course!

10

My alarm clock rang at seven o'clock the next morning. It felt like it should have been the middle of the night. I thought about William's phone call the evening before. He'd said one of the girls at the salon gave him my cell phone number, he hoped it was okay, and asked me to please not be mad. While I wasn't upset with them, it was certainly something I would need to address with the ladies. Giving out my cell phone number to *anyone* was not okay, and frankly, it surprised me that any of them would have thought it was. I had never come right out and told them not to, but I guess I didn't know I had to. I guessed wrong. At least the one time they gave my number out was harmless.

I spent most of the night tossing and turning in anticipation of the lunch I'd agreed to have with William, the constant movement making the heat of the still night air nearly unbearable. I finally gave up at one o'clock, turned on my bedside lamp, and read until I was relaxed enough to fall asleep. The last time I saw on the clock was two-fifteen. It would be a day for corrective makeup to cover the under-eye circles I would no doubt have going on.

I stretched, reaching my arms and legs as far as they could go, and then lay still, looking through the skylight window in the loft that houses my bedroom. Another sunny day sent a sliver of irritation through me. What I wouldn't have given to have a good thunderstorm to snuff out the heat. I typically loved the heat, but we've had too many hot, humid days in a row, and I was ready for a break.

I made my way downstairs to wake up Jack, who was already awake and ready to go.

"Where are you off to? I thought you were staying."

"Bryce called an hour ago, and there's an issue with a vendor that I need to tend to."

"He just misses you," I teased.

"I told him I'd come back, but only after you promise by your last dying breath and pinky-swear that you will call me the minute you hear something from the police about the circumstances of Velma's death."

"That's pretty drastic, don't you think? Swearing by my last dying breath?" I tried to suppress a grin.

"I'm serious, Melanie," he scolded. "I won't rest until I know you're safe."

"Okay, okay." I stuck out my pinky, linked it to his, then hugged him.

I got Jack out the door, watched as his taillights disappeared down the driveway, and went back upstairs to take a long, cool shower. By the time I applied my makeup—the eye concealer decidedly necessary—and fixed my hair, I felt like myself again. Claire often teased me about why I bother to wear makeup. "If I had your amazing skin, I wouldn't cover it up," she'd said umpteen times. Like she had any room to talk. Her mother was Native American and her father African American, which birthed in Claire the most gorgeous, dark-golden skin tone I'd seen on anyone in my life.

It took me nearly half an hour of trying to find the right thing to wear until I finally chastised myself for spending so much time on something I rarely give a second thought to. Some of what I found in my closet I didn't even know I had.

I finally put everything back and donned my usual—jeans and heels—and chose a ruffled, flowing orange tank top to dress it up a little. I slid in my standard hoop earrings—which I had in about every size and color—and still had twenty minutes left to enjoy nature time on the deck with coffee and the newspaper. Those twenty minutes passed all too quickly before I slung my bag over my shoulder and headed out the door. I made sure to lock both locks as last night's episode of the movement outside the window flashed through my mind. The movement probably wasn't even there, but my imagination decided it was.

When I pulled into the salon's parking lot, I instinctively looked for the little green BMW, disappointed when I saw the empty lot save for the white cargo van that was always parked in the corner on the end by the grocery store. I swear that thing had never moved since it parked there at least two years ago. But then, who else would even notice that? Had I not been so action starved and intrigued by the beamer, I probably wouldn't have noticed it either.

Claire reminded me last night that she wasn't coming in until two o'clock, so Maria, Connie, and Gina—if Gina even came in today—would be alone for a short time. For reasons I couldn't think of, other than faint speculation that one of them could have had something to do with Velma's death, leaving them alone left me a little uneasy. Especially since it appeared Buford had made more than one appearance to see Gina while both Claire and I had been gone.

My first appointment of the day was Ruth, an old friend of Velma's, who had canceled yesterday for reasons unknown. I was thrilled she had called sometime later and rescheduled. It would be a tight squeeze since I had another client half an hour later, but this time I was glad whoever scheduled it had done so, tight or not.

Maria and Connie waltzed in as I changed my Barbicide water to sterilize my combs and brushes. Maria's tiny frame was accentuated by a pair of black jeggings and a long, sleeveless black top with a Harley Davidson emblem on the front. Today her hair was down, her natural curls straightened, making the bleached white streak super visible. It always reminded me of a lightning strike amid black, ominous clouds. Her septum ring was back in place.

Connie had on a pair of white leggings, white gladiator sandals, and a long blue—and snug— shirtdress, a combination that didn't hide a single thing—or rather *things*—of her very full figure. Their differences in style matched the differences in personalities. Oddly, Maria and Gina had similar styles and personalities, yet they didn't seem to be very fond of one another. I had found the dynamics between the three of them amusing on more than one occasion.

"Hey, girls!" I called, trying to be cheery. Maria seemed a little more back to her old self, but Connie not so much. "Do either of you know if Gina is coming in today?" I wanted to know if I should worry that Buford might make an appearance in my absence.

"Who knows?"

"Haven't talked to her."

I was just about to ask which of them gave my cell phone number out yesterday, but it slipped my mind when I saw Ruth hobbling across the parking lot. My pulse quickened. A chance for some answers for my growing curiosity.

It took all of two seconds to see Ruth was all bent out of shape. Her eyes were wide, her breathing quick, and she was already sweating, my guess was from nothing other than nervous energy, not to mention the excess pounds she carried around. And whatever happened to her she hobbled as she was? She began talking before she even sat in my chair.

"You wouldn't believe what I heard this morning."

My pulse quickened. "Whatever it is, it looks like it's upset you." I quickly fastened a cape around her thick, sweating neck and brushed out her hair before bringing her back to a shampoo bowl. As I brushed, I continued to watch her in the mirror we both faced.

"I heard Velma might have been *killed*." The last word was a harsh whisper.

"I don't think we should be jumping to conclusions," I said to calm her down for fear that she would be the next to collapse in my chair. "It may have been a heart attack. Or even a stroke." I was getting good at this lying stuff. Too good. But the last thing I wanted was for everyone to think someone was killed in my salon. Even though I believe she had been. And how must people be looking at me, knowing it happened while the victim was in my stylist chair? I saw the way Corporal Matthews and Officer Straus looked at me. And telling me not to leave town. Like disappearing wouldn't make me look even more guilty. I needed to find out who killed her before I found myself behind bars, sharing a bathroom with other people, and cleaning toilets.

"Uh-uh." She shook her head. "No sir. Velma's never had a heart problem in her life, and she was healthy as a horse."

"Do you know that as a fact?" My pulse quickened even more.

"Yes, I do. I've known Velma for many years. We were just playing whist last week, and she was perfectly fine."

Whist was short for Minnesota whist, a card game so popular we just called it whist. "Who else played with you?"

"Last week?"

"Is it a different group of women who play each time?"

"No, dear. We only play with the same group." Her voice took on an edge of irritation that I would even ask such a stupid question. "One of us can't play, none of us does. That's the rules."

I lingered briefly on why she referred to "last week" then in answer to my question, but decided it wasn't worth pursuing. I couldn't help but wonder if that meant they would never play again. Because Velma obviously wouldn't be there anymore.

To maximize the little time I'd have her attention before rushing to my next client, I asked as we walked to the shampoo bowl, "Who all plays?"

"Me, Velma, Tillie, and Alice."

"Alice who?" I couldn't recall anyone by the name of Alice except a friend of my grandmother who had died a few years back.

"Alice Wilson. We wanted Rose to play, but she said she didn't have time. Or something to that effect." She waved a hand in dismissal. That my grandmother declined their invitation didn't seem to sit well with Ruth. Kind of sounded like high school all over again, and I cringed at the thought. "So we asked Alice."

Why does that name sound so familiar? "Hmm...I don't think I know an Alice Wilson, do I?" I held my breath in hopes she would give me more to go on.

"Well, how should I know?" She looked up at me with a grimace, my face directly over hers as I was finishing the final rinse.

I kept silent until I got her back to my chair and began combing the tangles from her fine hair. But finally I couldn't any longer. There was too much I needed to know. "Can I get you a cup of coffee?"

"Good grief, Melanie! I should think you wouldn't be serving anyone coffee anymore. That's what killed Velma. Your coffee."

I fought the urge to roll my eyes and tug on the section of hair I was wrapping around a roller. "Ruth, we don't know what Velma died from yet. It was likely from natural causes." Another lie because I knew in my gut that wasn't true at all. I was sure Ruth and Tillie knew that as well. And probably the rest of the town since the two of them knew. The glare from the corner of her eye showed me I was right. "Do you know of anyone who was upset with Velma for any reason?"

"Well, she was awfully quiet at whist last week. Was odd, I thought, because if there's one thing Velma wasn't, it's quiet. Seems she was thinking about somethin' pretty serious."

"Any idea what it would have been?"

"No, but she was just getting set to tell me when we were in the kitchen dishing up the dessert. Said it was something she wondered if she should tell Tillie or not cause she didn't want to hurt her but felt she had the right to know. Then she said she needed to think about it. I said, 'Well, Velma, what is it?' And she was just gettin' set to tell me, but Tillie came in huffin' about what was takin' us so long. So Velma, she just shut her mouth and gave me the look."

"The look?"

"Yes, *the* look."

I tried to figure out what *the look* was, but my next client came in the door, so I quickly ushered Ruth under the dryer. The rest would have to wait until I combed her out. But by the time I got her back to my chair again, I had yet someone else waiting for me, sitting in the chair next to mine, hanging on every word. Any conversation about Velma's death would have to wait.

At a quarter to twelve, I was finishing up my last client of the morning when I saw a patrol vehicle pull into the parking lot and next to the curb in front of the salon door. I watched as Corporal Matthews got out, adjusted his duty belt, shut his door, and took his time scanning the parking lot. I looked at what might be of interest and noticed the green beamer in the far corner. Corporal Matthews finally came through the door as I finished checking out my client. He waited for her to leave before strolling up to the desk.

"Ma'am?" He nodded his head ever so slightly.

"Melanie."

"Can we talk a moment? In private."

I looked at the girls. Connie openly stared as she tried to hear, and Maria focused on her client as she listened. Gina was unreadable.

"We can go in the office." I led the way hearing his shuffle behind me on the tile floor. When we reached the office, he closed the door behind him. "I take it you've heard something?"

"I have. We don't know anything positive and won't know one hunnerd percent until the toxicology results are in. But I can tell you the preliminary findings don't suggest the vic had any health issues. All of her organs looked perfectly healthy."

Vic. There he goes with that term again. I took a deep breath and let it out slowly. I sank into my chair and looked up at him. "I knew it."

"What exactly did you know?"

Oops. "Does this mean what I think it does?"

"We suspect foul play."

"Cyanide?"

"Possible."

"So the almond smell from the coffee wasn't a coincidence," I said more to myself than to him.

"Doesn't appear so."

We talked for a few more moments before he turned to leave but not before promising he'd be in touch. And not before asking me to keep our conversation under wraps, and again, not to leave town. "We wouldn't want to hinder the investigation if that's the way it's going to go. And leaving town — well, that would just make you — "

"Look guilty?" I finished for him, a combination of anger and fear bubbling to the surface like bubbles fizzing to the surface of a freshly poured glass of Coca-Cola. "Of course," I said. He opened the door, and before he could get out, I startled myself with the sound of my own voice. "Corporal?"

He stopped and turned. "Yes?"

"I was wondering if you could run a license plate for me."

"Do you know something you want to share with me, Ms. Hogan?"

"Not about this case, no."

"I can't just run a plate for grins."

"I understand. XMN-233. Just in case you change

your mind and are looking for something to do when you're not solving murders."

I swore I saw a look of amusement, faint as it was.

"I'll see what I can do."

11

William came through the door just as I began to think he was standing me up. Not that I would have minded, except for the hit my self-esteem would have suffered. In the time spent waiting, I dreamed up every reason imaginable why I shouldn't go, deciding it was only because it was outside of my comfort zone. I was fine traveling outside that space if I was the one in control or without time to entertain what could go wrong.

He carried in the most gorgeous vibrant orange and yellow flowers. Connie and Maria oohed and aahed over the beauty of them and continued as William carried them over to me, handing them to me with a smile that showed off brilliant white teeth revealing expensive dental work.

"They match your blouse perfectly!" Connie said.

"Are you ready?" he asked me as if Connie hadn't said a word.

"I am." I cursed my heart for fluttering wildly. "Give me just a moment to go put these in some water." My fingers brushed his as I reached for the flowers, and I felt my cheeks get hot.

"I assumed you would have a vase."

"We do. Claire gets flowers regularly."

"Oh, come on. I'm sure you get your share." His voice was smooth, reminding me of black velvet.

I smiled and walked toward the office, saying over my shoulder, "Maybe a couple of times."

I filled a vase with water and put the flowers in as they were. When I got back, I would take the time I didn't have now to cut and arrange them properly. I grabbed my shoulder bag, did a quick once-over in the mirror, and rounded the corner back to the salon area, where I saw William standing by my workstation.

"Looking for something?"

"Getting to know who I'm having lunch with." He smiled that dazzling smile yet again.

"Making sure I'm not a mass murderer?" I teased. "If I were, I wouldn't have it displayed in the open."

"Who's the little girl here?" He was pointing at a picture in the bottom right corner of my mirror.

"What would you say if I said she's my daughter?" I was testing.

"I would say you have a beautiful daughter," he answered, not missing a beat.

Either too good to be true or very good at lying. And I'm perhaps a bit cynical. "She's Claire's daughter," I confessed. "But I would take her as mine in a heartbeat."

"Do you have children?"

"No." My chest tightened. I saw the unspoken question in his blue eyes. "That's a story for another time. Maybe." I didn't want my inability to have children to chase him away as it did Cain. There might not even be a reason to tell him at all. Time would tell. "We should get going. We're running a little late, and I have to be back for a one-thirty appointment."

He crooked his arm, encouraging me to slip my arm through his. "Shall we?" He walked me to the most beautiful little sleek gray Jaguar and opened the door for me. I slid into the low bucket seat, the black leather feeling hot against the backs of my legs. He walked around the front of the car and slid in, the small vehicle holding us close, and I could smell his cologne, masculine with a hint of bergamot and leather.

"Gucci 'Made to Measure'?"

"Excuse me?" He looked at me, awaiting an answer.

"Your cologne."

He cocked his head slightly to the side, one corner of his lips curled into an amused smile. "Good nose." He put the car in drive and began coasting slowly.

"Where would you like to go?"

"Are you familiar with the area?"

"Perhaps a little. Not overly. Any suggestions?"

"There's a cute little café-type place close to here. Not the most attractive from the outside, but anyone who's from around here swears by it. The food is amazing, and they serve a decent wine."

"Then that's where we'll go. Tell me the way."

He began to expertly maneuver the little sports car out of the parking lot, and I noticed the all-too-familiar vehicle still in the corner of the lot. "Did you just get this car? It still smells new."

"It's not mine. I'm borrowing it from a friend."

"All-wheel drive, yes?"

"Correct."

"Three-forty or three-eighty?" His left eyebrow arched as he glanced at me. "Horsepower," I explained.

Now he raised both eyebrows as he cast a sideways glance in my direction, a bemused smile tugging at his lips. "Three-eighty. How is it you know so much about cars?"

I suppressed a smile, proud my knowledge of cars had come to good use. "My grandfather used to work on cars. When I was a little girl, I used to hang out in the garage with him, and he'd teach me things here and there."

"Sports cars?"

"No, mostly older models. Collectibles." My ego fed, I stopped showing off with my car talk to give him the remaining directions to the café.

We parked along the curb, a block from the café, the closest spot we could find. "Where are you from?" I asked as he opened my car door for me, giving me a hand as I crawled out.

"Here and there."

I chuckled. "That's pretty vague. Could you be a little more specific? I know you're not from around here, but that's all I know."

"And how do you know that?"

"Other than you telling me? You don't—how shall I say it—you don't exactly *fit in* around here."

When we reached the door, he placed one hand on the small of my back and opened the door for me with the other. I hoped he couldn't feel the beads of sweat that had dripped down my spine. There wasn't even the slightest breeze for relief.

"How so? I mean, how do I not *fit in*, as you say."

"Men from these parts are a little more—well, rugged."

"Paul Bunyan types?"

I laughed loudly, surprising even myself. "Yes, I

suppose so."

I led the way to a table in the corner, walking past several tables, carefully stepping over the shiny black shoe of a gentleman who stretched his leg into the aisle as I passed by. The table we landed at was out of the beaten path and as private as could be in a public place at lunchtime. He pulled a chair out for me, waited until I sat down, and then sat in the chair to my right.

"So you never told me," I said.

"Told you what?"

"Where you're from."

"I live in New York."

"Hmm..." I smiled. "A city boy."

He smiled back at me with intoxicating deep blue eyes. I marveled at how one person's eyes could take on so many different hues, depending on the moment.

"Yes, a city boy," he said as if the thought had never occurred to him before.

The server appeared at our table out of nowhere and stood close to William, clearly smitten. After telling us the specials for the day and getting our drink order, she lingered a little too long and finally left.

"You know people from this area then?"

"No. I'm here on business. That's why I was late in

picking you up. I was meeting with a client. So tell me." He smiled, and it melted my heart into a puddle. "What kinds of things do you like to do?"

"Other than my job?"

"Yes, other than your job."

The server appeared in record time with our drinks. I'd never been served so fast at this place. She looked star-struck as she stared at William, who seemed not to notice that she was practically sitting on his lap. She placed glasses of wine in front of us that William had ordered before painfully tearing herself away.

"Go ahead," he said.

Go ahead? His words, as innocent as they likely were, made me feel like I had permission to speak. Remnants of my marriage to Cain, no doubt. I felt a sliver of something uncomfortable. I tried to brush it away, chalking it up to nerves.

"Well," I finally answered, "I enjoy gardening and reading. And I dabble in poetry. How can one live on a lake in the country and not be drawn to express the beauty in poetry?" He sat back and watched me, his eyes twinkling. "What?" I suddenly felt self-conscious.

"I'm having lunch with a poet. I'm flattered."

"I'm not a poet. I just dabble in it, that's all."

"If you write poetry, you're a poet," he said, making it sound so simple. So true.

I took a sip of wine while I basked in that truth. "Well, then, if that's the case, then yes, I'm a poet." It felt good saying it. Like the admission validated my playtime. "And what do you like to do? In fact, *what* do you do? For work."

"I'm a private contractor and consultant."

"Private contractor and consultant for what and whom?"

"My degree is in business."

I took another sip of wine, pleased with the one he chose, and sat back in my chair. "So what do you do when you're not working?"

"That, my beautiful lady, is a question that remains to be answered. You see, it seems like I'm always working, so I don't have time to pursue anything else."

"That's not healthy." My fingers toyed with the stem of my wine glass.

"Maybe you can help me find some interests while I'm here then." That velvety smooth voice again, and my heart warmed. Or maybe it was the wine. Either way, it made me happy.

"How long are you here for?"

"I'm not sure yet. Until I finish the job I was hired

for."

"Ballpark figure?"

"I don't have one and couldn't even venture a guess." There was a momentary awkward pause. "So tell me about yourself."

"Not much to tell that you don't already know." *Or that I want to go into further. Yet.* "You know where I work, what I like to do—"

"Are you the sole owner of the salon?"

"No. Claire and I co-own."

"Yes. How could I have forgotten?" His mind seemed to churn with something he wasn't willing to share. He clearly didn't like to talk about himself. I found it to be refreshing from the view that I'd dated more than one too many men who wanted to talk about themselves entirely too much. And yet I wanted to know more about William.

"So tell me about the job you're working on while you're in town. What brings you to beautiful northern Minnesota? Other than the mosquitoes," I added, trying to make him more comfortable about opening up.

"Not much to tell."

"Work with me here. My grandmother would kill me if she knew I'm having lunch with a man I know absolutely nothing about. Much less get in the same car with him." I could almost hear her scold me, and for all I knew, maybe she'd have good reason to.

His head cocked to the side, and one eyebrow raised abnormally high. I found significant comfort in that. Knowing he wasn't perfect after all relieved some of the tension. I tore my gaze away for fear of appearing rude by staring. I noticed the gentleman whose foot I'd had to step over on the way to the table, now staring at me, his face expressionless yet his eyes cold. Discomfort needled me, and I looked back at William as he spoke.

"What happened to your parents? You said you used to hang out with your grandfather in his garage, and you've mentioned your grandmother, but not your parents."

"I never knew my father."

"And your mother?"

"Never really knew her either." We were getting into uncomfortable territory, and I looked around for the server, hoping she'd come to the rescue. Instead of seeing her, my gaze stopped on the man who still stared at me. He didn't even try to pretend otherwise. Despite the heat, I shivered.

"Is this topic off-limits?" I found comfort in the gentleness and sincerity of his voice. I tried to focus on that instead of the creep whose interest in me was unnerving.

"Not off-limits, just not exciting first date conversation material."

My face grew hot as I realized the assumption I'd made about it being a date. And not just *a* date but a *first* date. I looked for the server again. Until now she'd found every excuse to visit our table. "I wonder where our food is. I have to be back by one-thirty." The creeper was still looking at me, seemingly amused at how uncomfortable I was. "Will you excuse me?" I asked as I stood up. "I need to use the ladies' room."

"Of course." He quickly stood until I left the table, and I looked back as he sat again.

When I came back to the table, the man's foot just landed back out in the aisle again. I stopped, took a deep breath, let it out slowly, and turned to face him. His smirk was the last straw.

"Listen, buddy," I said, my voice quiet but steady. "I don't know what your problem is, but back off."

"Or what?" He challenged me.

Suddenly William's voice was behind me. "Is everything okay here?"

"I hope so." I kept my attention on the man, who was still sitting down and looking up at me. "Is everything okay here?" I echoed William's question as I kept my eyes trained on the man.

"Never better," he answered, the smirk barely visible but still there.

I went back to the table and sat down without waiting for William, relieved when he was right behind me.

"What was that about?" he asked.

"That man has been staring at me for too long."

"Maybe he means it as a compliment."

I knew William probably meant well, but my gut was telling me he was wrong. Not wanting to cause a scene and spoil a good time, I simply said, "Maybe," and let it go. "I hope our lunch gets here soon."

All it took was a glance from William, and our server was at his side. Not a minute after she left our table, she returned with our food and a refill on our wine. A refill I declined out of consideration for my afternoon clients if for no other reason.

On the way back to the salon, my phone buzzed with an incoming text message. I looked at the screen, seeing an unknown number. I tapped the screen to open the message. *I always appreciate a beautiful woman. I look forward to enjoying you more. Oh, and did I mention? Watch your back.*

I felt the color drain from my face, and for a moment it was hard to breathe. I noticed William's concerned look as I saw him out of the corner of my eye.

"Everything okay?"

"Yeah, just Claire wondering when I'm coming back," I lied, wondering if he bought it.

"Since it's one twenty-eight and you have to be back by one-thirty, tell her we're two minutes out." He bought it.

William took me back to the salon right at one-thirty, not a second earlier. I saw Claire's car parked next to mine.

"Want to come in and meet Claire?"

"No, I really should get back. Maybe next time?"

"Next time works." I had the car door open almost before we stopped and bent over to look back in the car. "Thank you for lunch." I closed the door and watched as he zoomed out of the parking lot, leaving me wondering where it was he had to get back to. I realized I knew no more about him now than I did prior to our lunch. The little sports car, in all rights, should belong to him because it fit him well—sleek and mysterious. But it wasn't William I thought about as I went back to work. I was sure I had a problem on my hands and needed to figure out why.

12

The next morning I arrived at my grandmother's house to help her with some gardening I'd promised her the evening before. She'd said weeds had overrun her flower beds, and as many flower beds as there were, she thought it would be more fun, and faster, if we worked at it together. I had to admit I loved these times together. It was during these times of working side by side and breaking for lemonade and whatever freshly baked goodies she'd made for the day that created my fondest memories of our time together. I knew I would need to update her on the latest news about Velma's death, too. I'd been trying to postpone it as long as I could, but it wouldn't be long before she heard it from someone else, and I couldn't let that happen. As it was, Ruth and Tillie were convinced of foul play without hearing it from Corporal Matthews. And sometimes those ladies can be more like the media than the media themselves— taking a quarter truth and running with it as full-on truth.

I wanted to get a start on the weeding before the sun traveled high in the sky, making it unbearable rather than just uncomfortable, so I planned to fill her in about Velma whenever we took our first break. I briefly filled her in on William when she'd specifically asked me about it since I'd mentioned to her yesterday morning that I was having lunch with a client. I could tell she wasn't as enthused with my account of William as I'd hoped she would be, but to her credit, she hadn't seen him yet either. Once she saw him, she would be as smitten as the server in the café. Okay, probably not.

My grandmother always saw the good in people, but she reserved judgment for any men in my life until they'd proved themselves. Thus far, none had done that to her standards. She had the maternal instinct Violet never grasped. If I continued to see William, I would need to bring him to meet my grandmother so he could prove himself to her.

Then again, maybe not. First, I didn't want to scare him away before anything even got started, and second, I didn't have a clue how long he was in town. Heck, *he* didn't have a clue. He must not have pets, or even houseplants, that needed tending if he didn't know how long he'd be gone. Unless he had a housekeeper. And if that was the case, that could be a whole other concern. One I wouldn't let myself entertain and grow right now.

My mind wandered as wild and out of control as

the weeds in the flower garden I tended to. I swore those little buggers grew as fast as I could pull them. By the time my grandmother called me in for her famous finger sandwiches and iced sweet tea, the myriad colors of flowers that thrived from her green thumb were refreshingly vibrant minus the weeds.

I slipped off my gardening gloves and swiped the sweat from my forehead with my forearm, surely leaving a streak of dirt behind. I used my old, torn once-white tank top to wipe my hands and the sweat from my face. I looked down and realized how it looked grayer each time I wore it to work in the garden. My shoulder-length brown hair that I'd recently pulled back into a severe ponytail now worked its way loose, tendrils sticking to the sweat on the nape of my neck. I reached for a sandwich, and Nana swatted my hand with a dishtowel.

"Hands!" she scolded.

"Yes, I have two of them," I spouted as I turned to the sink to scrub them, knowing what a stickler she was for handwashing before meals. Almost as much as saying prayers. Almost. Sometimes I attempted to eat without praying just to get a rise out of her. And it worked like a charm every time. But she knew I loved to tease her and was good-natured about it. Not so much so, however, that I would ever follow through with eating without praying first. I valued my life.

"And wash your face, too," she ordered.

Hands and face clean and prayers said, we took our plates to the little inlaid nook in the corner of her kitchen. There were French bay windows on three sides of the alcove for birdwatching and even seeing the occasional deer. The air conditioning felt like heaven on earth after working in the sun.

"Supposed to rain later this afternoon," I said as I absently looked at the sky off in the distance.

"Storm clouds are supposed to roll in by evening."

"Maybe a good storm will end this horrid heat spell."

"Plan on coming back here if it looks like it's going to get bad. We can go to the storm cellar."

"To protect you? I have a basement, Nana." I suspected she wanted the company because I knew she hadn't forgotten. It occurred to me then that maybe there was something else behind her request. I worried that perhaps she'd already heard about Velma.

"Sure, honey." She chuckled, her eyes recalling a memory. "Remember when—"

Nope, she hadn't heard anything yet. I breathed with relief. "I knew this was coming."

She shot me a look, and I groaned. "Don't be

rude," she said. "Now, as I was saying before you interrupted, remember when we had that string of tornado warnings over the course of a couple of weeks? One day I couldn't find you no matter where I looked. I finally found you under the bed in the downstairs bedroom."

I would never forget this story because she reminded me of it all the time. But I let her continue, knowing how she loved to tell it.

"You lay there with your blanket and that old ratty stuffed rabbit that was almost as big as you. You insisted you weren't coming out until summer was over, and would I please bring you some food and water." Her head tilted back as she laughed softly, her eyes sparkling with merriment. I noticed the once-fine lines at the outer corners of her eyes becoming more pronounced. "You were so dang cute."

I stared at her, eyes wide. "I was seven. You think a seven-year-old being scared half to death was cute?"

"Oh, honey, stop being so dramatic. It *was* cute. I wouldn't have let anything happen to you." Her eyes showed her thoughts were back in time, her smile exuding tenderness.

"Well, I'm all grown up now." I stood and did a little curtsy and gave her a half hug before sitting back down. "In case I haven't said so lately, thank you."

"For what?"

"For making fun of me, of course." I pulled a face at her. "Just kidding. For being my nana." We shared a smile. The words weren't coming easily, but I knew I had to tell her. "Corporal Matthews came to see me today."

"What on earth for?"

"Velma." She waited for me to continue. "Have you heard anything about the situation, Nana?"

"Not a word. I've been wondering when the funeral is going to be. Reckon I should probably go. Care to go with me?"

"You know I will." I covered her small hand with my own. "Corporal Matthews said Detective Wescott was assigned to the case."

"They don't think she died from a heart attack?"

"They won't know for sure until the toxicology results are in, and that can take weeks. But they suspect foul play." *Like I've known from the very beginning.*

I watched as her eyebrows knit together and the nearly constant smile faded to a dim remnant of one. "Do they know why?"

"I'm trying to find that out."

"Melanie Hogan, don't you go sticking your nose

where it doesn't belong."

"Nana, she died while she was in my chair. If she was poisoned with cyanide, which is what I know—suspect—"

"What makes you think it was cyanide poisoning?"

I might as well just lay it out there for her. She was much too wise for me to pull one over on her.

"Her sudden onset of symptoms, the short time from the symptoms until she died, and when I was cleaning up her coffee, I smelled almonds. And I did a little research. Gotta love technology." I watched her carefully for a moment. "There were only a handful of people in the salon at the time it happened. It had to be one of them. What other explanation could there be? And if it was someone that works side by side with me, or visits frequently, I need to find out who. And why. To clear my name if nothing else."

"Leave it to the police, Melanie." Her eyes begged me, and I scolded myself for causing her to worry.

"I'm only going to help them find out who it was." I placed my hand over hers again, noticing it felt a little frailer. I looked deep into those eyes I loved so much, the eyes that had comforted me too many times to count. "Nana, I'm a suspect. She died in my chair. This is something I need to do." Seeing I hadn't quite won her over yet but was getting close, I continued. "I'll be careful. I promise."

She patted my hand gently with her free one. Knowing Nana as I did, I knew that was her blessing.

I sat back and leaned my head against the back of the chair, my full stomach now slightly upset and churning. I gazed out the window at the birds that flocked around the cluster of bird feeders. Several red-winged blackbirds were squawking loud enough that I could hear them through the closed windows. A couple of bright orange orioles, and two blue jays, one bright-blue male and a pale, mostly ugly female, fought over a peanut in the shell. Hanging directly in front of the window was a hummingbird feeder that she kept filled with red sugar water. A tiny hummingbird with a bright green throat buzzed up and stuck its needle-thin beak into the hole to draw out some of the sticky, sweet water, its wings beating so furiously I could almost hear the humming sound and feel the vibration. It wasn't long before another joined, this one ruby-throated. They both hovered together for a few seconds and then zoomed off together.

I finally stood up, collected our plates, stacked them in the dishwasher, covered the rest of the sandwiches, and slid them into the refrigerator.

"What are your plans for the rest of the day?" she asked.

"Probably just go home and get some cleaning done. And work in my own flower beds once it cools down some. It feels good to have a Saturday off once in a while. A full weekend free is just like a vacation."

"Claire's working by herself?"

"Maria and Connie are there. And maybe Gina." I realized I never asked if Buford made an appearance yesterday in my absence.

"Do you have plans with your male friend this weekend?"

"He called and wanted to get together tomorrow for an early dinner, but Claire's coming out to the house. We're going to take the boat out and hang out on the lake all day." I had an old fishing boat I kept on my one small section of the dock and sometimes used the oars for rowing around the lake. Other than running, which I'd neglected of late, it was the only real exercise I got. Claire liked a variety of workouts, but I usually stuck to my one constant—running. Once in a while, I would row out in the lake, take a book, and lay and read, jumping in the lake to cool off as the mood struck. There was nothing as relaxing as floating on the water in the stillness of an afternoon, smelling the fresh lake air, hearing a fish jump here and there, feeling the hot sun. Especially during the week when most of the tourists were back in the city.

"You girls are good for each other." Nana came over and squeezed me. "And I'm proud of you for not canceling plans with your best friend because a man calls."

I pulled back and looked at her. "When in the world have I ever done that? Or what makes you even think I would?" I wasn't sure if I was surprised or insulted.

"You never have, and I don't for a second believe you ever would. That's one of the reasons I'm so proud of you. You have values, and you stick by them."

I felt relief flood through me. "I take after you with that." *And thankfully not Violet.*

She hugged me once more, this time a little tighter, and she walked me to my car. I had parked under the big oak tree when I arrived that morning and left my windows open so the air could filter. That way it wouldn't be so unbearable when I got in it to go. I waved at Nana and blew her a kiss before the dust was kicking up behind my car. We certainly needed some rain.

13

As I turned onto the main road, I could see the clouds building in the distance before me, and it looked like we might get more than just rain within the next few hours. I felt a surge of adrenaline course through me. I loved the thrill of a good storm, but they still can scare the wits out of me. Especially when I'm home alone. But I would never admit that to my grandmother.

As soon as I got home, I called Claire to check on things at the salon. She let me know Gina hadn't been in today but assured me that both Connie and Maria were there, so she wasn't alone. I wasn't sure if I should be relieved or worried that the two people who were there with her could be potential murderers. I told her to be sure and close up before dark and keep her phone close by. After confirming our plans for tomorrow, we hung up. I set out to work in my garden, reasoning that I could do housework once the rain moved in.

I got nearly everything done that I had set out to do before the clouds rumbled with thunder, the lightning not far behind, letting me know it was too close to be safely outside any longer. I set the hoe and my gardening tools alongside the porch, slipped out of my canvas kick-around shoes, and left them on the front porch for the rain to wash. I jumped at the next crash of thunder and hightailed it inside to take the fastest shower of my life. I knew enough to know water and electricity didn't mix. I didn't want to be the first case for everyone to talk about around here, and I wasn't quite ready to meet up with Velma yet. Besides, having someone find me naked on the bathroom floor wasn't on top of my list either.

I quickly stepped in the shower before the water warmed, the cool water running dark with dirt and sweat. I heard the faint tone of an incoming call on my cell phone above the water streaming over my head while rinsing the suds from the second shampooing, but I decided not to take the time to answer. If I was going to get out of the shower before the storm hit its peak, I only had a minute, two tops.

I turned off the water and reached for my towel just as the thunder rumbled and cracked so loudly I wondered if it split my house in half. A small scream escaped my lips as my heart pounded a mile a minute. Geez! I haphazardly hung my towel and threw on a pair of cotton shorts and a thin, loose T-shirt. I ran a comb through my still-dripping hair, opting not to risk running the hairdryer after that last crack of thunder. Thank goodness I frequently light candles, because just as I lit the nearest one, the lights went out.

I carried the candle around with me as I unplugged all the major appliances, something my grandmother taught me, and I made my way upstairs to my cozy little reading nook in the loft, swiping up a few more candles along the way. This would be the perfect time to settle in with a good book and read by candlelight.

As I climbed the stairs and walked past the slanted windows that ran alongside them, I looked out at the lake. When I moved in, I had opted not to hang curtains on these windows because it seemed a shame to cover up the beauty of nature that lay beyond the window. But in times like this, I wished I had something to close, especially when the next ribbon of lightning bolted a little too close to the window, making me leap and skip the last two steps entirely. The wind was whipping and howling, and the big silver maple that was usually so beautiful turned ugly as the branches slapped the side of the house.

I made a quick call to my grandmother to let her know all was well and that I was staying home.

Oh poo! I left my phone downstairs. The thought of going back down wasn't at all appealing, but I knew how worried she'd be if I didn't call. I decided to be a big girl and bravely made my way back down to find my phone. The lightning cut a clean, sharp line through the sky alongside the window again, illuminating the lake as if it were on fire. *What was that?*

I strained to see what caused the movement I saw just before the bend in the lake. Who in the world would be on the water at a time like this? Even the city folk would know it wasn't safe to be on the lake during a storm of this caliber. There were no tornado warnings out in the nearby area, but the wind and lightning could be deadly to someone on the water.

I stayed rooted in place as I watched, the next bolt of lightning coming nearly on the heels of the last, allowing me to see that nothing or no one was there. And if something or someone had been, there wouldn't have been time to move that quickly. I relaxed a bit and realized I had been holding my breath, making it feel like my heart was pounding in my ears.

I finished my trek to grab my phone and checked the lock on the front door as I passed by, taking the steps back up to the loft two at a time, careful not to spill the wax from the candle I clutched. I set it down on the little rustic oak table beside my reading chair and covered my legs with a sheet I kept draped over the back of the chair. As far back as I could remember, I had found safety in covering with a blanket. At least my legs. And when the heat didn't allow for that in the summertime, a bed sheet worked miracles.

I sat back in my chair, curled my legs underneath me, and called my grandmother, talking just long enough to let her know I was fine before I settled in with my book. I knew there wasn't a possibility of falling asleep with the candles burning because my adrenaline was doing a fine job of keeping me alert.

Forty-two pages later, the storm had settled considerably, and the ceiling fan I kept on twenty-four-seven began to turn slowly again. The lamp on my reading table flickered on. I closed my book and crossed over to the window, my breath catching at a gorgeous double rainbow that seemed to rise from the lake and stretch across the sky. Even though two hours passed since the storm started and dusk began to settle, the sky appeared somewhat lighter now.

I noticed some branches were down, and the wind had pushed my fishing boat tight against the shore, but all in all, the damage was minimal. In the morning I'd have to get out and survey the rest of the yard.

I blew out my candles, stretched out on my big four-poster log bed, and lay in the near-dark room as my mind decided it was time to wander. *Really? Now?*

I remembered the phone call from when I was in the shower. When I called my grandmother, I hadn't looked to see who it was. I reached for my phone, clicked on the lamp on my nightstand, and saw an unfamiliar number. But the voice on my voicemail was becoming more and more familiar. I smiled to myself as my stomach fluttered. William.

14

I awoke to the sun shining brilliantly through the skylight in the loft. I stretched, walked over to the window that faced a big clump of birch trees, opened it wide, and drank in the freshness of the morning air after the rain. Everything, including the hardwood floor, felt damp with the high humidity.

The surface of the lake sparkled like millions of diamonds scattered in the sunlight. What a glorious day this was going to be. Claire planned on coming out later in the morning to spend most of the morning out on the lake. I'd have to throw some fishing poles in the boat and cast a few lines in. I'd take the fish to my grandmother's to cook since her efforts at teaching me how to fry fish hadn't quite been successful. *Someday I'll get it*, I kept telling her. But I think she stopped believing that and was just happy when I brought the fish and myself to her doorstep.

Typical for Claire, she arrived precisely fifteen minutes late. But since she carried a cooler of tropical wine coolers and bottled water, she could have been two hours late and I wouldn't have cared.

I unlocked and opened the door for her as she breezed past me, leaving in her wake the succulent scent of lime and coconut from her suntan lotion.

"Mmm!" I moaned. "You need to let me use your suntan lotion."

She turned back to me and stooped to hug me. "Of course you can." She stood and grinned at me. "I see some huge branches fell in your yard last night. The storm must have hit harder here than at my house." She took off her wide-brimmed straw hat. "I'm hungry. What d'ya got to eat?"

"You want me to *make* something?" To say I was surprised would be an understatement.

"That would be a no!" She scrunched up her nose. "I was hoping more along the lines of purchased from the grocery store."

I picked up her hat and tossed it at her. "Starve then." She picked up an apple and a banana and shoved them in her beach bag. "My cooking is getting a lot better, ya know. My grandmother's efforts are beginning to pay off."

"You don't say." I could hear a smile in her voice.

By eleven o'clock we loaded ourselves with—and balanced rather well—lawn chairs, coolers, fishing poles, life jackets (not that we would wear them, but to keep in the boat just in case—of what, we didn't know), and snacks.

"Remember when we used to use lemon juice in

our hair?" she asked, laughing.

I groaned at the painful memory. "How could I forget? I remember all too well the orange color your hair took on, and mine just got dried out."

"Being hairstylists, you'd think we would have known better."

"You'd think, wouldn't ya? I also remember—" I stopped dead in my tracks as I looked ahead.

"Remember wh—?" she stopped abruptly. I turned to look at her watching me, her eyes wide with concern. "Mel, what's wrong?"

"Claire, how strong would the wind have had to be to do that?" I pointed to the boat.

Her gaze followed my pointing finger, and she looked at me with confusion. "I don't know what you're referring to."

"That!" I snapped, instantly regretting it. "How could the wind last night completely push a fishing boat up on the shore? I'd tied it to the poles at the end of the dock." When I looked from my window this morning, I could tell it wasn't where it should have been, but this was far from what I even thought. I remembered the boat I saw on the lake the evening before in the height of the storm.

"Maybe the wind was stronger than you thought it was. I mean, there are some mighty big branches down in the yard."

I debated with myself whether I should tell her about what I saw the night before. But truth be told, I wasn't even one hundred percent sure I saw it. I mean I thought I did, but fear can play tricks on the mind, and it's not like I wasn't just a little freaked out about the storm and the lights going out. I decided to tell her since she probably thought I was all kinds of crazy right now anyway.

"I could have sworn I saw someone on the lake last night and couldn't believe someone would be so stupid to be out there on the water in such a storm. During the next lightning strike, I looked again, and they were gone, so I figured I just imagined things."

"That, or maybe some rambunctious teenage kids from one of the nearby resorts took it for a joyride. City kids don't exactly know the dangers of it out here. Trust me. I'm from the city, remember?"

She was probably right. I relaxed some as I looked at her. She still had a lot of city in her with her fashionable straw hat, and her shorts and T-shirt would look like plain old shorts and a T on anyone else. Yet it made Claire look like she stepped right off the pages of *Vogue*.

"You're right." Yet...well, something just remained unsettled in the pit of my stomach. My intuition seemed to be warning me about something. I had to figure out what it was. Despite the discomfort of the unknown, it brought an odd flutter of excitement at the thought of solving the problem. And that in itself was a little unsettling since it went totally against my character. It wasn't clean, clear, or orderly.

I set down the rest of the things I'd forgotten for a moment that I was still holding. "Come on, city girl. Help me get this boat back in the water so we can float and have some girl time away from the salon."

Claire, excited as a little girl on Christmas morning, dropped the rest of her things and took a firm grasp on the boat. I was proud of how easily we slid it into the water, just we girls, and I belted out the words from the song "I Am Woman, Hear Me Roar" by Helen Reddy.

"What the heck are you singing?" Claire laughed, shaking her head.

"Don't tell me you don't know that song. It's a classic!" I stared at her, my jaw hanging open, eyes wide in disbelief.

"You're older than me," she reasoned.

"Not *that* much! Honey, we are going to find that song for you to listen to." After some thought, I said, "Hey, did I lock the door when we left?"

"I think so."

"I don't think I did." I contemplated going back up to check, but since we were already loaded up (lawn chairs on the shore for when we came back) and ready to oar on out, I put the thought to rest. "Let's get a move on, my friend." I jumped in the water by the shore to push the boat out, just far enough so the bottom of it was off the muddy floor of the lake. The cold water skimmed my thighs, and I climbed over the side and onto one of the wooden bench seats.

The weather couldn't have been more perfect. The sun was high in the sky, its warmth kissing our skin. The water's surface was smooth as glass, and each stroke of the oars sent out the gentlest ripples, the prow of the boat cutting silently through the surface. It was so beautiful and serene that neither of us spoke for fear of ruining the tranquility of the moment.

Claire leaned slightly over the side of the boat, reached her hand in the water, scooped some up, and let it trickle through her fingers.

"Why don't we do this more often?" I wondered aloud.

"We're always too busy."

"Well, that's gonna have to change, isn't it?"

"We say that, but as soon as we get back to shore, the magic will burst like a bubble. Pop!"

I jumped. So much for the tranquility. I chuckled to myself. She was so darn cute and innocent. She was like the little sister I always wanted and never had. Being an only child wasn't all bad, but it would have been nice to have a sibling with whom to share life and get into trouble. As it was, whenever I got into trouble, I didn't have anyone else to blame.

"Do you think you'll ever have any more kids, or is poor Sydney going to be an only child?"

Claire looked at me and scrunched up her nose. "You and I are both only children, and I don't think we turned out so bad."

"I didn't anyway." I grinned at her.

She reached over the side of the boat, scooped up a handful of water, and splashed it my way. "Oh, look!" I pointed my finger to a turtle's head that was sticking up above the top of the water, staying completely still. If I hadn't been aware of what was around me, I wouldn't have even seen it. As soon as Claire saw it, she squealed as if Syd had been the one to see it. The turtle's head quickly disappeared under the water. "Way to go. See if I point anything out to you again."

"Who knew turtles have ears?"

"The deafest man could have heard you, Claire." I couldn't help but laugh at her.

"So what's the latest with Mr. Hot Stuff?"

"He called when I was in the shower last night, but I missed it. I was in too much of a hurry to get done before lightning struck me."

"What did he want?"

I was at a loss for words as I stared at her. "Earth to Claire. I just said I missed his call."

"I heard you," she said. "But didn't you call him back?"

"No. I was already in bed when I got his message. Plus there was still some lightning in the area."

"What were you thinking?"

"That a man isn't worth getting struck by lightning over."

She looked at me as if I were a sandwich short of a picnic. "What were you thinking going to bed while it was still storming, genius? What if a tornado would have hit?"

"The major threat had passed. But by that time, it was too late to call anyway. Besides," I added, "he wanted to do something today, and I already had plans with you."

"You could have canceled—"

"Absolutely not! And miss this?" I gestured as if I were none other than Vanna White from *Wheel of Fortune*. "Seriously, there's no way I was going to cancel out on our plans. We don't get to do stuff like this nearly enough."

"Maybe you guys could get together this evening for dinner or something."

"I don't know. We'll see."

"What are you not telling me?"

"Nothing, why?" My voice didn't even sound convincing to me.

"I know you. And you're thinking about something. Don't you like him?"

"Sure I do. What's there not to like?"

"You'll have to do better than that, my friend. What is it?"

I slipped out of my T-shirt and shorts, down to my swimsuit so I could get some sun. I lay my beach towel on one of the wooden bench seats and lay down, wishing I would have thought to bring cushions to lie on. I made a pillow with an extra towel and rested my legs over the edge of the boat. It was quiet until I realized Claire was still waiting for me to answer. Except I didn't know how.

"Well?" she pressed.

I made a sun visor with my hand and looked at her. "I don't know. He's so amazingly gorgeous and very kind..."

"But?"

"There's something—I don't know. I can't put my

finger on it. He seems so secretive. And I don't know if I want to trust again. It's a big risk."

"Well, for starters, other than talking at the salon, you've only been out with him once, right? And didn't you just meet?"

"Phrasing it that way makes me feel just plain stupid."

"I wouldn't say *stupid*, but maybe you need to lower your expectations a teensy-weensy bit."

"Your honesty kills me sometimes." I chuckled, laid my head back, and closed my eyes.

"Well? Think about it. You're not exactly Ms. open, ask-me-anything-you-want-to-know either. You're pretty closed."

"Are you trying to make me feel better? Because I think you're gonna have to try harder than that."

"Stop the sarcasm," she ordered. "I'm serious."

"It's just—I don't know, maybe you're right."

"Of course I am," she touted, obviously pleased with herself. "Let's celebrate my wisdom with a wine cooler."

I snickered. "Yes, let's."

My eyes still closed, I heard her rummage in the cooler, and I bolted upright when the ice-cold bottle settled on my stomach. Claire laughed so hard she snorted, which, as always happened, set us both into a fit of laughter. We finished our wine coolers in less than fifteen minutes, talking about nothing important, and then opened a bottle of water. We each lay down on our respective wooden benches.

Not a minute after getting settled, she said, "Melanie?"

"Yeah?" I asked, my eyes still closed as I drank in the warmth of the sun sinking deep into every muscle.

"I hafta pee."

I shook my head and chuckled. "Of course you do."

"Kidding."

"You're a brat." I relaxed back to my state of bliss.

Three hours, two sunscreen applications, and another wine cooler later, both sun-kissed and more relaxed than I'd been in a very long time, we got our things together and headed back for shore. I briefly thought about my door, wondering again whether I had locked it when I left, but as quickly as the thought entered my mind, it left again. I wasn't going to find something to worry about today. Or as my grandmother had told me more than a few times, *Don't go borrowing trouble, Melanie.*

"Are you gonna call Will?"

"William."

"That's what I said."

"You said 'Will.' He let me know in no uncertain terms he doesn't like to be called Will."

"What a stuffed shirt," she mumbled just loud enough for me to hear. "Fine," she shook her head. "Are you gonna call *William*?"

"I don't know. Probably."

Probably turned into a yes. Shortly after Claire hustled her still-bubbly self out to her car, eager to get home to video chat with Sydney, I picked up my phone and hit the call-back button from his voicemail the previous evening. I received his voicemail recording and felt butterflies at the sound of his voice. I left a brief message and hung up. Just as well. I was desperately in need of a shower to wash off all the sunscreen I had lathered on throughout the afternoon, something to eat, and a good movie. I had my evening all planned out. And then my phone rang.

15

William met me at the door of my favorite restaurant that serves impressive Cajun grilled walleye. He gave me a half hug, and my cheeks blushed as he grazed one of them lightly with his lips. I had agreed to dinner on the condition that I meet him at the restaurant rather than have him pick me up. I needed to get to know him a little more before letting him know where I lived. My home was my sanctuary, and I didn't want anything interfering with that. As it was, the restaurant was close to my house, and it wouldn't take a rocket scientist to figure out where I lived from here.

Per usual, I wore jeans and heels, dressing up the jeans the slightest bit with a white, sleeveless, gauzy blouse over a white tank top to show off the golden tan I'd picked up today. I added a shimmering lotion from Victoria's Secret that had a subtle sparkle in the evening light for an extra touch. Nothing too fancy yet something with a little jazz. I had pulled my hair back into a loose braid, wisps of hair falling around my face.

William placed his hand gently on my upper arm and expertly steered me to the table at which he'd already gotten settled as he waited for me.

"Have you been waiting long?" I asked, surprised when I saw his half-empty glass of whatever it was he was drinking.

"Not too long," he answered as he pulled my chair out for me. He waited for me to sit before he gently pushed in my chair. He walked around to his chair and sat down, ever the gentleman.

"You look nice," I said, doing my best to sound casual. "Nice" was a gross understatement, but I was playing it cool. In truth, he looked absolutely gorgeous in a cornflower-blue silk shirt that made his blue eyes do an exotic dance. He'd left the top two buttons undone, revealing the slightest glimpse of sparse chest hair, and he'd rolled up his sleeves to just below the elbow. He had on a pair of white, perfectly pressed linen slacks and tan leather Jerusalem sandals. The man had impeccable taste; I had to give him that.

"What would you like to drink?" He signaled for the server.

"Whatever you're having is fine."

"Water?" His eyebrows raised, a smile played on his lips.

I chuckled. "Maybe something a little stronger." By now the server was at our table. "I'll have a diet

Pepsi, please," I said. I glanced at William to see the corners of his lips curl up; his eyes twinkled mischievously.

"That strong, huh? Think you can handle that?"

"I'll do my best." This dance going on between us caused my heart to beat a little faster, and butterflies fluttered in my stomach.

The server placed a menu in front of each of us. He ran down a list of the specials with as much enthusiasm as my monotone college history professor. He'd probably run through the specials dozens of times already tonight. After finishing his painful recitation, he left us on our own again.

Our enjoyable banter was disturbed by the server, and now it was uncomfortably quiet for a moment too long before William finally broke the silence. "So what did you two ladies do today?"

"Nothing but enjoy some girl time."

"You don't see enough of one another at work?" The way his voice raised an octave toward the end of his question, he seemed somewhat surprised.

"It's different there. We're business partners at work, friends off duty."

"You're not friends while on the clock? Being in business together can ruin a friendship."

"Yes, we've been told that by many people. With

good intentions, I'm sure. But it hasn't worked that way with Claire and me. Our friendship is above anything else, but it's just that we're in a different frame of mind at the shop," I explained. "At home hanging out, we can just be us."

"Do you ever disagree about business?"

"Sometimes," I answered honestly, remembering our last disagreement. Claire had wanted to try a whole new line of hair care products and discontinue a good portion of what we carried. She thought we needed to get a little more fun and liberal, and I felt we needed to stay status quo because our sales proved what we were doing was working. "Why rock the boat?" I'd asked her. And she'd accused me of being too conservative, telling me I needed to waver out of my comfort zone if even with one toe.

"Where did you go just now?" William interrupted my traveling thoughts.

I pulled my mind back to the here and now. "Just thinking about our last disagreement. Mine and Claire's."

"What was it about?"

"Nothing exciting, so I won't bore you. Let's talk about you."

"What about me? There's nothing to talk about."

"What exactly do you do?"

"I told you. I'm an independent contractor and consultant."

"And you majored in business, I know. But can you expand on that? Just a little?" I held my thumb and forefinger close together.

"Probably. But as you told me just a moment ago, it's nothing exciting, so I won't bore you."

I watched him carefully and tried to read him. I couldn't. "Do you have children? Married?" I asked him, only half-joking, but wanting to cover my bases. The question caused him to choke on the drink he'd just taken. "Are you sure that's just water?"

His cheeks colored slightly. "Maybe it shouldn't be just water. This feels like an interrogation."

I'd struck a nerve. Was he trying to cover up something? Oh my gosh, he *was* married! Which only meant I needed nothing less than a direct answer.

"Well?"

"No, Melanie. I'm not married." Relief washed over me. "Are you?"

"Not anymore."

"But you were."

"Yes."

"You said you have no children?"

"Nope." My stomach did another somersault as it did the first time he'd asked that question. "Kids aren't in the cards for me." With everything in me, I hoped he'd leave it alone at that and not press further. Luck was on my side.

"Tell me about yourself, Melanie. What is your last name?"

I thought a moment before deciding it was a harmless enough question. "Hogan. As in Hulk."

I felt my cheeks get warm and flush at the lame connection. The socially awkward days of my youth reemerged after I'd finally overcome that hideous time in my life.

"Where are you from?"

"My mother." Yup, I really said that. I'm sure I winced visibly at not only my undeniable sarcasm but the mistake of my own humor. "Not really."

"Yes, I remember you mentioning your mother. Your grandmother raised you, yes?"

"That's correct." I looked down, averting my eyes from his probing gaze. I took a drink from my diet Pepsi, wishing I'd ordered something stronger and wondering if it would be an obvious sign of weakness if I ordered one now. Finding a shred of bravery from somewhere within, I looked up at him. He was watching me, studying. I wondered if he was enjoying my discomfort and quickly realized I was simply overly sensitive. He was only being kind and considerate. And probably as much at a loss as I was right now about how to recover this conversation seamlessly. How quickly it turned from an exhilarating dance to a dance in which neither of us could quite find the beat.

"What do you say we talk about something a little lighter," he offered gently. "My apologies for making you uncomfortable. That wasn't my intention."

I realized then, as I suspected a moment earlier, that I was being overly sensitive. "No, no. That's fine." I waved my hand in dismissal. "It's nothing. Really. I'm just not used to anyone wanting to know about me." His eyebrows raised in question. "Most dates I go on, the man talks incessantly about himself, and by the end of the night, I'm in a stupor."

"So you go on a lot of dates then?"

"Not a lot, no."

"How long have you been divorced?" He sipped his water, his pinky slightly extended.

"Five years." The server came back to let us know our dinner would arrive shortly and asked if he could get us another drink. Here was my chance to order a glass of wine to help me relax, and I grabbed the opportunity. William followed my lead and ordered a top-label scotch on the rocks.

"Can I ask what happened?" William leaned

forward, leaning his arms on the table, his hands cupped around his water glass. My breath caught as I looked into his laser-sharp blue eyes, the color of his shirt, which seemed to cut right through me, making me feel too exposed.

"My ex decided I wasn't who he thought I was," I half-lied. William looked at me and patiently waited for me to continue, his eyes conveying a gentleness that could have moved me to tears had I let it. But I didn't, and I wouldn't. "He wanted children, I couldn't have them, and he had already fathered a child with another woman before we were sure I couldn't have any. End of story," I gushed, bitterness seeping from my explanation.

The server set our drinks in front of us, and I took a gulp of wine, grateful for the relaxing warmth spreading through me.

His hand reached across the table and covered mine. "His loss," he said quietly. "I never wanted children myself."

I dared to look in his eyes again. They'd made a 180 degree turn and were warm and tender. And yet — well, I didn't know. I couldn't put my finger on it. I casually sat back in my chair, my hand naturally pulling out from under his. "So tell me about your week," I said lightly, shifting gears. "Any big plans?"

"Other than hopefully seeing you again?" He sat back and took a drink. "Just work."

"Here in the area?"

"Of course."

"Since you don't have a clue how long you are going to be here, I wasn't sure if you are working here this week." I took a smaller sip of wine, studying his eyes to see if they'd changed. Or if I was reading something completely off. They stayed warm. Friendly. "How long do you usually stay in one location?"

"Until the job is done." He watched me as I continued to try to read him. "Why all the questions?"

"Why not?" My response ruffled his calm demeanor. Just a little. But who could blame the poor guy? I was trying to figure out what had gotten into me, but that could take a good long while, and I didn't have enough time to do that right now. This was how I would expect Violet would behave, and the thought made me shudder, touching every vertebra as it rippled down my back. And yet I couldn't seem to stop myself. I was a train derailed and heading for a crash. Anxiety made an unwanted appearance. I took a slow, deep breath to make it disappear, something that had worked miracles once I'd learned that simple little trick.

"I'm not trying to be difficult, William. Truly, I'm not. It's just that you've dodged all my questions. Maybe if you answered a few, I wouldn't ask so many."

He smiled, amused. "You may be small, but you have a powerful punch."

"I'd like to think of it as wise. If we're going to see each other again, I would like to know who you are. If even just a little bit. I don't know anything more about you now than I did the first day you walked into my salon."

"Don't you think that's an exaggeration?"

Something about his tone bothered me. It almost sounded condescending. Proof that I needed to know more about him. Enough to see if I was misreading these moments.

"Not by much." I sat back, inhaled deeply, and said, "Look, it's just that you ask me all these questions, but you're unwilling to answer any. Makes me wonder if you're hiding something."

He laughed in a way that made me wonder if I had been overreacting after all. "I've got nothing to hide, Melanie. But I don't want to chase you away by talking too much. Or by answering one of your questions unsatisfactorily." He looked at me for a moment, as if he were choosing his next words. "It feels like you're setting me up to fail by answering a question wrong. Maybe if you made them multiple choice, I would have a better chance."

My eyes, heavy with shame, looked down toward my glass, my fingers playing with the stem.

"When you ask a question, I will answer to the best of my ability. Deal?"

I nodded. "Deal."

I looked up and surveyed the room around me. Suddenly I froze, and time seemed to stop. At a table in the corner, a table hidden in the shadows so that I almost missed him entirely, sat the man from the café two days before. Our eyes met, and I saw him smile. An unfriendly, evil grin that turned my blood cold. I wanted to think I was mistaken, that I couldn't see that clearly in the dim lighting, but there was no mistaking that look.

"Are you okay?" My attention snapped back to William and the concern I saw there.

"William, that man—the one from the café the other day. He's over in the corner table to the left behind you." I kept my voice low and my head down, not wanting to see the man's face again.

"Where?"

I looked up to see William turned, looking in all directions behind him. And to see the once-occupied table now empty.

"William, he was there. I swear. I'm not imagining things." Not only did I sound desperate for him to believe me, I *was* desperate.

"I believe you, Melanie. I do. But he's not there anymore."

"Maybe he's in the restroom. It's just around the corner from the table he was at."

"I'll go check it out." He took the napkin from his lap and laid it on the table. I watched his back as he strode with purpose toward the restroom, reappearing seconds later. "There's only one other man in there, and it's not him."

"Are you sure? Did you get a good look at him?"

"As good as a man dares to look at another man in the restroom without getting punched out." Despite the seriousness of the moment, I couldn't stop a chortle. "But unless the guy from the café was a short man about seventy, mostly bald with a few gray hairs, he's not your guy."

I breathed deep and sat back. I wasn't sure if I should feel relieved that he was gone or concerned that he was here to begin with.

"Melanie," his voice was gentle, "maybe he was just in the same place at the same time."

"Twice?"

"Stranger things have happened."

I knew he was right, but throw the threatening text message into the mix, and it yielded a whole different theory. But I didn't want to get into the text with him. Not now. I needed to sort things out first. With Claire if I was going to sort them out with anyone.

"Another glass of wine?" He signaled the server to our table.

"No, thank you. I've had enough." *In more ways than one.* The server appeared, cleared our plates, and left again. "I think I just need to go home. Feels like I'm getting one of my headaches again."

"Too much wine? But you only had one glass." His eyes radiated concern, his brows furrowed.

"Probably a combination from too much sun and the wine." *Not to mention the creeper.* "Claire and I had a couple of wine coolers out on the boat."

He reached for the check. "I'll take you home."

"That's very kind of you, but I have my car."

"You can leave it here, and I can bring you back here to get it tomorrow."

That authoritative voice again, and I wasn't in the mood to deal with it. But then again, maybe I was only irritable because of the oncoming headache and the events that unfolded tonight.

"I'll be fine. Promise," I added when he appeared

skeptical.

"How about if I just follow you to be sure you get home okay, and then I'll call to check in on you tomorrow? Now's not the time to be proud and not let someone take care of you."

Realizing there was no harm in his suggestion, and so he would feel better, I acquiesced. "That's fine. I've already had one accident; I certainly don't need another."

He stood and came around to my side of the table, helping pull my chair out for me. "You've been in an accident? Nothing too serious, I hope."

He cradled my elbow, steering me out of the restaurant. "It was. But I'm fine now." I could sense his concern. "Really, I am," I insisted. His concern was truly touching.

He opened my car door for me, placed a quick, almost formal peck on my cheek, and closed my door once I buckled in. And true to his word, he followed me until I turned into my driveway. With a quick honk, he zoomed off into the night.

16

Monday morning I awoke to the sound of birds squabbling in the tree right outside my bedroom window. The gray, overcast sky held the promise of more rain. I stretched and lay still for a moment, testing to be sure my headache was gone. They were getting fewer and farther between, but they could still knock me down and out for an entire day if I didn't catch it in time.

Confident it was gone, I got up and walked across my small loft and looked out at the lake. The air looked hazy as if there was a thin layer of white, wispy gauze hovering over the water. It made it look so serene and beautiful. A couple of loons floated on the lake, occasionally dipping under the water and resurfacing seconds later. I heard one call through the open window, the sound that only loons can make. It sounded almost eerie sometimes, but this morning it added to the tranquility. The grass was wet with morning dew. On the far side of the lake, a sailboat sailed slowly and gracefully, taking advantage of the gentle morning breeze before the rain inevitably began falling.

Since I had Saturday off, I went into the salon for a

while today to get some bookwork done. Saturdays are typically too busy to get any housekeeping items done anyway, so I knew Claire wouldn't have done it. Besides, she hated the tediousness of bookwork.

Still in my thin cotton nightshirt and sleeping shorts, I took my coffee and the newspaper out on the deck. The beauty of living in the country—I could wear anything I wanted out here, and no one would be around to see. I eased myself into an Adirondack chair and stretched my legs out in front of me, resting my feet on the black wrought iron railing that surrounds my deck. I loved the curlicues in the railing because they held my feet in place just so. I left my cell phone in the house so the outside world wouldn't interfere with the solitude I enjoyed and craved in the mornings. The simple pleasures of life on the lake.

I had just begun my second cup of coffee and started my morning devotional reading when I heard knocking on my front door. Who in the world could that be? Nana never just dropped by unannounced because she never knew when I would be here. Claire? Or maybe Jack was in town. Either, they'd seen me look worse than this, so when I opened the door and saw William standing there holding flowers, my hand instantly flew to my hair, setting it loose from its ponytail.

"William!" I could feel my face flush. "What brings you here?"

"You didn't answer your phone, so I was worried."

Naturally. The man worried more than my grandmother.

"Come on in." I held the door open and stepped back so he could get past me and into the kitchen. "Coffee?" I reached for a cup without waiting for his answer. My self-consciousness disappeared. This was my house, after all, my own space. And he did come by unannounced.

"Please." I felt his gaze on me as I poured him a cup and handed it to him. "Why didn't you answer your phone?"

"I never take my phone outside with me in the mornings. It distracts from the beauty of serene country living. I silenced it, too."

"I was worried."

"You worry too much. I told you last night I was fine." I met his eyes and smiled, trying to make up for the edge in my voice. And if he heard it, he didn't show it. His eyes didn't show much of anything this morning, which left me feeling the need to read him. Again. I knew I hadn't been an active participant in the dating scene but wondered if getting to know a man was supposed to be this hard. "Would you like to join me out on the deck with your coffee?"

"It would be my pleasure."

He followed me toward the back of my house and out onto the deck. He stood and silently took in his surroundings. If I didn't know better, he even looked relaxed. I smiled to myself and leaned my head back on the chair, taking in a deep breath of the fresh air. He sat down in the chair next to me and silently watched the lake, taking a sip of his coffee. I studied him from the corner of my eye.

"I can see why you love it here," he said quietly. "I'll bet the sunsets are amazing."

"Yes, they absolutely are," I agreed, seeing a romantic side to him emerge.

"Maybe I could come out here and watch one with you sometime."

"Sure."

"Tonight?"

My head swiveled in his direction, yet I wasn't sure why his self-invitation surprised me. "If it rains all day, there won't be a sunset."

"Tell me about your accident. The one you mentioned last night."

"I know which one. I've only been in one," I said. "But there isn't anything to tell because I don't remember hardly anything about it."

"You don't remember the accident?"

"You sound surprised."

"It just seems that —"

"I suffered a brain injury and was in a coma for a few days. My memory is sketchy at best."

"What, if anything, do you remember?"

"I lost a day or so prior to the accident and some after I woke up."

"Do you think you'll get them back? Your memories?"

"The brain is a strange thing. Some days it seems like something I see or hear will trigger something; snippets that I can't be sure are fact or fiction."

"Like what?"

"I wake up at night sometimes in a cold sweat like someone is chasing me, and then I crash. The only thing is I can't see who it is or why I'd be running."

"Go on," he encouraged.

"You don't need to worry, you know." I turned my head to look at him, startled by the gentleness I saw there.

"I realize I don't need to, but I do." He drained the last of his coffee and looked directly into my eyes as I watched him. "Is there anyone else in your dream?"

"Sometimes my ex-husband is with me, but most

of the time I'm alone."

"So the details vary?"

"Slightly. I just wish…" I trailed off.

"Wish what?" His voice was low, husky.

"I wish I could figure out why I have the same dream." I looked out at the lake again. "I mean, is it a dream or a memory?"

"What do the doctors say? About getting your memory back. Do they think you will? That might be helpful."

"It's possible, but after this long, probably not likely. I think that's what bothers me the most. How can I put these dreams to rest if I don't know what's triggering them?"

"When is the last time you had this dream?"

"About a week ago."

"Did you see or hear anything out of the ordinary that day?"

I tried to recall my day again, gave up, and shook my head. "No. I've been tempted to try a hypnotist, but the thought of someone else having control over my thoughts is unnerving."

"Yes, you are controlling of your surroundings."

I half-laughed. "And you're either rude or direct; I haven't decided which."

He chuckled. "I suppose I deserved that one."

"Yes, I suppose you did." I had to admit it was fun to joust with him verbally. A large raindrop fell on my hand and looking at the color and weight of the clouds directly above us, I realized the bottom was going to bust open soon, heaving large amounts of rain. "We best head inside extremely fast," I said as another drop fell, followed by several more. By the time we stood and picked up our coffee cups and I grabbed the newspaper off the little rustic table beside the chair, we barely made it through the door before it poured.

I ran up to the loft to close the window I had left open earlier and threw on a light, loose sweatshirt. It wasn't cold, but the humidity from the rain brought a slight chill with it, and I loved sweatshirts. I briefly checked my hair in the mirror, ran a brush through it, and started back downstairs, unable to see William when I reached the bottom. I turned the corner to go into the kitchen, and there he was, staring at something that was lying on the counter.

"What are you looking at?" He startled and turned toward me, looking like a boy caught smoking behind the shed. I craned my neck a little to see what had captivated his attention.

"Just passing time until you got back down here. Did you get the window closed in time?" His smile warmed me.

"Just barely. Breeze is blowing hard enough to push the rain in through the window."

"San Diego."

"Excuse me?"

"Your sweatshirt."

"Oh," I said, spreading my arms out and doing a full circle. "Compliments of my ex-husband. Actually," I added, "had I not taken it, I wouldn't have it. His new wife would."

"I take it you didn't come out ahead in the divorce."

"I'm still a little bitter," I said and sighed. "I'm working on that."

"My ex got everything but the clothes on my back."

"I'm going to assume that's a slight exaggeration. Did she have a good lawyer?"

"Hell, she *is* a good lawyer."

"What a pair we are, huh?"

"The lesson I learned from mine is don't marry a lawyer. It's easier just to find one when you need one."

"I would offer you another cup of coffee, but I need to change and head into the salon for a little while."

"I thought you said you were closed on Mondays."

"I have some bookwork to catch up on. And some other things I need to do." *Like calling Corporal Matthews to see if there's any more news on Velma.*

He turned to place his cup in the sink and wrapped me in a hug that felt strangely stiff and awkward. He turned for the door, where he stopped, his hand on the doorknob. "Just curious, did you live in San Diego?"

I tilted my head. "You are a curious man, aren't you?"

He shrugged, smiled, and turned, opening the door. "Apparently."

"No."

He turned back to look at me once more. "No what?"

"No, I've never lived in San Diego. Honeymoon. That's where my accident was."

"Oh." And he was out the door. I stood staring at the back of the closed door, a sliver of interest arising as I peered out the window to see what car he was driving today. Not the sleek little Jaguar that belonged to his friend, but a dark-green BMW. More than simple curiosity piqued my interest.

I made a mental note of the license plate number.

All of a sudden, something felt off. Or was I just being hypervigilant since Velma's death and the man who sent me the less-than-friendly text message? It was only a week ago that I told Claire I wanted some excitement in my life. I may have just found it. Little did I know at that moment how I would long for peace and quiet once again.

17

I spent most of the rainy morning at the salon doing some bookwork, deep cleaning, and flipping through some hair books. I've had the same hairstyle for far too long, and I was ready for a change. I sat in my client chair at my station looking through books and watching the rain fall outside, now in sheets, waiting for it to stop, or least slow down before I headed home.

I crossed over to the large windows that lined the front of the salon, and I scanned the sky in search of some sign of clearing. A car in the far corner of the parking lot caught my attention. Since the parking lot was full of cars from the other businesses in the center that were open on Mondays—all except ours, actually—I nearly missed it. I focused on the vehicle next to the white van—a dark-green BMW. My heart started beating faster. I waited for a minute and then reached for my cell phone. My curiosity was beyond piqued.

The line rang and rang until finally he answered, voice gruff and distracted. I nearly didn't recognize it.

"Yes?"

"William?"

"Well, hello there." His tone changed immediately. "To what do I owe this honor?"

"Is this a bad time?" I kept my sights glued on the BMW, straining to see something, anything.

"Absolutely not. It's a pleasure to hear from you. A surprise but a pleasure nonetheless."

My heart fluttered a bit. "I just wanted to extend that invitation to catch a sunset from the deck. Tonight won't be good since it's raining, but what does your schedule look like for the rest of the week?"

"I'm not sure how to answer that because I don't know how much longer I'll be in town for this job."

"Oh." I tried to mask my disappointment. "It's wrapping up that quickly?"

"It may be. I'll be back, but I don't know precisely when."

The door opened on the BMW. My heart began racing, and then the door closed again. "Another job coming up?"

"If not for work, I'm hoping for pleasure." My heart fluttered again. Darn it anyway. I was trying to solve this whole weird car puzzle, and he was distracting me from that. "Dinner tonight?"

"I have to swing by my grandmother's on my way home, and I'm not sure how long that will take." I didn't *have* to swing by Nana's, but I wanted to. There was something I need to talk with her about. "Tomorrow?"

"Tomorrow works perfectly. I'll be looking forward to it. Six-thirty? I can stop and pick up dinner."

The door to the BMW opened again, and I waited, my heart beating faster, my breathing seeming to stop. At this rate, I was likely to pass out from either a rapid heartbeat or a lack of oxygen.

"Melanie?"

"Yes, I'm here. Six-thirty is perfect. I can make dinner if you prefer. But truth be told, people aren't all that crazy about my cooking. Those people being Claire and Jack."

I heard him chuckle. "I'll stop and pick something up. Besides, after working on your feet all day, the last thing you'll want to do is cook dinner."

"How thoughtful." Despite being distracted, his consideration truly touched me. The door to the BMW opened wider, as well as the passenger door. Dang tinted windows.

"Melanie? Are you there?"

My attention was jolted back to the phone. Again. "Yes! Sorry…" I stammered. "What did you say?"

"I asked if you have any requests. For dinner."

"Whatever you pick up is fine."

"Okay, then. Tomorrow at six-thirty it is."

We hung up, my eyes never leaving the BMW. The driver finally got out, and I wasn't sure if I felt relief or further curiosity. He was a tall hulk of a man. So much so that I was surprised he could unfold out of the compact car so effortlessly. He smoothed his suit, leaned over and said something to the passenger, and closed his door, the passenger closing her door simultaneously, deciding to stay in the car. And now I was *really* curious. For entertainment if nothing else. I wanted to tell Claire about the half-solved mystery of the dark-green BMW. But I had to know who the woman in the passenger seat was first.

I rifled through my purse and found the business card that would hopefully give me some answers. I pulled it out and ran it between my fingers for a moment before reaching for my phone.

The line rang and rang until I thought it was going to roll into voicemail. But an answer stopped it short.

"Corporal Matthews here."

"Corporal, this is Melanie. Hogan." As if he'd dealt with more than one Melanie in the last week.

"Ms. Hogan. Do you have something for me?"

I heard chattering in the background, and a man yelled some obscenities above the din of voices. Either there were a lot of angry officers in the room or he was at a jail. Either sounded equally frightening.

"No. I was hoping you had something for *me*." The noise stopped abruptly, and the line got quiet. I wondered if he hung up the phone. "Corporal?"

"Yeah, I'm here. I had to step out of the room. What was I s'pose to have for you?

"You said you'd try to run the license plate for me."

"Oh. Yeah, I did that."

I waited until a sliver of irritation rifled through me. Seriously? Was he going to make me ask? I waited another moment. Yup, I guess he was. "Well? What did you find out?"

"It belongs to a Sampson Wilson."

The name got my attention. "Sampson Wilson?"

"Yeah. The name mean anything to you?"

"No," I lied. "I was just trying to place it." And in all fairness, it wasn't exactly a lie. I didn't know Sampson Wilson. Wilson was a common name around these parts, after all, so that Alice's last name was Wilson could be purely coincidental. Though my gut was telling me it wasn't. "Any more news on Velma's case?"

"I can't discuss an open investigation, Ms. Hogan. Besides, I'm not the one doing the investigation. Detective Wescott is."

"I see." I scrambled to come up with some way to get information. "So he's the one speaking with anyone who may have information about Velma's death?"

"Yup. Anything else?"

"No. Thank you."

"Okay then, you have yourself a nice —"

"Wait!" I stopped him. "I guess there is one more thing. Could you run one more plate for me?"

"Ms. Hogan, no offense, but I'm not your personal —"

"BFW-431," I interrupted. "Just in case you change your mind." Silence. "You never know, it could have something to do with the case." I wasn't ashamed to manipulate the situation to get what I needed here.

"As could every other car in the parking lot where you work." I heard him sigh into the phone. "I'll pass it along to Detective Wescott."

"Thank you." I smiled to myself. "Have a good day, Corporal."

"Yup. That's the plan." And the line went dead before he'd have to answer yet another question.

I stared at the phone for a moment and took a quick field trip. I looked through the card catalog of client information, found the one I was looking for, plucked it out of the stack, picked up my shoulder bag and my umbrella, and headed out to my car.

The puddles of water that filled the potholes in the parking lot were a disaster waiting to happen. Especially in my high heels. I bravely took my eyes off of the ground and looked to the corner of the parking lot, a white Camaro now parked where the beamer had been. And all it took was that one moment for me to nearly fall to my death when I stepped down and landed square in the middle of a hole. I caught my breath and cursed. Not only had I nearly broken an ankle, but now I was soaking wet with muddy water. Thank goodness William hadn't been around to see that graceful move. Or my grandmother to hear my choice language.

I entered the address into my Garmin GPS and began my quick jaunt. My adrenaline started pumping at what I was about to do. I knew this town like the back of my hand and found what I was looking for in no time at all. 2751 Oak Street.

I left my car running as I sat still for a minute and looked at the house. It was a large, yellow house that reminded me of buttercream. The white shutters on the upstairs windows were closed mostly, and the blinds on the main floor windows were closed. The concrete steps leading to the front door were cracked, and a black iron handrail that ran alongside one side of the steps leaned a bit too much to be of any support should anyone need it. If it was for looks only, the house would look better if it were gone completely. I opened my door, then my umbrella, and began walking up the sidewalk. I looked at the neighboring house, just off to the left, and breathed with relief when it looked like no one was home.

I put my hand on the front door handle to see if it was open, my heart beating furiously. Locked. I stepped back and looked around me, hoping no one was watching. I felt like a panther on the prowl, stalking its prey. I crept around the house to the right side where a gate led to the back yard. I touched the handle on the gate.

"Can I help you?"

I jumped and stifled a scream, feeling my cheeks turn hot. I inhaled sharply and turned to see an elderly woman behind me, her hair in rollers, rain cap keeping them dry, an umbrella for good measure.

"Velma was my aunt," I said, sure I was about to get struck down for lying. "I forgot my key, so I was hoping someone else from the family would have left the door open." It's true what they say. When one tells a lie, it's easier to tell the second to cover the first.

The woman's face looked pitying. "I'm so sorry for your loss, dear. Velma was a good woman."

"How well did you know her?"

"As well as neighbors do. When she was gone, I watched her house for her. And we talked when we were outside working in our yards, but...well, that's the extent of it. Other than the day she died."

"You saw her that day?"

"Sure did. I went over to her house to give her a piece of mail that got mixed up with mine."

"Did she seem okay?"

"As okay as she ever has been. She didn't seem sick none if that's what you mean. She was eating healthy, I remember that. That woman was always eating somethin' or other."

"How long did you stay?"

"Just long enough to give her the mail and for her to get somethin' for me from the other room."

"What did she get for you? If you don't mind my asking."

"Not at all, child. It was a letter from my nephew. Said it got mixed in her mail. She'd a never give it to me if I never come to her," she huffed. The more she talked about Velma, the angrier she became. I had to keep her talking. The truth is often revealed through anger.

"Did she have a lot of company?"

"Hardly none at'll. I really didn't see anyone much

over here. Once in a while, someone would show up, but they never stayed long. Velma could be…"

"Could be what?"

She eyed me as if weighing whether she should continue.

"Demanding. But I'm sure that doesn't surprise you a bit, being related and all."

"No, not a bit," I said. *Huh. Finally, some truth had come from my lips. Now if only that truth shall set me free.* "Have you seen many people at the house since her death?"

"Just one person, but I try not to be a nosy neighbor, you know."

"Do you know who it was? The person who was here?"

"No, can't say that I do. But like I said—"

"You're not a nosy neighbor," I finished for her. I wished she would have been a little more like Velma and knew everyone's business. I think she probably was, but she didn't want me to believe she was a busybody. "Just one more question, if you don't mind. Do you remember what kind of car the person was driving?"

"Hmm…" I watched her closely as she tried to remember. "I think it was a little green something or other. I'm not too familiar with cars, y'know." She seemed miles away as she thought about something, and then her eyes widened as she inhaled, the thrill of remembering a forgotten piece of information that she apparently thought was crucial. "It was just like Alice's son's car!"

I felt my breath catch in my throat. She was right if she thought it was important. It was exactly that. I reached my hand out to shake hers. "Thank you, Mrs. — what did you say your name was?"

"I didn't." She shook my hand, hers feeling cool and frail in my now-sweaty palm. "It's Mrs. Wilson."

"Wilson?" I could hardly believe what I'd heard. There had to be some mistake.

"Uh-huh."

"Are you any relation to Alice?"

"She was married to my brother. He died sometime back, you know."

"Thank you, Mrs. Wilson. You've been a tremendous help." *You have no idea how much.*

Her eyes shone with pride. "Glad I could help, dear."

Hmm. Coincidence? I thought not. I peered around the corner of the house and watched as she made her way back across the yard to her home. Mrs. Wilson. That was certainly interesting, now, wasn't it?

As soon as she disappeared from my line of sight,

I let myself in through the gate and looked around the back yard. The screen door looked like it could be open, and my hopes lifted. Maybe, just maybe, someone left the door open.

Sure enough, to my delight, it opened, the hinge whining from the humidity. The inside door was ajar as well. I pushed it open slowly, wondering what in the world I was doing. But I couldn't stop myself. And was it really considered trespassing if there was technically no one living here? And who would press charges anyway? It didn't appear anyone visited. Except for the mysterious little green car Mrs. Wilson had mentioned. The same kind her nephew owned. Her nephew couldn't have been William, so he was off the hook in my book.

Stairs leading to the basement were immediately off to my left as I entered the house, and the smell of mildew wafted up to greet me. And the unmistakable scent of mothballs. I tiptoed further into the kitchen and saw the dirty dishes, absent of any trace of food, still sitting on the counter from the breakfast Mrs. Wilson had obviously caught Velma in the middle of eating. I made my way into the living room, darkened by the closed blinds. I was tempted to turn on a lamp, but I didn't want to alert anyone passing by that there was someone in here. Besides, I didn't want to touch anything and leave my fingerprints behind, just in case. In fact, I was surprised they hadn't dusted for prints yet. That was the first thing they did in the television crime shows.

I turned down the hall that led to some bedrooms, finding the one that used to be hers. I tiptoed — unsure who I was trying not to disturb — into the adjoining bathroom and peered into the medicine chest. Other than the typical medicinal staples like Tylenol, allergy medicines, and a stock supply of antacids, there weren't any other medications. I walked back out to the kitchen and looked at the bottles above her sink. More Tylenol, antacids, and a nasal spray. I looked in the living room one more time to see if there was any mail with return addresses. I pulled my cell phone from my bag and touched the app that turned on the flashlight. I shined it on the table that sat beside a chair that appeared to be used often. The arms were stained, and the impression of her backside was imprinted on the seat cushion.

I focused my light on the table and froze. There, among used tissues, a navy-blue button, several round wooden toothpicks, and atop a crocheted doily, was a four-by-six photo in a frame. Tucked in the frame's corner was another image. I couldn't believe what I saw!

18

Nana had just begun cooking dinner minutes before I walked in the door. She met me with a tight squeeze that nearly took my breath away. For such a petite woman, she certainly was strong. In more ways than one. She had gone through so much in her life with Violet, and yet she was the strongest woman I knew. She'd never let it wear her down, and I envied her that.

"You're just in time," she beamed.

"For what?" I asked, not sure I wanted to know the answer.

"For a cooking lesson."

I dropped my things in the nearest chair and pushed up my sleeves to wash my hands. "You mean you haven't given up on me yet?"

"Never." She winked at me, her eyes twinkling.

I loved coming to see her. No matter how bad my day was or how terrible life seemed at the moment, walking through that door and into the warmth of her home made everything else disappear. I don't know what I would ever do without her. Just the thought of it made me shudder.

"So what are we making?" I asked.

"Wild rice hotdish and glazed carrots. And I could use your help in glazing some pecans for a salad."

"Huh. The woman's raised me for nearly forty years, and she still trusts me in the kitchen," I muttered. I swerved to miss the dishtowel slap on my rear end I knew was coming.

"Get glazing, child." She knew glazing pecans was something I could do with minimal supervision.

We fell into a comfortable silence for a few moments, my grandmother focusing on draining the wild rice so she could boil it yet again, and me thinking about what I saw in Velma's house and trying to make sense of it. I decided to wait until we got the hotdish in the oven before telling her about it. Nana stopped what she was doing and called me over to the window. "Honey, come quick. Look at this magical sight."

I laid the wooden spoon on the rooster spoon rest and crossed the kitchen to stand by her side. Past her flower gardens and across the field was the most glorious rainbow in shimmering red, blue, green, and purple hues. I almost expected a leprechaun to pop right out of the earth beneath it. Neither of us dared to break the beauty before us by uttering a single word. I was afraid to breathe for fear I would disturb the moment.

Finally, as the colorful ribbon slowly faded, we reluctantly turned back to the food preparation, looking at one another as if we'd just witnessed a tremendous secret miracle. God's message to just us.

"I went out with William last night." I focused hard on the pecans as I awaited her response.

"And?"

"And he stopped by this morning for coffee." I could feel her gaze hot on me as she drained the water from the rice. "No, he didn't stay overnight. Give me some credit."

"I didn't say a word."

"You didn't have to."

I looked at her from the corner of my eye and smiled at her. I finished the pecans and spread them out to cool on waxed paper.

My job complete, I sat down on a wooden stool by the counter where she was now peeling carrots. I got back up and walked around the center island, took the peeler from her, and began stripping the carrots of their skin. It was one of those weird things that turned my stomach unless I didn't think about what I was doing while I did it. But it was also another one of those things she could trust me with unsupervised in the kitchen.

"What is it you want to talk about, dear?"

I stopped peeling and looked at her. I didn't know why I was surprised. She usually knew what I thought before I even did.

"There're two things."

"Start with one." Her voice was so quiet yet filled with authority. Something only she could pull off.

"I had another nightmare this past week."

She stopped what she was doing and looked at me, her brows furrowed with concern. "Did it reveal anything more?"

I started peeling again. "No. I wish I knew what triggered them."

"How long has it been since you had the last one?"

"About six months. When I stayed here for two nights in a row afterward."

"Come." She took my hand and led me to the table where she turned my chair to face hers before I sat down. "Melanie, I'd like you to consider my suggestion of seeing someone."

"Instead of William or in addition to?" I could tell by her stare she didn't appreciate my attempted humor.

"These nightmares will not go away until you figure out what's causing them. You and I both suspect they're from the accident, and they usually follow your headaches, but wouldn't you like to know what's triggering them so you can put it to rest?" She took my hands and held them in her own. I looked down at her hands and compared them to mine. They were almost identical, and I found comfort in that.

"The thought of seeing a therapist makes me feel like—well, defective. Like I'm just like Violet."

"Oh, Melanie," Nana squeezed my hands and shook her head slowly, her eyes twinkling. "You couldn't be more different than her. That fear is something you could use outside help with. You're stuck and need to get past it, dontcha know."

"Who gets past their mother not wanting them? What kind of woman turns her back on her child?"

"Someone who doesn't understand the magic of motherhood. You need to stop expecting from her something she's not capable of giving."

"So it's my fault?"

"Stop twisting my words. No, it's not your fault. Not even the slightest bit. It's *her* loss. And someday she'll come to realize that."

"It's already too late." I sounded like a petulant child, but I didn't care. Not now.

"Now, about these nightmares. They're always about someone chasing you and then you get into an accident, huh?"

"Yes."

"And the rest sometimes changes. As far as who's in the dream, what you're doing in the car right before the crash—"

"I'm always on my cell phone trying to call 911. But the person who answers the phone is always different. Sometimes it's my lovely less-than-faithful ex, sometimes it's the 911 operator who can't hear what I'm saying, even when I scream, sometimes it's a strange man's voice. Heck, sometimes I can't even make a sound come out of my mouth."

"This last one you had—who answered your call this time?"

I allowed my mind to travel back in time, trying to remember the details. All of a sudden, my eyes grew wide. For a moment, I couldn't catch my breath. "Buford," I whispered. "But then—it's kind of like it went to William. It seems all jumbled up."

"I assume you'd met him by then?"

"Buford?"

"William."

"That day." Thoughts raced around in my head as I tried to piece them together. "What do you think that means?"

"I think it means you should take my suggestion and see someone to help you work through this."

"That's what I'm doing now. With you."

"A professional. Someone smarter than me."

"There is no one smarter than you." I leaned over and gently kissed her cheek. "Have I told you how much I appreciate you?"

"Not today," she beamed.

"Well, let's not spoil it then."

"Melanie Hogan!" she scolded, and we laughed. "And?"

"And what?"

"You said there were two things. It's another good forty-five minutes until dinner anyway, so talk."

"You sure are a bossy woman." I sat back in my chair, bracing for her reaction that was sure to come when I told her what I did before I appeared in her kitchen.

"Time's a-ticking, child. Talk to me."

"Promise you won't get mad at me. Oh, forget it," I blurted out. "That's a dumb thing to expect."

"What did you go and do?" Her eyes narrowed.

"I paid Velma a visit. Well, not Velma, but her house."

"Why do I think I will not like what comes next?"

"Cause you won't." At least I was honest. "You'll never guess what I saw."

"Probably not. But tell me anyway."

I smiled sheepishly at her. "I did a little

195

investigating. I didn't see a stitch of medication in her medicine cabinet or above her sink where there were some other over-the-counter medications. Just run-of-the-mill stuff you'd expect to see in everyone's home. Or not to see, whichever way you want to look at it. I know she was murdered."

"Who else was there?"

"No one."

She took a deep breath. "Who let you in then?"

"The back door was open."

"Melanie Hogan, that's trespassing, and you—"

"Didn't get caught. Besides, is it a crime if no one is living there and the door was open?"

"What if someone saw you?"

"Someone did. Her neighbor. But she thinks I'm Velma's niece."

"Hmm. And I wonder where she would have gotten that idea?" She could see right through me, and I knew it. "You're lucky the police didn't see you there. If they're investigating a suspicious death—oh, good heavens, child, tell me you didn't touch anything. I don't want to be bailing your scrawny little bottom out of jail because you've interfered with an investigation."

"My fingerprints aren't on file, so they wouldn't have anything to match it to even if they found them."

"Melanie, you're getting in over your head."

"You'll never guess what was on the table beside her chair in the living room."

"No, I probably wouldn't. But you're going to tell me."

"Aha! So you're just a little bit curious, too, huh?" I grinned.

"Well, go on and tell me already. You can't leave an old woman hanging."

"There were two pictures. One was an older picture with two adults and a child with an uncanny resemblance to Maria, who works in my salon. The other was a more recent picture of the same adults, an older Maria and Buford Woods." I stood and began pacing. "Nana, Maria acts like she doesn't even know Buford. I mean, she knows of him and said she'd seen him a time or two visiting Gina while I've been gone, but never once has she intimated that she knows him beyond that."

"That is strange, indeed. What do you make of it?"

"I don't know yet. I need to talk to Maria. And Connie. The two of them seem to get together occasionally outside of work." I was pacing again but couldn't stop. "Know what else? The neighbor's last name is Wilson."

"Does that mean something?"

"The woman who played cards with Velma, Tillie, and Ruth is Alice Wilson. And the license plate I asked Corporal Matthews to run for me on that green BMW I keep seeing around is registered to a Sampson Wilson. And this Mrs. Wilson said Alice Wilson was married to her brother."

"Granddad's friend that died," she said to herself while looking at me.

"Who?"

"I admit that's odd, but Wilson is a common last name around these parts." It was almost as if she hadn't heard me, or she was trying to avoid answering the question.

I forced myself to sit down again and look at her. "Nana, you know some Wilsons?"

"Your grandfather had a friend named Samuel Wilson. But he died years before your granddad did."

I stood and got my shoulder bag, blindly reaching in until my fingers found the object of my curiosity. I placed the picture on the table in front of my grandmother, and her nearly constant smile faded. "Tell me you didn't—"

"I can't tell you that because I did." I pointed at the man in the photo. "Did granddad's friend look like that?"

She laid one palm on her cheek and gasped, "Goodness gracious, almost exactly like that."

19

By the time I got home, it was after nine. It was a rare day that Claire and I didn't talk to each other at least once, but this had been one of those days. William had called when I was at my grandmother's, but I didn't want to take my attention away from her, so I let it go to voicemail.

I pulled into the garage and turned my car off before I listened to his message. I couldn't help but wonder why I waited to hear it. Was there something more to it than I simply didn't listen to it yet?

After listening to him confirm our plans for the next evening, I closed the garage door and meandered to the house, stopping to gaze at a lone star that escaped from the mostly cloud-covered night sky. Not having an attached garage was the only thing I didn't like about my house. But I loved everything else so much that it was a sacrifice I was willing to make. Someday I'd do something about it, but it wasn't a priority right now.

I turned the key in the lock and let myself in, relieved to be back home. A shiver cascaded from head to toe from the chill in the air from all the humidity, so I kicked on the furnace just enough to make it comfortable. Growing up, we always had to keep the thermostat at a specific temperature to conserve energy and save money, but that was one thing that I didn't carry with me when I left home.

I kicked off my shoes, made a cup of tea, grabbed a lightweight blanket and my book, and curled up on the couch, leaning against the arm. I had just gotten settled in when I heard a loud thud outside. I startled and bolted upright. My ears perked up, listening for something else. Several moments later, with no sound other than the distant yelling and laughing of children, probably from one of the nearby campgrounds, I settled back in to read.

It wasn't even ten minutes later, and I heard another sound, this one more of a screech. What the heck? I wasn't typically afraid of going outside in the dark, but when I got up to look and noticed how it was exceptionally dark tonight with the clouds still layered in the night sky, I decided I wasn't thrilled to go exploring. I couldn't even see the one star now that I saw twenty minutes ago. There was no hint of moonlight whatsoever. Only blackness.

I opened the front door and peered through the screen door, holding the handle tight with one hand. It was then that I discovered why it was darker than it usually was under a cloudy night sky. The bulb in my yard light had burned out. "Of all times," I muttered. I was positive it had been working last night, but the more I thought about it, I couldn't be completely sure. I turned on the porch light just in time to see a startled raccoon by the trash can, its eyes reflecting eerily yellow from the porch light.

"Guilty!" I said aloud. I grabbed the flashlight I kept on the side table by the door and went outside to set the garbage can back upright that the little critter overturned. Cute as they were, they were a nuisance. "Scoot!" I shouted and shooed him away. If I didn't set the garbage can back up and secure the lid, I would have a bear visitor during the night that I could do without.

I had just gotten the cover tightened down when I saw movement out of the corner of my eye. I spun around, expecting to see another raccoon, hoping with everything in me it wasn't an unwelcome bear, but nothing was there. "Now I'm seeing things when it's too dark to see anything at all," I said under my breath. A sure sign it was time to get some sleep. My evening of reading wasn't meant to be after all.

***

Tuesday morning I overslept, which is something I

never do. Well, I guess I can't say *never* since I did today. I had one of my darned nightmares again, and by the time I could finally get back to sleep, I saw the first signs of the sky turn a shade lighter as morning drew near. It unsettled me I'd had another so soon after the last. My head spun with thoughts of what the trigger could be.

I stood and stretched before I made my way to the window to look out over the lake. A fine, misty haze hovered over the water. But even that didn't snap me out of my funk. Maybe it was time to take my grandmother's suggestion after all. I made a mental note to make a few phone calls as time allowed between clients today.

Without taking time for a cup of coffee, much less to read the paper, I showered and headed out the door to get to work. My hair was still wet, but it wasn't like I was going somewhere that I couldn't do something about it.

I was pleasantly surprised when I turned in the parking lot to see Claire's car already there. After last night, I wasn't crazy about being alone. Not only that, but I couldn't wait to tell her about my trip to Velma's and to run my dream by her. I wanted to know what she thought about it. As naive as she could be and often was (a very endearing quality in her, I must admit), she was also one of the most intuitive people I'd ever known.

When I walked into the office, one look at her showed me that *I* needed to be the one to listen to *her*. I dropped my shoulder bag onto the floor in the corner, my eyes meeting hers.

"I don't mean this in a bad way, but you look pathetic."

"Is there a good way to take that?"

"Of course there is." I smiled gently. "What's going on? Anything I can help with?"

"I doubt it," she pouted.

"Try me."

"Syd called me last night crying. She has the flu. She's homesick and wants to come home."

"So go get her."

"I can't."

"Sure you can. I can tell your clients you had a family emergency and reschedule them."

"No, I *can't*." She sniffed. "My parents took her to my aunt and uncle's in California, and I have someone coming here to fix my windshield today."

"What happened to your windshield?"

"I woke up this morning and found one whole side smashed. I could hardly even see to get here this morning."

"For crying out loud, Claire," I gently scolded her. "Why didn't you call me to come and pick you up?"

"Because I needed it to be here so I can be around when they get out here to fix it."

"Well, you're lucky you got here without crashing, you goof."

She sniffed again, and I thought it likely she was going to cry. "Can I come hang out with you after work? We could have a slumber party." Her eyes pleaded with me.

"Of course you can. But it won't be just you and me if that's okay." Her silence invited me to explain. "William is bringing dinner, and we're gonna watch the sunset over the lake."

"Well, that would be awkward. How about I don't." Her shoulders slumped slightly.

"How about you do. And if you think it will be awkward, I will reschedule with William."

"You would reschedule a date with Mr. Hottie for me? I'm flattered." She sat up a little straighter, her shoulders tucked back. She was obviously feeling quite proud of herself. "But no, I won't let you do that."

"It's not a matter of you *letting* me, it's a matter of me telling you that's what I'm going to do."

"Okay, don't cancel with him. I'm coming so I can

meet him and give you my professional opinion."

I laughed and walked around the desk to give her a squeeze. "That, my dear friend, is a deal." I began folding towels from the dryer as I told her about my trip to Velma's and what I found. When I finished, her eyes were enormous, round saucers one could drown in.

"What the heck were you thinking? Oh wait, don't answer that," she gushed, "because you weren't."

"I need to know what happened to Velma, Claire. And I don't want to believe it was someone we work with every day. The problem is, cyanide—well, that stuff's fast-acting, and I'm not sure it would have been able to be given to her anywhere other than here."

"That's disturbing," she said, eyebrows knit together.

"Very."

"No wonder you're having your dreams again. It's not like nothing's goin' on around here." The bell jingled. "We will continue this." She sounded more motherly now than earlier when she was talking about Syd.

"Yes, ma'am." I made a mock salute as she left me folding towels to check in the customer.

I had one hair color appointment after another

most of the day, along with a few of my regular older ladies who still insisted on the blue hair rinses and back combing that would give me the wildest headache if anyone tugged on my head that hard. Their heads must have been made of brick back in the day. And speaking of heads, it was past four-thirty when I realized I hadn't made a single call to inquire about therapists for the headcase I was becoming. Or always had been, and my grandmother was just too kind to say as much. It would have to wait until tomorrow. It wasn't like one day would make a difference anyway.

The rest of the girls had left already, so Claire and I finished cleaning up before she called to check in with Syd while I did the deposit.

"I'll swing by the bank to drop off the deposit in the after-hours slot if you stop and pick up some wine for dinner."

I had squeezed in a call to William earlier to let him know Claire was going to us.

"Deal."

When I was ready to leave, Claire was still on the phone with her mother and Syd. I waved dramatically to get her attention, mouthed *see you in a few*, and left. Lo and behold, what I'd come to call *my* car, was parked straight out from the grocery store, a few spaces down from the white cargo van that had become a permanent fixture in the parking lot.

I slid into my car and rolled down the windows to allow the air to cool off the interior that was still so hot from the sun I thought I could probably fry an egg on the dash. I circled around so I could drive close enough to the mystery car to see which one it was. What would be the chance that maybe it was yet a different car? When I saw it was the license plate I'd given to Corporal Matthews, which he hadn't gotten back with me yet, I decided to follow up with him first thing in the morning. Just to give him a gentle reminder. Very gentle. I didn't want to make him mad so he refused to look it up for me. If he hadn't looked it up yet, I could always move around him by asking Detective Wescott. Of one thing I was sure, I was going to find out who it belonged to.

The image of William's car he'd had at my house popped into my head. What would be the chance that it was the same one? And if so, why? The problem was, I was so taken aback that I'd completely forgotten to get the license plate number. Hopefully he had it tonight so I could compare plates. If it was a match, he and I had some talking to do. Or he did, anyway.

I had just started driving away when I glimpsed

movement through the darkly tinted windows. Great! And I, in all my brilliance, had my windows rolled down! Even though my windows weren't tinted nearly as dark as this car's were, having them up would have offered me *some* visibility protection. Too late now, assuming the occupant even noticed me at all to begin with. Just because I saw movement didn't mean he or she was looking at me.

I looked away with the if-I-don't-see-you-you-can't-see-me mentality of a two-year-old child and pulled out of the parking lot. I hung a right at the light, which brought me along the backside of the parking lot, where I saw the little car slowly edging out of its parking space. I zoomed off toward the bank, wondering if I would see the mystery man get out of the mystery car in front of my house this evening.

Before I left the bank, I pulled my hair into a ponytail and rolled the top down on my car, letting the breeze play with my hair, working strands loose that I finally held back and out of my face with one hand, elbow resting on the door. What a beautiful evening this was. The sky was a combination of crimson and pink in the distance before me. *Red sky at night, sailor's delight*, my granddad used to say.

I turned onto the side road that led to my house

and glanced down the side dirt road along the cornfield, my adrenaline pumping and my heart beating faster in anticipation of what I might see. Nothing there. I had all I could do not to laugh. I had myself all worked up over nothing. Claire was right. No wonder I was having my nightmares and headaches again.

20

Claire pulled in not even five minutes after I got in the house. I was glad we would have a few minutes before William arrived. His reaction when I told him Claire would be joining us was interesting, to say the least. He'd never tried to put the moves on me, which in itself seemed odd. Not that I thought I was a catch, mind you, but why would a man keep coming around if he didn't intend on showing — or getting — some sort of affection? Or at least some sign that it would be forthcoming. An old-fashioned gentleman, perhaps? Yet he didn't strike me as the old-fashioned type. And he certainly wasn't a southern gentleman. Maybe Jack was more his type, and he thought of me as nothing more than a friend and a way to meet Jack. But there was still the question of why he'd want to spend so much time with me if that was the case. Maybe I'd been misreading his interest.

I met Claire at the door, and she quickly and lightly brushed her cheek against mine as she breezed by me.

"No more broken windshields?"

"Nope. It's weird." She set the wine bottle on the

counter and turned to me.

"What is?"

"That someone would intentionally damage someone's property."

I rolled my eyes. "You are so naive it's almost cute."

She made that little sound she did when she was perturbed. The one she made with her tongue against the roof of her mouth. Almost a "tsk."

I couldn't help but laugh, and she scowled. "Claire, it's called crime. You live in town. It happens."

"But it's a safe neighborhood."

I lifted one hand, palm facing her. "No need to get defensive. I know it's a safe neighborhood. But when you live in town, it means more people. More people means a higher likelihood of something happening."

"You don't have to get sarcastic." She pouted for a second before getting back to her perky self, forgetting all about her window. "So fill me in on Mr. Hot Stuff."

"Mr. Hot Stuff has changed names to Mr. Mysterious."

"Ooh!" She grinned with excitement. "Do tell."

"It's complicated."

"Try me. I think I'll be able to understand."

Now who was the sarcastic one? I was rubbing off on her. She grabbed an apple from the counter, tossed it in the air, caught it perfectly with one hand, and crunched into it. She could be such a smart aleck. And I loved that about her.

"I'll wait to tell you what I think until—" We both reached for our phones simultaneously when we heard the ring tone. I lifted my phone for her to see the lit screen. "Hi William, are you almost here?" Claire's eyes sparkled with interest as she watched me listen to William.

"Well?" she inquired before I had even set the phone back down. She reminded me of a five-year-old kid who was waiting for her mom to tell her whether she could go outside and play with her friends.

"He got caught up with work and didn't think he'd be able to make it."

Now she looked like the little girl whose mother told her, no, she *can't* go out and play.

"It's because of me, isn't it?"

"My guess would be yes." Her shoulders drooped slightly, so I quickly continued. "But in a roundabout way. Let's pour a glass of wine and go sit on the front porch, and I'll tell you what I'm thinking." Claire reached for the wine glasses, and I snagged the corkscrew. "Want me to make you something to eat?"

"That would be a no," she said, nose scrunched.

"Come on. You exaggerate my lack of cooking skills. It's not that bad."

"Says you. Can we just have cereal?"

"Cereal and wine? What a disgusting combination!"

"Still beats your cooking," she said sheepishly.

"Whatever." I threw her a nasty look, and she giggled, sounding like a schoolgirl.

"I know that look. It means I won."

"Pretty proud of yourself, huh?"

"Yup. I'll get the cereal out."

"I'll get the strawberries out of the fridge."

"There! See? Wine goes beautifully with strawberries."

I shook my head slowly. "Hopeless," I muttered.

As we each balanced a full cereal bowl in one hand and a glass of wine in the other, we carefully walked ever so slowly as if we were balancing them on our heads, and made our way out to the front porch, each taking a seat in the wicker rockers.

Claire sighed as she sank in one. "These things are so comfortable. We should use them more often."

"Mm-hm."

"Why don't we?"

"Because the lake's on the other side."

"But the trees are on this side, and they're beautiful too. Especially in the fall."

"Then we'll sit out here in the fall, okay? Geez, girl. We sound like an old married couple."

She smiled that satisfied I-won-again smile that made me forget how old she really was.

"I love these sunflowers you have here." She leaned over and touched the velvety, mustard-yellow petals of the sunflowers in the vase between our chairs, spilling milk from her bowl in the process.

"Now the coons will be up on my porch tonight. As if they need any further encouragement. Thanks."

"My pleasure."

Neither of us said another word for a few minutes but stayed quiet and content as we ate our exotic dinner. Claire belched loudly, and I laughed despite the shock that something so disgusting could come out of something so pretty. "Good thing William wasn't here for that one."

"He'd be impressed." She smiled, obviously pleased with herself. "So give me the scoop on him, anyway."

I turned to face her, sitting sideways in my chair, wine glass in hand, one foot resting on the edge of my chair. "I don't know how to say it without sounding like I'm off in left field somewhere." She remained quiet, which was odd for Claire. "Ya know that dark-green BMW that we've seen in the parking lot of the salon?"

"I think so."

"Remember? You noticed it a few days ago."

The fog cleared from her memory. "Oh yeah!"

"Well, that car keeps showing up everywhere. It's been in the parking lot numerous times —"

"Are you sure it's the same one? There has to be more than one dark-green BMW in town."

"There's at least two that I know of. Possibly three. I asked Corporal Matthews to run the plate for me on one of them, and it's registered to a Sampson Wilson. There's another with a different license plate."

"Who's that one registered to?"

"I don't know yet. I asked Corporal Matthews if he'd run that one for me, too."

"And?"

"I don't know. He wasn't thrilled about it, but he didn't say no. I'm going to call him tomorrow to see what, if anything, he found out. If he hasn't checked yet, then I'll call the detective who's working the case on Velma's death. To complicate matters even more," I added, there's been a dark-colored BMW parked on the dirt road just down from here twice now. It's been too dark to tell for sure if it's dark green, but it looks like it is."

"Maybe the owner of one of them lives down that road."

"Unlikely. There aren't any houses where it's parked. Houses on that back road are few."

"Hmm."

I watched as she appeared to turn things around in her mind. "I don't want to assume every car is a suspect, as the corporal inferred when I asked him to run the second plate, but I don't want to regret being naive right now either." I kept my eyes trained on her as she mulled things over. "And the other day when William showed up, what was he driving?" Her eyes got huge, and her jaw dropped open. "Yup! A dark-green BMW."

"Do you think maybe he's stalking you? Mel, you need to call the police!"

"And say what, exactly? That I've been noticing a green car wherever I go? They'll send me to the loony bin."

"At least you'll be safe there." I thought she was teasing, but with Claire, who knows.

I stared at her with her eyes wide and her mouth hanging open. "No, thank you. I'm going to sort this out myself."

"I'll help." I could see a mixture of excitement and

fear bubble up in her eyes.

"I would appreciate that. Another set of eyes will help."

"Hey! We could be like real private eyes. I'll be Sherlock, and you can be Watson." She laughed.

"Not! We don't know what we're dealing with here."

"I know taekwondo."

"Yeah, you're one tough lady."

"You have no idea. You can keep the sarcasm."

"But it's the one thing I'm so good at."

"So do you think it's William who's following you?"

"I honestly don't think so. Some of the odd happenings have occurred when I was with him. I think it's the creep from the café and again from the restaurant. I just wish I knew what he drives. I need to find out."

"What if it's not him?"

"Don't know. He obviously got my phone number somehow."

It was getting darker outside. I felt a slight chill in the air, and I shivered. But I couldn't distinguish whether it was from chilly night air or the unknown that not only lay before me but seemed to come to meet me. I looked at Claire, sitting comfortably in her shorts and tank, feet bare.

"What happened to your security light?" She looked up at the light that usually began illuminating slowly by this time of evening.

"Went out. I was gonna call the utility company today and let them know to replace the bulb, but I was so busy I forgot. I'll have to do it tomorrow." I drained the last of my wine and set my glass down on the stone-top table that sat between us. "So how's Sydney? Is she feeling better?"

Claire's eyes lit up at the mention of her daughter, but when she talked about her, I could hear the wistfulness in her voice. "I miss her so much," she breathed. "I couldn't imagine my life without her. I just wish she could have known her father. She would have loved him so much."

I saw a tear glisten in her eye. I stayed quiet until she had talked herself dry about Syd. Finally, she stopped, yawned, looked at her watch, and jumped up. "I gotta go. It's late, and I have a busy day tomorrow. Jack's coming tomorrow again too, right?"

"Supposed to, but I haven't heard anything from him confirming, so I don't know." I stood and scooped up the wine glasses while Claire took the cereal bowls. The screen door slammed behind me. Two minutes later, she headed out the door, and her taillights disappeared down my driveway.

I locked the door, turned off the porch light, and began closing up the house to head upstairs for some light reading before bed. I no sooner got settled back against my pillows, my book opened to the page I had left off on the evening before, and I heard a clanging outside on the porch. The raccoon had found Claire's spilled milk. I groaned, waiting for him to go away. I wasn't about to get out of bed when I'd finally gotten comfortable. Next, I heard what sounded like a car door. Had Claire forgotten something?

This time I got up and went downstairs to investigate whether it was my four- or two-footed friend. But by the time I got there and turned on the porch light, the critter was gone. Dim taillights faded in the dust at the end of my driveway. Both had already left. I thought about calling her but decided to wait and talk to her in the morning.

21

When I pulled up to the salon the next morning, I saw Claire's car already there. She'd beat me to work. Twice in one week. I was in for a shock, however, when it wasn't just Claire's vehicle in the parking lot. Two police cars were parked in front of the door, and Claire was talking with one of them. "Now what?" I groaned. They couldn't possibly think Claire had anything to do with Velma's death. She wasn't even at the salon when it happened. I parked so quickly I nearly gave myself whiplash. I grabbed my shoulder bag from the passenger's seat and jogged to the salon door where the congregation of people camped.

Claire was visibly upset, so I attempted to lighten things up despite being worried half to death. "What'd she do, officer?"

"Very funny," Claire retorted. "Officer, this is Melanie Hogan, co-owner of the business." Her eyes narrowed at me, and she added, voice quiet and tight, "And the one I've been trying to call for the last half hour."

It must have been Corporal Matthews's day off, as well as Officer Straus's. The officer on duty today reached his hand toward me. "Hello, ma'am."

"Melanie," I corrected him, shaking his hand. "So what happened?" I asked no one in particular. I looked around to survey the activity going on inside the shop as another squad car pulled up. "Claire?" I demanded, beginning to panic.

"Someone broke in and made a mess of the place—"

"Through a window?" I looked around her to see which one was broken.

"That's the weird part. No broken windows and the lock hadn't been tampered with."

"That doesn't make any sense. How did they get in then? Did you forget to lock the door when you left last night?"

"No!"

"Take it easy, Claire. I'm not blaming—"

"What would you call it?" she snapped. She exhaled loudly. "I'm sorry, Mel. But I swear I locked the door. I *know* I did." Her voice was riddled with guilt.

"I believe you." She looked at me warily. "I do!" I insisted. "I'm only trying to figure out how someone could have gotten in without damaging the doors or windows."

"Does anyone else have a key?" the officer asked,

looking from me to Claire and back to me again.

"No," we said in unison.

"No other employees work here?"

"Three others, but they don't have a key."

"Any chance one of them could have gotten hold of one of yours and made a copy?" he asked me.

"Anything's possible, I suppose." I thought about it for a second. "But I don't think they would."

"Why?" he asked.

Good question. One of them may be a murderer, and you don't think they'd steal a key? "What motive would they have? I doubt they'd want to destroy the place unless it's a sick way to get a day off. Besides, they're nice girls." *But are they?* Everything was becoming so uncertain.

"Famous last words," he muttered.

I skirted around them and went into the shop, surprise slapping me cold when I assessed the damage that surrounded me. The most disturbing was my shears, the blades spread apart, the tips of each stabbed into the wood. The culprit carved a message into my station top with them first and wrote the same warning on my mirror with hair dye. Red, no less. *Leave well enough alone or else.* Or else what? I wondered. This was madness!

"Why does that seem like a threat?" I whispered to

myself.

"Probably because they meant it as one." I jumped a mile at the sound of another officer's voice behind me.

"Geez!" I wrapped my arms around my waist. "Give a girl a little warning."

"Sorry, ma'am."

"What is it with you people and calling me 'ma'am'? It makes me feel like a hundred years old." I breathed out long and heavily. "I'm sorry, Officer" — I looked at his name badge—"Mahoney. I'm just on edge."

"Understood. No apology necessary."

The first officer I had spoken with outside the shop now stood beside me as I tried to make sense out of a message clearly meant for me. "Your friend there said someone has been following you?"

I shot a look at Claire, and she shrugged and mouthed, "What?" I shook my head, irritated with her honesty at the most inconvenient times. "I don't know if someone has been following me or not. The same vehicle just seems to frequent the same places I do."

"What kind of car? Make and model."

"A dark-green BMW. But I'm sure it's nothing," I added all too quickly. "Corporal Matthews ran the plate for me, and it belongs to someone I've never heard of." Well, it's not *entirely* a lie, I rationalized. Here was my chance to get the second plate run since Corporal Matthews obviously thought it was too much below him.

"Like the one that's out there now?"

I looked in the direction he was pointing, and sure enough, there it was. Parked next to that same white cargo van.

"Yeah," I said, completely distracted now as I watched the car, straining to see if anyone was moving around in there. Because of the distance and the tinted windows, it was impossible to see. I couldn't even make out the license plate number from here.

The officer left my side and strode across the lot toward the car. I watched as he got closer, looked at the license plate, and talked into the radio connected by a clip to the shoulder of his uniform. He hesitated for a moment, wrote something down on his notepad, and walked to the window on the driver's side. I watched as he knocked on the window, and a moment later he was talking with someone through the driver's side window. A few seconds later, he walked back over toward the salon, whispered to another officer, and then made his way over to me.

"Who was it?"

"I don't know how to tell you this ma'am—Melanie—but it isn't one person, it's two. And they were just getting their day off to—shall we say an invigorating start," he stammered, his cheeks tinting.

"What did the man look like?" As much as I knew it wouldn't be, I needed to hear it wasn't William.

The officer blushed again as he averted his gaze from me, but not before he failed to suppress a smile. "Which one?"

It took a moment to sink in. "Gotcha!" I smirked at the officer's embarrassment. "The license plate, was it BFW-431?"

"Yup. That the one you been seeing?"

"One of them, yes."

"There's more than one?"

"The other one is the one that belongs to someone I've never heard of. This is the one I asked Corporal Matthews to run for me, but, apparently, he had better things to do with his time."

"Melanie?" I heard the screech of Mrs. Grover's voice calling me from outside.

"My first appointment for the day," I explained to the officer. "I'll be right back." I excused myself and went to meet Mrs. Grover to tell her we needed to reschedule her appointment, at which she balked.

"Oh dear! But I have my book club tonight."

"I really am sorry." I put my arm around her, steering her back toward her car. "I'm sure your book club ladies will understand."

"But I'm hosting it," she argued, as if that would help her case.

"Look, why don't you try coming back later today. We should have all of this cleaned up and done by then, and I can squeeze you in between my other clients."

"Well..." she pondered the suggestion, but her disappointment was evident. "I guess I can try."

I opened her car door for her, hurrying her along. Sweet lady, but seriously? Her hair wasn't my primary concern right now, book club or not. It occurred to me she hadn't even asked what happened to the shop. I wasn't sure she even noticed anything was amiss.

As I watched her pull away, I saw a familiar little silver Jaguar pull in right where Mrs. Grover had been just a moment prior. I watched as William got out of the car.

"What's happened? Are you okay?" He placed a protective hand on my back.

"Someone decided they wanted to get inside the salon after business hours," I answered, my voice laced with sarcasm. I turned and walked toward the shop, and William fell into step beside me.

"Sorry I didn't make it out to your house last night."

"No problem. Claire and I had a good time."

"Did I miss anything?"

"No. Just girl talk." I glanced at him from the corner of my eye. "What did you end up doing?"

"I didn't finish up with work until nine or so, so I just went back to the hotel."

"Oh." I knew I was less than cordial, and I couldn't even put my finger on why, other than my concern that someone broke into my business. And so far we couldn't see that anything was missing, just damaged. The shears were the most disturbing part to me. Right up there with the message in red hair dye.

He stopped and turned me toward him, the soft warmth of his hand against the clammy gooseflesh on my upper arm. "Are you upset with me?"

I looked directly into those piercing blue eyes and sighed. "William, it's not you. I've got bigger things to worry about right now." I extended my arm toward the salon and the officers working the scene. "As you can see, we have a minor crisis going on here. That's all I can process for the moment."

He took a step back. "This coolness feels more like

an assault against me personally, Melanie. If this is about last night, I told you I'm sorry." His voice was curt, but really, who could blame the man after I just nearly snapped his head off. "You're making me stand in the corner, is that it? And for how long will I need to be there before I'm free to come back out?"

"No." I sighed again. "I'm the one who's sorry." I was behaving like a brat, and I knew it full well. As well as I knew that, sadly, I wasn't able to develop a relationship with anyone at this time in my life. I looked up and met the unmistakable hurt in his eyes. "I have to get back in there and see what I can do about getting the business back up and running, or there will be a lot of ladies and gents inconvenienced at the hand of some idiot."

"It's a good thing it happened after hours, and you weren't here. Things could have been much worse."

"I never took you as the glass-half-full kinda guy." I gave him a half-smile, letting him know I was okay. "I'll talk to you later, okay?"

"Certainly." He stepped toward me, laid his hands gently on my shoulders, and kissed the top of my head. "I'll call you."

I turned and saw Claire watching us. I realized I couldn't read her expression, and that was a first.

22

By the time the police finished their work in our shop, it looked worse than it did before they started. Things were all over the place, including the ever-elusive fingerprint dust, and it took Claire and I most of the day to clean up the mess. The only break we took was before we even began, and that was to hang a sign on the door and call our respective clients to reschedule, claiming an emergency, which wasn't exactly a lie. I contacted Maria and her clients and then called Gina. Claire called Connie, who she said was horrified and stated she thought maybe it was time she looked for a job somewhere else. Who could blame her after the last few days? Maria, though, didn't sound overly surprised, and I immediately wondered if she had something to do with it but just as quickly told myself that it was a ridiculous thought. But was it? She had been keeping a secret about knowing Velma, after all. And what was the connection between Maria and Buford? They obviously knew each other, which she had been keeping mum about as well.

Gina didn't pick up her phone, so I left a voicemail for her, uncertain if she had been planning on coming in today anyway. In the voicemail, I asked her to call her clients since I didn't have any of their information.

We blasted up the volume on the stereo and listened to the likes of The Beach Boys, Carrie Underwood, Audio Adrenaline, and Nirvana, covering every genre of music we could think of. The only person allowed in was the locksmith, who we called to change the locks even though they weren't damaged or tampered with. If Claire didn't leave the door unlocked, that meant someone had somehow gotten hold of a key, which in itself was disturbing. If Claire and I were the only two with a key, how could that have happened? Unless —

"Know what just came to mind?" Claire interrupted my train of thought. Whatever she was thinking about clearly upset her. We had finished cleaning up, the last CD had stopped playing, and we had just sat down in the office. I looked at her eyes, huge and shadowed with horror.

"Tell me."

"Melanie, your house is keyed the same as the shop!"

"Oh my hell, that's right," I murmured, more from irritability than fear.

"I told you —"

"I'm fully aware of what you told me." My mind

raced in circles before I pulled it back together. "It's unlikely whoever got in here would know that," I reasoned. "And if they did, it's too late now." I stood, grabbed my shoulder bag, mindlessly brushed away some stray strands of hair from my face that had fallen out of my ponytail, and began punching in the numbers to the locksmith again. "Hopefully I'm not too late."

I jogged to my car, phone to my ear, unaware Claire was following right behind me until I heard the passenger side door opening. She got in, buckled up at the same time she closed her door, and ordered, "Go!"

After giving the locksmith my home address, I hung up the phone and spun out of the parking lot and onto the highway. "What are you doing?" I asked, suddenly remembering she was right beside me.

"Going with you, what does it look like? I'm not letting you go alone in case someone is there."

Her statement amused me. "What in the world are you going to do? You wouldn't hurt a spider."

"Only because they crunch when I step on them. It's disgusting."

I couldn't help but chuckle, weary with exhaustion and fear. Though I didn't want Claire to know that.

"Mel, about William—"

"What about him?" I hadn't thought about him most of the day.

"Do you trust him?"

"As much as I trust anyone, I guess." I glanced at her, hoping she would continue. Claire's intuition was exceptionally spot-on most of the time. "Do you?"

"It's just a feeling I have."

"A feeling? You'll have to do better than that."

"Weird things have been happening since the first time he came into the salon."

"True that," I muttered with more than a little sarcasm. "But he didn't know Velma, wasn't there when she died, and neither vehicle is registered to him."

"And what about the one he was driving?"

"I don't know." I sighed, swerving into the lane next to me to get around a car that was insisting on going the speed limit. I wasn't exactly high in the patience department right now. "Coincidence?"

"You don't believe in coincidences."

"He said it belonged to a friend. Maybe it's not a bad idea to give him the benefit of the doubt."

"At this point, I don't think you can afford to give anyone the benefit of the doubt."

I stole a glance at her. "Does that include you?"

Neither of us spoke until I couldn't stand it anymore. "Stop staring at me. I can feel you burning a hole right through me."

"You're not taking this seriously. And you didn't answer my question."

"You didn't ask me a question; you made a statement." I swerved again, and Claire grabbed the dash with one hand, the door with the other.

"Wishing you would have driven your own car?" I glanced at her as I accelerated again.

"It crossed my mind."

We rode the rest of the way in silence until I turned onto the country road that led to my house. "Look down that dirt road when we pass to see if any cars are sitting there."

"Cars as in plural or a particular car? Say a dark-green BMW?"

"Either, or."

I slowed slightly and turned my head to look down the long, lonely road despite telling her to.

"Nope," she said, craning her head to continue looking after we'd passed. "I didn't see anything."

"Me either." But something was amiss. I just couldn't put my finger on what it was. A chill rippled through me, and I shivered, grateful Claire wasn't looking in my direction when I did.

I pulled up in front of the garage door, not bothering to pull in. We both got out and ran up to the house, Claire taking the porch steps in one giant leap with her long legs.

"Did you do the hurdles in high school?" I asked, not really expecting an answer.

"Nope. Dance line."

"Of course you did," I said over my shoulder as I unlocked the door, grateful it was still locked.

Once inside, we each went in different directions so we could take in the full scope of my small and humble log home. Seeing nothing out of the ordinary on the main level, Claire bounded the steps, two at a time, to the loft, me trailing right behind her.

"Nothing missing, right?" she asked, breathless. Given her obsession with working out, I knew it was from nervous energy rather than exertion.

"Not that I can tell." I opened my closet door and stood rooted in place, staring at nothing but my clothes that remained untouched. Something was off, though. I could feel it. But what the heck was it? I turned in a slow circle to take in the rest of my room, my desk, my reading chair, my—that's it! I hesitated for a moment then crept over to my nightstand. Someone pulled the drawer out the tiniest bit. Next to the nightstand, the mattress had the faintest indent where someone would have sat and tried to cover it up. I stood completely still, unable to even breathe as I looked down at my bed and nightstand.

" —is it?" Claire's voice jarred me back to the fact that she was in the room with me. "Melanie?"

"Someone was here."

"But I thought you said nothing is missing."

"It's not."

"Then how do you know?"

I looked over at Claire, her face contorted in confusion. "Look at this."

She came and stood beside me. "Look at what?"

"Claire, you keep a journal, right?"

"Of course I do. But what does that have to do with any of this?"

"Where do you keep your journal?"

"The same place everyone probably does—"

"In your nightstand, right?" I asked, interrupting her.

"Yeah. Why?"

"Someone was in my nightstand." I pointed at it and turned to see if she was finally catching on. She wasn't. "My nightstand drawer is slightly ajar." I pulled it open and saw my journal askew. "I prove my point." I pointed to the bed. "Someone was sitting right there."

"Melanie, we need to call the cops," she whispered.

"I can't prove anything at this point. Once I have something to substantiate my claims, I'll call the police."

"If someone is after you, Mel, it's too dangerous to do on your own." Her voice shook. "I don't like it. You at least need to report the creeper from the café."

"It was twice in a public place. They'll just say he was there at the same time as me. Coincidence. Besides, I won't be doing it on my own." I looked at her. "You'll be helping me."

"Me?!" Her voice squeaked.

"Yeah. We'll be careful. I promise." I kept my eyes trained on her, waiting for what seemed an eternity.

"Fine!" She exhaled, defeated. "But if you do anything stupid…"

"Really? Since when have I done anything stupid?"

"Like just now when you said you're going to do this on your own like she-woman."

"I'm not on my own, remember? I got you. And we're going to sort this out if it's the last thing we do."

Claire groaned and rolled her eyes. "Please don't say that. Because it just might be."

I gave her a half squeeze and said, "Come on. I'm staying at your house tonight."

"Finally, you're talking some sense." She turned and hustled down the stairs.

I turned to follow behind her but turned back. "Go downstairs and wait for the locksmith. I'll be right there. I'm going to grab my toothbrush and clean clothes so we can leave as soon as he's done." I walked into my bathroom and caught the faintest whiff of a familiar scent, which I couldn't place. Where did I know that from? It was a perfumed scent mixed with a hint of cigarette smoke. Uneasiness followed. Buford was a smoker.

23

As soon as the locksmith left, I called my grandmother to tell her about the burglary at the shop, deliberately leaving out the part about the visitor at my house. It would serve no purpose except to cause her undue worry. I swore Claire to secrecy.

I took a quick shower before we left my house, and when I came back downstairs, clad in a light sleeveless T-shirt and shorts, my hair still wet, Claire had all the drapes pulled in the living room, and she was curled up in the corner chair. I couldn't help but laugh.

"What?" she asked. "I'm not about to take the chance of your stalker watching me."

"*My* stalker?" I hadn't thought of it that way. "I just need to figure out what he wants from me so I can put a stop to it. Then he'll leave me alone."

"Don't you think we should have the cops dust for prints? Maybe they'll find something on your nightstand."

I shook my head. "He's much too clever for that. There wasn't a single print left behind at the shop."

"I suppose."

She was so hesitant I wasn't sure she hadn't

already called the police when I was in the shower. "Tell me you didn't already call them, Claire." When she didn't answer, I narrowed my eyes at her. "Claire?"

"No, I didn't." She sighed. "You told me not to."

"I don't want them out here making a mess of my house like they did the shop. And I don't want them going through all my personal stuff. Besides, all they would do is tell me to be sure to lock my doors, give me a business card, and tell me to call if I notice anything out of the ordinary. Of course I'm going to keep my doors locked, but that didn't keep the intruder out the first time."

"I suppose you have a point. But I still think it's a mistake not to let them know so they can file a report."

"All that will do is create paperwork on their part and wasted time on ours."

"Just out of curiosity, what makes you think it's a he?"

Good question. One I had to think about for a moment before answering. "I guess I don't know. But it's not too likely a woman would stalk another woman. Or I wouldn't think so anyway." But now that she had raised the question, I realized I wasn't so sure about the gender. I guessed I was sure it was going to be the bearded creeper from the café. "Come on. Let's go."

By the time we got to Claire's, it was dusk but still hot and humid. This summer had had no mercy on us. The air insisted on sweltering, and it felt like I hadn't even taken a shower. In fact, despite driving with the windows down, my hair was still damp.

While I made up my bed on the sofa, Claire called Syd to say goodnight. I crossed the spacious room to look out the window at the streetlights almost all on by now. My anxiety lessened as I watched a family down the block trying to find a lost softball. Or at least I assumed it was a softball since they were all carrying softball mitts and shuffling their feet around in the grass looking for something lost.

I saw a car down the street that seemed oddly familiar. I turned off the living room light and closed the curtains. I peeked through a sliver of an opening on one side. The thought popped out of nowhere to call William. Claire was right. Too many weird things had been happening since he'd come to town, including the creeper. Was he up to something? And if so, why, and why me? I definitely caught a whiff of cigarette smoke in my room and William wasn't a smoker. Of that, I was positive. Even so, I had to know.

I reached for my phone and punched in his number. It rang four times before going into voicemail. I left a brief message for him, looked out the window again, and saw the car had left its post. Perhaps my mind was running away with me, and I was making something out of nothing. I was turning every vehicle into a suspect, as the corporal had hinted at.

My phone rang, causing me to jump a mile. I looked down to see William's name and number on the display.

"Hi, William." There was a lot of noise in the background, so much so that I had a hard time hearing him. I pressed the phone closer to my ear. "Where are you?"

"Jaxon's."

"Alone?" I was almost afraid of the answer and wished I hadn't asked. Had he met someone else while he was in town? And who could blame him with the way my life was shaping out to be. I would run as fast as I could if the shoe were on the other foot. And I wasn't up for a relationship right now, anyway. Or so I kept telling myself.

"Meeting with clients." His voice got louder as he tried to talk over the noise. "I saw I had a missed call from you, but I obviously couldn't hear my phone in here."

Claire entered the room and watched me as she sat on the turquoise sofa. She reached for a peach and turquoise throw pillow and hugged it to her chest.

I felt silly thinking William had anything to do with any of this. He wasn't in a car at the end of Claire's block two short minutes ago. Jaxon's was at least a twenty-minute drive from here. "I don't want to bother you. I was just calling to say hi."

"I'm so glad you did. It's always good to hear your voice." My heart melted, if even just a little, and I felt like a schoolgirl with a crush. As soon as I hung up, I realized Claire was still watching me, frowning.

"Let me guess," she said with as much enthusiasm as a rock. "Boy wonder?"

"Yup. And until you have a reason not to like him, I think you're being completely unfair."

"Probably." She sighed. "Guess I'm just trying to find an answer to what's been going on."

"Such a committed gal you are," I teased her, and she tossed her pillow at me and grabbed an identical one, pulling it to her chest again.

"You don't have to sleep on the sofa, you know. You would sleep better in Syd's room."

"That's her space. I don't want to take over when she's not here to have a say in the matter."

"You know as well as I do she wouldn't care if you slept in there. In fact, she'd be thrilled that her aunt Melanie used her room."

"All the same, I'm fine on the couch." Somehow, I felt safer on the couch, knowing I could hear better if anyone tried to make a middle-of-the-night entrance.

We stayed up and talked until midnight, striving to devise a plan on how to proceed regarding the unwanted guest at the salon and my house. I was eager to have my home be mine again and not a crime scene. I needed it to be my sanctuary again.

Early the next morning, I carefully and quietly folded my blanket, laid it and the pillow at the foot of the sofa, and went home to shower again. It was so hot in Claire's house last night, and she wouldn't let me keep any windows open for fear someone would snatch me up during the night. She should be so lucky.

I showered and dressed in record time so I could be sure to have time to sit on the deck with my coffee, my notebook to scribble some poetry, and the newspaper. I spent most of the time just looking out over the lake. The beauty of it was always breathtaking and something I never quite got used to. I wouldn't give up my usual routine and the serenity of my mornings because of some moron trying to disrupt my life—for what I had yet to figure out.

As I sat there, however, my mind wandered all over the board and would not stay focused. What in the world did this person want? Was it a client? Buford? Cain? Even Maria, Connie, and Gina came to mind. I'd proven it wasn't William. My mind traveled back as far as I could remember, trying to think of any potential suspects, male or female, thanks to Claire's question about how I knew it was a male. Was I looking at it all wrong? Was it a woman? Maria, perhaps? My mind was coming up blank. I couldn't think of anyone that would have a grudge against me for anything. But if it didn't have to do with A Cut Above, what could it be? Was it one of Cain's goons? But if that was the case, that again begged the question—why? Not that he was a stand-up husband or even a great man, for that matter, but this went far beyond what I believed he was capable of. Or even interested in. His current wife? But doing something like this just put me right back in his life when all either of them wanted was to live their lives without me in it.

I began questioning everything he had done, every business trip he went on, trips we had taken together. Unless—could it have something to do with my accident? I knew it was a stretch, but I had never remembered exactly what happened. Could I have done something to someone without remembering, and now that someone was getting revenge? I saw that in a movie once. In a movie on the Lifetime Movie Network I watched a long time ago, a woman cut a man off in traffic, and he stalked her and tried to kill her. "This is why you don't watch TV anymore, Melanie. You forget it's fiction," I muttered in the stillness. Maybe it was all connected to my disturbing dreams. Surprisingly, I didn't have one last night. I fully expected to, but maybe sleeping over at Claire's was a good deterrent.

Whatever the case was, I wasn't getting any poetry written or any reading done. The newspaper was yet unfolded, my coffee nearly untouched. This was getting me absolutely nowhere. I may as well head into work. I grabbed my heels and my shoulder bag, locked up, and headed for my car, still parked in the drive. I was almost to the car door when I turned to check my house one more time to be sure I'd locked it. That way, if anything should happen, I would know for sure that it wasn't me who left the door unlocked as I had questioned Claire about with the shop.

Satisfied that both locks were secured, I zoomed out of my driveway, windows down, sunroof open, cranked up the volume on my Kutless CD, and drove my happy little self to work, hoping I wouldn't pull up to the same scenario as yesterday. Although, I was reasonably confident that whoever it was wouldn't do the same thing twice, two days in a row. He or she had to be smarter than that. And yet, when I pulled into the parking lot, I realized I had been holding my breath. I exhaled with relief when all was quiet.

I spoke with Jack yesterday, who let me know he wouldn't be able to make it until today, which was for the best anyway. I had teased him he always had a way of getting out of work, and this time he finagled his way out of cleaning up the mess. But he insisted he was going to stay at my house for a couple of nights to be sure I was okay. Like he was a threat to anyone. Claire was more intimidating than Jack, and that wasn't saying a whole lot. I felt so incredibly blessed and lucky that I had such amazing, loyal friends.

I locked the salon door behind me, and halfway to the office, went back to recheck it. This had to stop. I was developing OCD, for crying out loud. I mentally scolded myself and resolved to trust myself more. How in the world was I going to solve this mess if I was turning into a mess?

I no sooner got settled at the desk when I heard Claire's key in the lock, the little bell jingling to announce her presence. I didn't hear her footsteps coming my way, so when she rounded the corner into the office and I didn't even jump, I smiled. The small things that made me happy.

"What are you so happy about?" she asked.

"What do you mean?"

"You look either pleased to see me or guilty. Which is it?"

"Happy to see you, of course."

She dropped her bag on the floor and plunked down on the chair across the desk from me. "What time is Jack coming in today?"

"Around five. He's going to be staying at my house for a couple of nights. Wants to be sure I'm safe." I snickered.

"Jack? What would he do to an intruder? And why the smirk?"

"Because I thought the same thing. About you, too."

"Hey! That's not fair," she complained. "I can be one tough cookie."

"I've known you for a long time, Claire Davis, and 'tough cookie' is not how I'd ever describe you. Cute as a button, and I'll even give you sassy. But tough cookie? Not so much."

"Whatever." She gave me a half-smile, narrowing

her eyes at the same time.

I chuckled, shook my head slowly, and stood. "Let's get this day rolling, my friend."

"I'm gonna run next door to the grocery store and get a muffin. Want one?"

"Of course," I answered. "When have I ever turned down a muffin? Especially for breakfast."

"Or lunch, dinner, or anytime in between. I don't know how you do it."

"You have no room to talk."

"Yeah, but I work out. Like a lot."

"I run."

"When's the last time you ran?" she challenged, hands on her hips.

Okay, she had me on that one. I shrugged. "A while."

Not even ten seconds after she left, I heard the bell above the door jingle. "Don't tell me you need money," I called out.

"No, I don't," came Maria's voice. Just who I was dying to talk to.

24

I walked out to the salon and saw Maria setting her things down at her station.

"Got a minute?" I asked.

"Sure." I waited a beat until it was clear she had no intention of giving me her full attention. Or any at all for that matter. Instead, she continued getting her hair cutting things ready for the day and then began fixing her hair.

"How are you doing? With the whole thing with Velma. And now with the salon yesterday." I desperately hoped she didn't hear anything unusual in my voice. That would shut her down for sure, and I needed information.

She shot me a sideways glance. "Fine. Why?"

"Seeing someone die isn't easy to handle."

"I'm fine." I tried to listen for what she wasn't saying but got nothing at all.

"Is there anything you need? Do you have a support system?"

"I've talked with Connie about it."

"Did that help?"

"Yup."

She was making this anything but easy, making

me ask question after question. Too many more, and she would surely question my motive. "Okay." I stood up. "I just wanted to check in with you."

"Are you doing the same thing with Gina and Connie?"

I felt my face get hot. I was so busted. "I'm not sure what you mean." I was such a terrible liar. But I sure had been practicing a lot, so soon I should be all too good at it.

"Checking in with them."

"Of course. Why?"

"No reason."

I waited a fraction of a moment longer and turned to walk away. I got halfway to the office, stopped, and turned toward her one more time. I had to know. "Maria?"

"Yeah?"

"Has Buford Woods been in lately?"

"Who?"

She was really going to play this game? "Buford Woods."

"I dunno. Why?"

"No reason," I mirrored her from a moment ago.

"Maybe Gina would know."

"Yeah. Maybe."

What was she hiding? And why? She was quickly

becoming a suspect in my mind, and I didn't like how that felt.

From my desk in the office, I heard Maria puttering around in the salon and soon heard Connie's voice, the two of them murmuring, too quiet for me to hear what they said. I contemplated making the bold move of going out there and blatantly inserting myself into their conversation but quickly decided that was a stupid idea if ever there was one. The conversation would come to a dead halt. Should I hide a recording device? Now I was sounding just plain desperate.

The bell jingled again, and I watched the open office door, expecting Claire to come through it. What was taking her so long anyway? I opened the desk drawer to look for something and jumped when I heard a familiar voice. Just not the one I expected.

My breath caught at such a gorgeous sight, and I smiled. "William?" He was holding a bouquet of the most vibrant blue-violet irises I'd ever seen. I was more of a daisy and sunflower kind of girl, but I had to admit the flowers he extended toward me were beyond beautiful. "What are these for?" I took the flowers from him and instinctively put them up to my nose and realized I'd never smelled an iris before. It smelled faintly of grape. It even made my mouth water.

"Falcon Prides."

"Excuse me?" I looked at him over the top of the bouquet.

"That's the name of this specific variety."

"Oh." The man knew his flowers. "They're beautiful. Thank you!"

"It's a peace offering."

"Yeah?" I heard my voice go up an octave higher at the end of the one short syllable. "For what?" I braced myself for the answer. Had he done something I was unaware of? Had he been with someone other than a client at Jaxon's?

"I had this feeling I was in the doghouse."

Now I was confused. I turned to get the recently empty vase that the brilliant orange flowers he brought not too many days ago once occupied. "Did I do something to make you feel that way? Or did you do something you want to tell me about?" I held my breath in anticipation of what he was about to say.

"I thought maybe you were still upset with me for being a no-show the other night. Yesterday morning you didn't seem too happy with me."

I rolled my eyes as I filled the vase with water, my back to him. What did I expect? That he was going to admit that he'd been out with someone last night?

Besides, it's not like we were exclusive, even if he had gone out with someone else. We were simply enjoying one another's company while he was in town. Well, *mostly* enjoying our time. Too many questions about too many people, and the questions tumbled around in my brain like laundry rolling over and over in a clothes dryer.

"It's fine." I turned to face him and smiled. "Really. Claire and I had a great time with just the two of us." I heard his footsteps light on the floor behind me as I walked out to the salon and set the vase of flowers on the front reception desk.

"May I invite myself over tonight?"

I busied myself with arranging the flowers to avoid meeting his eyes. "You could..." my voice trailed off as I searched for the right words.

"But?"

"But my friend Jack is staying with me for a few days."

"Jack as in Jackie?"

"No, Jack as in Jack."

"Should I be jealous?"

So he didn't know Jack. There went my recent question of whether it was Jack with whom he was interested rather than me. I had planned to ask Jack about it when I saw him later. Guess I wouldn't need to now. I felt a sense of relief. "You could, but it wouldn't do you any good." I smiled at him. "Jack is the one who has the display of clothes and jewelry over there." I nodded toward the brilliant display. "Next to Claire—and my grandmother, of course—he's my dearest friend."

"Exactly how dear?"

"William—Hmm...do you realize you've never told me your last name?"

"Scott."

"Scott who?" My eyebrows arched.

"That's my last name. Scott."

I chuckled at my inept ability to communicate sometimes. But I would never have thought of Scott as a last name. "William Scott," I said, trying the name on for size. "In answer to your question, William Scott, Jack is a very dear friend, and only a friend." Amused, I turned to look at him, daring to meet his eyes with mine. "Are you jealous?"

"Perhaps."

"Like I said, you're welcome to stop by, but it will be the three of us. Probably four if Claire comes by, which I suspect she will."

"Sounds like a full house."

"Yes. And you don't like that much," I mused.

"How about lunch today?"

I stepped around to look at the appointment book to see if anything had been canceled that I was unaware of. Nope. I looked harder to see if there was anyone scheduled for longer than what it would take, hoping. I heard a muted *tap, tap, tap,* surprised to realize I'd been absently tapping the pencil eraser on the open page.

"If you want to bring something here about two o'clock, I can spare a half-hour, and we can eat in the office. Or even out back on the picnic table if it's not too hot." Claire and I kept an old red wooden picnic table out back in the grass and a picnic basket, complete with red-and-white-checked tablecloth, at the ready in the office in case we had time to relax. It didn't happen much, but when it did, it was nice.

"Would I get more time if I schedule a haircut?"

I couldn't tell if he was joking or not. "You just had one." I laughed. "And no, you wouldn't. I have a new client scheduled for an hour at one-thirty. It's a man; a man's haircut never takes me that long."

Claire breezed through the door, breaking the spell of the banter between us. I looked around and saw that Maria and Connie had left as well. Probably someplace they could gossip some more and be sure I wouldn't be able to hear. *Paranoid much, Melanie?*

"We have company so early?" Claire asked. She

looked at William as she passed him, giving him a smile that didn't quite reach her eyes.

What in the world was up with her? I was almost embarrassed about her barely civil behavior and wondered if I should apologize for her. Maybe it was fear of being left out if something transpired between William and me.

She waved the bag in the air and called over her shoulder, "Muffins are here, Mel. Come eat it while it's still warm."

Instead of making it even more awkward, I kept my mouth shut, determined to ask her when he left. I walked him out to his car with confirmation that he would be back at two o'clock sharp.

On my way back into the salon, I caught sight of Connie and Maria walking from behind the building.

I felt a pang in the pit of my stomach, but waved, forced a smile, and called gaily, "Where you girls been?"

"Out back on the picnic table."

"Glad someone's getting good use of it." I waited for them to catch up to me and caught the smell of cigarette smoke when they did. "Connie, I thought you quit."

"I did." She looked away, but not before I saw the heaviness of guilt in her eyes. "For a while." She looked down at her feet and then up at me again. "If I don't smoke, I resort to my next drug of choice. And that drug isn't healthy for my love life."

"Which drug is that?" Maybe I was taking the same one without realizing it.

"Food." She sighed. "And then all those people who say I'm voluptuous," she ran her hands from her head down to her thighs, "will say I'm just plain fat." Now she formed a circle in front of her with her arms and puffed out her cheeks.

I laughed. "Smoking's a hard habit to break. Or so I've heard," I hastily added. "I wouldn't know personally."

"Of course you wouldn't," Maria said under her breath.

"Meaning?"

"Just that you're health-conscious is all."

Such attitude! I bit my tongue and counted to five before speaking. "That would be Claire who's the health conscious one. Do either of you know if Gina is coming in today?" Gina kept her own appointment book, so I never knew. As long as she paid her booth rental on time, neither Claire nor I worried about when she'd be in. Until now. Now I wanted to know so I could keep track of my surroundings until I'd gotten some answers to questions I had. I was becoming a bit of a control freak.

"I don't know. Maria, have you talked to her?" Connie asked.

"Why would I talk to her?"

Oh, I don't know. Maybe because you're hiding something? I thought. As I looked at her now, the white stripe in her hair reminded me more of Cruella de Vil than the lightning in a dark storm cloud. "We'll find out soon enough. By the way, have either of you spoken with your clients that were in here the day Velma died?"

"No." Connie was first to answer. "Mine is coming for a nail rebase tomorrow, though."

"What time?"

"Two, I think."

"Maria, have you talked to your client?"

"No."

"When is she coming in again?"

"She's not."

My heartbeat picked up. "Why not?"

"She moved."

Bingo! "Out of state?"

"Probably. It was last minute. Said her daughter needed her help."

I made a mental note to check the client files for her phone number, hoping she had a cell phone and wasn't like some of our older ladies who hadn't kept up with the times by getting one. While a house phone would probably be disconnected, the chances of a disconnected cell phone was less likely.

"See you guys inside." I turned to finish the ten steps to the front door but stopped and turned back toward the girls on step three. "Connie, if you're serious about kicking the smoking habit without turning to food as a pacifier for withdrawals, I will cover the cost of seeing someone to help you quit. Whatever insurance doesn't pay, just give to me."

"You'd do that?" Her eyes were huge, and her mouth dropped open.

"Yes, I would." I smiled at her and turned to finish the ten steps to the front door as I heard Connie's voice behind me.

"Wow, thanks, Mel! You really are the best."

Take that, Maria. I felt my cheeks get hot with shame. Was that why I made the offer to Connie? To throw it in Maria's face? Had I stooped to that level? I'd like to think not, but in all honesty, I couldn't be sure. Not anymore, and that bothered me. This whole thing was turning me into an ugly person. It almost felt like I was transforming into Violet. Yikes! Now there was a frightening thought. I had to get to the bottom of this. And fast!

I headed straight to the computer to access the client files. I had no sooner logged in when Maria and Connie came in and stood beside me, one on either side. I guessed it would have to wait. Just as well, because my first appointment had just come in.

25

Jack pulled his car in front of the salon at precisely five o'clock. I had never known anyone in the world as punctual as he. Gina came in for a few hours, and Connie had left for the day. Maria was just finishing up her last appointment. Claire had just finished a color and was singing to the music that piped through the speakers. I had just taken my last client for the day back to the shampoo bowl. It had been a grand day once my dear, loyal friend got out of her funky mood by some coaxing on my part. I was just about to give up and decided I would try one more time by spraying her with my water bottle. And that was all it took to get her laughing like she was Syd's age.

I was combing through the wet hair of my freshly shampooed client, Tillie Tilbury, and listening to her tell me about her son-in-law, who worked out of town more than he was home with his wife, Tillie's daughter Charlotte, and their two children. My attention traveled in and out while she was talking. It felt like I was on a mental obstacle course. Her story made me think about William. Maybe he had a family somewhere waiting for him to come home after working hard out of town. He said he didn't have kids when I asked, but if he did, would he tell me the truth? I realized I took him at his word for whatever he told me, a dangerous move for someone I didn't know well. A man who cheats on his wife wasn't exactly trustworthy and wouldn't be forthcoming with that information. We had done nothing to qualify as cheating in society's standards, but it would have been according to my standards if he was married. Yet one more thing I'd chosen to worry about. I realized I had even bigger trust issues than I'd ever thought I did.

" —car, Mel?"

My mind skidded back to the present as I heard Tillie's voice. Good thing, too, since I had just finished working through the tangles and was about ready to make the first cut.

"I'm sorry?"

"I asked you if you got a new car."

"Not since the last time you were in. I got it quite a while ago." I sectioned off her hair, glancing at her in the mirror she faced. "Why do you ask?"

"I thought you had a sassy little Nissan." She let her chin drop toward her chest, her eyes remaining focused on my reflection in the mirror as I cut the hair at her nape.

"I do. Which car are you talking about?"

"The sexy little silver Jaguar." She reminded me of one of those little string puppets, her head bouncing up when she opened her mouth to talk.

I snapped my head around to look outside the large window in front of the salon. "Where do you see a Jaguar?"

"It's parked out front, close to where you usually park." She turned to look out the window as if to prove to me it was there. "Hmm, now isn't that strange." She frowned. "I swear it was there."

"I believe you, Tillie." It wasn't like William had the only little silver Jaguar in the world. I swiveled her chair so she faced forward and smiled at her in the mirror from behind her. "But in any case, I still have my Nissan, and it suits me just fine."

Jack came back from running to the grocery store to pick up some pizzas for tonight's dinner. "Did you see a Jaguar in the parking lot?" I asked him over my shoulder while I continued to cut Tillie's hair. I did my best to sound casual, confident I was successful when he didn't pause before answering.

"Didn't pay attention. Hope you like whole wheat crust because that's what I bought."

"Yummy," I retorted under my breath, loud enough for Tillie to hear. She laughed, and I stopped cutting long enough for her to sit still again. "Did you at least get some good toppings on it?" I asked him as he disappeared into the office.

"Of course," he called out to me. "Turkey-Roni and dairy-free cheese."

"Why don't we just eat the cardboard it comes on? Might be tastier."

Claire let out a hoot. "I'm with Mel on this one, Jack."

Jack peered out from the office. "If you two ladies would like to poison your bodies with junk food, you'll have to do it on your dollar. I'm not contributing to your bad habit."

"Claire, how much money ya got?" This time everyone laughed except Jack, who glared at me over the top of his glasses before retreating into the office again. Good thing he knew how much I loved him.

Speaking of poisoning. "Tillie, how are you doing with Velma's death? Any idea when her funeral is going to be?"

"Whenever her son can make the arrangements. My son said he'd help him, but he said he wants ta do it hisself. Our boys know each other, you know."

My attention heightened as I hung on her every word. "No, I guess I didn't know that. Where does her son live?"

"He moved away a few years ago, so I don't know

where he lives now."

"Did he ever come back to visit her?"

"Nope. That boy's trouble if ever I saw it." She *tsked* her obvious disapproval. "My son said the same thing. That boy is no good."

"When's the last time your son saw him?"

"Year or two ago. He saw him in town, and do you know that boy never stopped to see his mother? What kinda child does that?" He wasn't exactly a child, but that fact didn't seem to matter to Tillie. "Reminds me of my son-in-law. Now that boy is surely a heartache to his mama."

Jack came out and did some cleaning up and rearranged his display. My mind traveled while Tillie continued her incessant talking, now about things that had nothing to do with where my mind was. Which was half an hour back. I finished styling Tillie's hair, walked with her to the front desk to check her out, and sent her on her way with a hug. I watched her walk to her car.

I continued thinking about the conversation we had about her son-in-law and about the mysterious car she saw parked where I usually park mine. Since the whole weirdness with the green BMW began, I had started parking in different spots so I wouldn't be as predictable as I usually was. My grandmother had always told me it was a good thing to do anyway. She'd told me several times that because I lived alone, I needed to be cautious and aware of my surroundings. She suggested taking different routes to and from work, making frequent checks in my rearview mirror, especially when I got closer to my house, and changing up any routines that had me out and about, including where I grocery shop. Of course, I gave little thought to that advice until now, but I hadn't told her that.

"I hear William came by to have lunch with you today," Jack said as he was working on his display.

"Yup." I cleaned my station, wiping everything down.

"I hear he doesn't much care for Claire," Jack added.

I stopped and turned to look at him and then at Claire, who was doing a fine job of pretending not to hear the conversation. But knowing her as I do, I knew she was tuned in to every single syllable. "Huh, wonder who would've told you that? Because if it's Claire" —I glared at her— "she gives him a reason not to. Besides," I added indignantly, "It's Claire who doesn't seem to like William."

"How am I responsible?" She looked at me, eyes wide with an innocence that I saw right through.

"Aha! I knew you were listening!"

Jack made his famous tsk of disapproval. "Ladies, puh-lease stop your bantering."

"Well, why would she say it's my fault that William doesn't like me? Besides, I never said I don't like him. Not exactly, anyway. It's just that I don't know who we can trust right now. And him being a stranger and all, well..." her voice trailed off.

"Yeah, we wouldn't want to give a stranger the benefit of the doubt, would we?"

"Stop that this instant," Jack scolded me, his eyes twinkling with unshared laughter. "I swear —"

"No, don't swear. It would hurt my virgin ears." My sarcasm was less than endearing, but at the moment, I didn't care.

Jack scowled at me, his eyes shooting darts over the rim of his black-framed glasses. "As I was saying —" he cleared his throat dramatically — "you two are more like sisters than business partners."

"We're not just business partners, we're friends," Claire and I piped in unison, an admission that melted some of the tension in the room.

"And we're not just your everyday run-of-the-mill fair-weather friends. We're besties," Claire added.

"Besties?" I stopped what I was doing and stared at her. I'd never heard that term before.

"Clearly, you don't have a little girl to teach you the cool words."

"Nope, I've got you." I belted out the words to the tune "I've Got You, Babe!" using the broom handle for a microphone, sounding every bit as good as Cher, I was sure.

"Apparently, you think you're a better singer than you are," Jack said.

I sprayed him with my water bottle, the most-used weapon in our salon. I was relieved when I saw it narrowly miss Claire's client, who was standing at the front desk paying. After she left and the door closed behind her, I turned out the lights.

"Come on, gang. Let's get to my house so we can eat that stuff Jack calls pizza."

We stayed huddled together until Claire locked the door, which I tugged for good measure, and we headed to our respective cars to form a caravan out to my house.

I was so focused on mentally replaying my conversation with Tillie that I hadn't even thought about the mystery car or any of the other unsettling events until I pulled in my drive. I looked in my rearview mirror and saw Claire close behind me. Another vehicle that had been between her and Jack zipped on by too fast for a side road, clearly impatient with our leisurely pace, and then finally Jack turned in. I couldn't help but smile. What a fine evening we were going to have. I only wished I would have thought of inviting my grandmother. Not that she would have come, but she may have surprised me. There was always tomorrow evening since Jack would still be here.

26

As soon as we got in the house, I turned on the oven before setting down my things. Jack carried his bags to the spare room, and I escaped upstairs to change into my usual sweat shorts and a T-shirt so I could kick back and completely relax. Claire opted to stay in her work attire, which, being a maxi dress, albeit vibrantly multi-colored, was nearly as comfortable as a nightgown. And she totally rocked it, as she did anything she wore. She took off her signature scarf, though, letting her wild curls spring free.

When I got back downstairs, Jack was putting the pizza in the oven. I looked around for Claire and spotted her in the living room.

"What in the world are you doing?" I asked in disbelief.

"Closing the curtains. What does it look like?" She was reaching to pinch together the slightest gap at the very top where the two curtains met in the middle.

"Claire, that's the beauty of living in the country away from everyone. I can leave them open and enjoy the outdoors without worrying about anyone looking in. And that includes watching the moon and stars after dark."

"Yes." Claire turned to look at me. "Under normal circumstances. But yours are hardly what I would call normal lately."

"Claire—"

"Melanie, in case you forgot," she interrupted me, sounding more like a mother than a friend five years my junior. She turned toward me, hand on her hip. "Everyone is not staying away from you out here."

I grumbled, more at the inconvenience this person placed on my lifestyle than at Claire. I knew she was right, but I didn't have to like it. And I didn't. Not one bit.

"Stop pouting," she said. "Until this bozo quits harassing you, a few safety measures aren't too much to do. It's not forever."

Not liking my independent lifestyle threatened, I was more determined than ever to figure out who this person was and find out why he focused his unwanted attention on me. I was glad it was cooler today. Not only was it more comfortable not sweltering to death, but it made me just a little less irritable. A good thing for Claire and Jack.

We all three sat cross-legged on the floor with our pizza and iced tea. Well, Claire and I did. Jack sat all prissy on the chair, claiming it was too hard to get off the floor these days. I think he just didn't want to wrinkle his slacks.

"Jack, Claire has a dress on, and she's even sitting on the floor."

"It's not my fault she's not acting like a lady."

"Jack!" Claire yelled, trying unsuccessfully to sound angry.

"Just because you girls choose to sit where most people walk doesn't mean everyone else is prone to doing the same. I walk on the floor and sit on chairs."

"Jack Dancy, has anyone told you how stuffy you are?"

"Has anyone told you how unflattering those shorts are to your behind?"

"No sir!" I argued. I stood and turned my backside toward Claire. "Claire?"

"Mel, you know I think you have a cute behind, but I gotta agree with Jack about those shorts."

"Whatever." I sat back down. "I like them and will be sure to wear them every single time one of you is here."

"Well, I certainly hope you'll launder them occasionally," Jack said.

"Launder?" I asked, trying not to laugh, the sound erupting anyway. "I don't know about you, my friend, but I wash my clothes, not laaaunder them," I said, drawing it out dramatically.

Our bantering was comfort food for our souls, and it was exactly what I needed right now. We continued to banter until the pizza was gone, our souls and our stomachs full. Claire picked up the plates and discarded them in the trash (the beauty of using paper, though not for the landfills, and Jack rarely allowed me to get away with it), Jack refilled our glasses with iced tea, and we settled in, this time Jack getting more comfortable as well. He even went so far as to take off his jacket. Yup, I couldn't let that one go. I teased him. He would have been let down if I hadn't, after all. I was sure of it.

"Okay, crew," I said. "It's time for a collaboration of the mega minds."

"About what?" Claire asked. I'd gotten to know Claire like an open book I'd read countless times. I watched as she settled in, her eyes glittering in anticipation.

"Who killed Velma, and who it is that's been making a nuisance of himself in my life. And why to both questions."

"Why do you assume it's a *he*?" Jack asked.

I gave him a did-you-seriously-just-ask-that look. I didn't like being asked a question I didn't have the answer to.

"Well?"

"Claire asked me the same thing, and I don't have an answer. Intuition."

"That's hardly dependable."

"Thanks for the vote of confidence." I lifted my glass, cheering him.

"I'm just saying, if you have your mind set that it's a man, you could be completely overlooking critical clues. When Velma died, it was only women in the salon, so if your theory stands correct, that's proof positive that the women you know aren't innocent."

"There's just too many things that lead me to think this stalking thing is a man."

"Not one and the same, then, obviously."

I looked at him without saying a word while I pondered what he had just brought up. "Never thought about it until just now. All I know is my bet for the stalker is the creeper." I filled Jack in, realizing I hadn't talked to him at length since then.

"I think Buford's involved somehow," Claire said, wholly convinced she was right. "The guy is a sandwich short of a picnic. Or William."

Jack finally spoke up after chewing on every word we'd said so far. And knowing Jack, even mulling over things that we hadn't said. "Something doesn't make sense with that theory."

"Which one? And why?" I asked, more than a little intrigued.

"About William. Because if he were going to do something to you, he's had ample opportunity without having to sneak around."

"True," Claire admitted reluctantly.

"What are you thinking, Claire?" I knew she was thinking something and unsure if she should say it out loud.

"Well...maybe he's trying to woo you before going in for the kill." Her eyes flew open wide, and her perfectly colored cheeks turned crimson. "I—I mean..." she stammered, "I didn't mean kill as in *kill*." She made a stabbing motion with her hand like she was auditioning for the movie *Psycho*. "I meant kill as in what his intention is. And that's not to kill. But to—"

I reached over and touched her hand that was still in midair. "Claire, you're in a hole. Stop digging."

"You know what I meant, right?"

"Yes," I assured her. "But it's not William."

"How can you be so sure?" she asked.

I wanted to answer her question, but I couldn't. Because it was based on a feeling. And even I knew how stupid that sounded. My feelings hadn't served me well with what was best for me. I finally sighed, long, drawn-out, and ran my hands through my hair. "I can't."

Jack said, "Mel, you're too close to the center of this to be objective."

"How about we end this roundtable discussion and pop in a movie? You guys up for it?"

"I'm in." Claire sounded all too delighted to get away from the subject at hand. "But I'm going to go call Syd first to say good night. I can't wait for my little bug to be back home with me." She wrapped her arms around herself. She walked up to the loft, grabbing her phone off the end table as she did.

I stood in front of the cabinet that held all of my movies, my eyes scanning them. "Any requests?" I asked Jack, glancing over to where he was sitting, engrossed in reading a text.

"Not a chick flick," he answered, miles away, preoccupied as he began typing what I assumed was a response. I looked at his furrowed brow and stopped skimming the movies to give him my undivided attention.

"Everything okay?"

The light on his phone showed an incoming message that captured his attention again. He finished reading, typed a quick response, and tucked the phone in the pocket of his linen jacket that lay draped over the back of a chair. "So what did you decide?"

"You agreed to watch *Terms of Endearment*."

"I so did not!" he countered. I could tell he wasn't entirely sure he hadn't.

"Anything you want to talk about?" I asked gently.

"Nah."

"You know I'm here for you, right? I mean, should you decide you want to talk."

"Of course." He smiled that smile I loved so much. The one that made his eyes soften and crinkle at the corners ever so gently. The one that showed a half-moon of the whitest teeth ever. "Thanks."

"Thanks for what?" Claire asked, bounding down the stairs. "What'd I miss?"

"You missed Jack say he wants to watch *Terms of Endearment*." I looked at him, smiled, and winked.

"No sir!" Claire's eyes were wide with disbelief.

"No sir," I agreed.

A sudden loud, sharp bang from the front of the house sent us all up in the air a mile. We all looked at each other, eyes wide.

"What was that?" Claire whispered.

"You ladies stay here, and I'll check it out."

"You'll do no such thing, Dancy," I retorted, my voice a sharp whisper.

Probably looking like something out of a *Three Stooges* episode, we held onto each other and made our way to the kitchen window that faced the front of the house where the noise came from. We heard another noise, though quieter than the last, and cautiously peered out the window through a sliver of an opening in the curtains. We all three stared at two sets of translucent eyes reflecting the light, looking right back at us. The culprits of the racket were becoming nightly visitors. This time, though, there was a whole family of them. Perhaps a mama showing her babies how to get into a trash can. As they tried to get inside, the entire metal can tipped over and sent the cover scattering. They were likely just as startled as we were. I was sure that every raccoon in the surrounding hundred-mile radius was out to get me.

None of us could move as we breathed in sweet relief and watched the bandits move swiftly into the blackness behind the garage. "Geez! Jumpy much?" I asked no one in particular, exhaling all the pent-up fear. "This whole thing has got us all in a frazzled mess."

"Speak for yourself," Jack replied, a picture of calm. "I knew it was those pesky critters all along." I saw him smile before he turned to walk back into the living room. "Now how about that movie?"

"*Jane Austen Book Club*?" I asked.

"That one I think I can do," he agreed.

27

I was the first to wake up. I tiptoed to the kitchen as quietly as possible to make coffee, careful not to wake Claire, who had stayed the night on my sofa. The floor felt nice and cool beneath my bare feet. As quietly as I could, I filled the coffee pot's water reservoir, added an extra dose of good strong French roast grounds, and turned it on to brew. With three of us, there would be no Keurig this morning, but real, fresh-brewed coffee. As the machine hissed to life and the stream of hot coffee began its slow trickle to the bottom of the pot, the aroma wafted through the kitchen right beneath my nose. I think I just might have drooled. Fresh-brewed coffee was one of my absolute favorite smells in the world, ranking right up there with the smell of early morning autumn air and fresh-cut grass. Thinking of them now awakened whatever part of my brain may have still been sleeping.

I felt refreshingly calm and at peace this morning. And so grateful. The three of us had had such a fun time watching the movie last night, and Jack made us promise if we ever started a book club, he would get to be in it. But he also made us promise it wouldn't be

Jane Austen novels we read, but something a little less relational. Men. As I waited for the coffee to finish, my mind replayed the conversation.

"Like what, *Little House on the Prairie*?" I teased him.

"Are those books even around anymore?" Jack returned, clearly surprised.

"Those books will always be around. They're classics."

"I would call them classics," he had argued.

"They most certainly are." Claire had come to my defense. "Sydney has even asked me to read them with her."

"And that makes them a classic?"

"Yup," Claire had insisted.

I smiled to myself and poured a premature cup of coffee from the half-full pot expertly so that I didn't spill a single drop onto the hot plate. Waitressing skills were like riding a bike. Once you learned the tricks, they never left you. I replaced the pot to finish catching the rest, took my cup out to the front yard, and perched on the top step. The concrete was cool on the backs of my thighs. I wrinkled my nose at the overturned garbage can, the cover a few feet away. When would I learn to get heavier cans? And lids that firmly attach. I certainly hoped the little rascals got something worthwhile out of the mess anyway.

I looked at the mess on the ground, noticing some raw meat scattered around the cans. I couldn't for the life of me think of where that would have come from. I hadn't cooked meat in such a long time. I shivered despite the early morning sun shining down on me. I wanted to believe the coons carried it here from a neighboring campground but thought it highly unlikely. Someone visited me last night; I was sure of it. As much as I hoped it was a prank from kids visiting the area, I honestly didn't believe that.

I looked around me, scanning for anything that appeared out of place or like someone might have been here. I stood on legs that felt like Jell-O and walked over to the mess. I bent over and studied the disgusting piles of goop, my stomach turning from the smell. If these pieces were still here after the coons feasted, how much had been dumped here to begin with? I looked for anything that would give some sign of who might have done this. Other than a partial footprint, not enough to give me any idea about size or tread, there was nothing. I stood and carefully surveyed the area in all directions around me. Of one thing I was sure, there was no one here now except me and the two sleeping beauties in the house. Despite wanting to fill them in and see if either of them heard anything last night, I kept it quiet for just a few moments longer while I processed the possibilities. So much for enjoying the serenity of the morning. Why someone had it in for me was still the million-dollar question.

I plunked back down on the steps. A tiny chipmunk, cheeks full, began climbing up the side of the steps, quickly scurrying back the way he came when he saw me move. I heard my cell phone ringtone through the screen door behind me and winced. Darn! I had forgotten to silence the ringer, and now it was too late. Claire was one of the lightest sleepers I knew, and it would surely have woken her by now. Surprisingly, not even the noise from the coffee brewing woke her. She must have been exhausted.

I waited, expecting her to come out behind me but half hoping she wouldn't yet. As much as I loved her company, right now I wanted to be alone with my thoughts and the little critters scampering around the yard. And my insatiable curiosity of who was out to get me. I had to admit, it was more than just a little unsettling. It was interesting how the daylight made things so much less ominous than the nighttime. It was easier to feel a false sense of security and safety during the daytime.

I looked at the lawn in front of me, the droplets from the fresh morning dew making the blades of brilliant-green grass look picturesque. As much as I hated spiders, the webs laced throughout the grass glistened, looking darn near beautiful.

I set my coffee mug on the concrete beside me, leaned back on my hands, and stretched my legs out in front of me. I leaned my head back and closed my eyes, inhaling deeply, slowly. Not ten seconds later, the door opened behind me, and I felt Claire's presence hunker down beside me.

"Mornin'," I said, keeping my eyes closed.

"Top o' the mornin' to ya," Claire replied, her tone letting me know she was smiling and happy.

I tipped my head back up, opened my eyes, and looked at her. "How was your night?"

"Great. Once I fell asleep anyway."

I cocked my head to the side. "Couldn't fall asleep? Why?"

"I couldn't stop thinking about our conversation."

"Well, that narrows it down for me."

"Your sarcasm is out of control. You know that, right?"

"Yup. Be a little more specific." I smiled and wrapped my arm around her shoulder, giving her a quick squeeze. "What conversation?"

"Mel—I just can't shake the feeling that—well, that—"

"Take another drink of coffee and try again," I teased.

"I just don't think you're taking this whole stalking thing seriously. And I worry about you."

"On the contrary," I answered quietly. I pulled my legs in, my feet directly beneath my knees, and leaned slightly forward. I studied my toes, noticing the peeling coral polish. I picked at it, stopped, and sat up straight to look at Claire, studying the overturned garbage can.

"Gross! What's that stuff on the ground?"

"Raw meat."

"From where? We had pizza last night."

"I know." I was hoping not to have this conversation with her, knowing full well she would freak out on me.

"Where did it come from?"

"Good question."

I felt Claire's stare hot on me. "Are you saying what I think you are?"

"Depends on what you think I'm saying."

"Melanie Hogan, knock it off."

"I think we had a visitor last night." My voice was quiet.

"This has gone far enough. You're gonna call the police today. If you don't, I will."

"I'll call." I turned my head to see her staring at me. "I promise." Satisfied, she went back to looking at the gift that had attracted the raccoons. "Wanna help me pick that up?"

"Not really." She wrinkled her nose in disgust. "But I will."

I leaned over and nudged her with my shoulder. "You're such a good friend. But I'll do it."

"Make Jack help you."

I chuckled.

"What?" she asked.

"I'm visualizing Jack in one of those white Tyvek suits, complete with shoe covers and gloves, careful not to get it dirty."

Claire chuckled, and after a moment, it got quiet again. "Are you scared?"

I took a deep breath, followed by a drink of coffee, keeping the cup in my hands. "A little. I'm trying to focus on Velma's murder and solving that. Keeps my mind occupied. Not only that," I added, "it might be nice to know if we have a murderer among us at the shop."

"Have you told your grandma anything that's going on?"

"As little as I can. I don't want her to worry."

"Hm."

She took a sip of coffee, and we each got lost in our own thoughts, staring into the open ground before us. But I knew it wouldn't last long because my sweet Claire can't stay quiet for long. And true to form, she piped up even sooner than I thought she would.

"Maybe you should stay with her for a while. I mean, just until we figure out who's doing this. And why."

"I've thought of that. But I don't want to draw whoever it is over to her house and put her in any danger. Jack will be here for another two nights. After he leaves, I'll reassess, okay?"

"Okay. You could always stay at my house after Jack leaves." I didn't say anything. "You know that, right? Besides, I think it'd be kinda fun." She had that silly grin on her face. "It'd be like a grown-up slumber party. You could sleep in Syd's room until she gets back."

"Yeah, I know that. And I thank you. But do I really want this person to disrupt my life?"

"If it means keeping you safe, then yes. You do."

"Thanks for telling me what I want. And I appreciate the offer, Claire. Truly, I do. But just in case we don't find out who it is, I don't want Syd to be in any danger. I'd rather stay here."

"Mel, you're so darn pigheaded." Her emotional explosion took me off guard. "That's a bonehead move, and you know it." If Jack wasn't awake already, he would be now.

"I know you think William is guilty. Of what, I'm not even sure *you* know. It seems like you just want him to be guilty of something. We have no proof whatsoever that he's behind any of this. Exactly the opposite." But I could tell I hadn't convinced her. "Claire, think about it. What motive does he have? Every crime has a motive behind it. And things have happened when he and I were together. Like one of the times I saw the green beamer. And the creeper in the café and again at the restaurant."

"Your investigator skills suck." She was pouting, and now I was amused.

"Investigator," I mused, knowing I was driving Claire crazy. "I kinda like that."

Behind us, the screen door whined as it opened. "Who's investigating what?"

I turned to see Jack standing there with a cup of coffee. "Nice hair, buddy."

Claire looked up at him. "Good thing you know a good stylist or two."

Jack was unimpressed by our teasing. He ran a hand through his hair. "Are you going to answer me or what? What are you investigating?"

"What do you think?" Claire threw me an accusatory glare. Wow! She could be so sweet with Jack and then turn dark toward me.

"William's trying to get a hold of you, Mel." I looked at him as he read the unspoken question in my eyes. "Your phone's been ringing."

"Screening my calls?"

"His name and number were on the display. I could have answered it if you'd preferred."

"Naw. He'll call back. Or I'll just call him on my way to work."

"What time do you ladies have to be in today?"

"Nine."

"It's eight," he said after I looked at my bare wrist. "Better get going."

"Good thing we don't have to get our hair done before work, huh, Mel?"

I rifled my hand through Claire's unruly hair. "Yeah, good thing."

I briefly filled Jack in on the unsettling visit last night. I watched as his brows furrowed, his lips forming a tight line as he thought about it. The only thing that appeased him was when I assured him I would call the police today to make a report.

"What are you gonna do with yourself today?" I looked up at him as he set down his coffee cup and extended a hand to both Claire and me, pulling us up.

"Pick up your trash," he answered drily.

Claire and I exchanged a look of shock and said in unison, "You are?"

Huh! I couldn't say I was disappointed, and I wasn't about to talk him out of it. Instead, I leaned in and kissed him on the cheek. "Thanks."

"Uh-huh. You owe me, Hogan."

Thirty minutes later, Claire and I were hightailing it out of the driveway, kicking up a little driveway dust as we turned onto the road. Claire zoomed right on by the car I saw from the corner of my eye down the old, typically vacant dirt road. And even though it wasn't the green beamer I'd seen in my world lately, something struck me as oddly out of place. A shiver shimmied down my spine, and the skin on the back of my neck tingled. I slowed ever so slightly and looked until the trees obscured my view, swerving to miss a squirrel that nearly just took its last breath had I not looked at that exact moment. I saw Claire's brake lights go on as she slowed down. She probably saw me swerve, and that made me especially glad I hadn't killed the squirrel in front of her. She would have had nightmares for days. She can't handle a dead spider, much less a dead rodent.

I let the wind from my open window dry my hair, planning to pull it back into a ponytail or braid when I got to the shop. I waved a hand at Claire as she turned off to go to her house to take a quick shower and throw on some clean clothes. I already knew I'd be impressed with how good she would inevitably look even though she only had minutes to accomplish it. Some people had all the luck. And the genes.

Sure enough, only thirty-five minutes after I got to work, Claire waltzed in looking like a million bucks and like she spent at least an hour getting ready rather than the twenty minutes she would have had time for.

"Syd called on my way in," she said, a smile plastered on her face. "She misses me."

"Why is that new?"

"It's just nice to hear her voice on the other end of the line. And she said she misses you too," she added over her shoulder as she disappeared into the office.

"I think I miss that little stinker a whole lot more than she misses me," I called to her. And there was a whole lot of truth to that. It may just be the two of them, but they were family. I had no one. Well, I had my grandmother, but that was different. The idea of adoption fluttered its way into my mind again, like a butterfly trying to rid its cocoon. I tried to dismiss it as the crazy notion it was. Again. It was a battle I had with myself whenever I felt void of something. Usually, I couldn't even figure out what that something was. I just knew it left a flashing neon "vacant" sign across the expanse of my heart.

"Why's it so quiet in here?" Claire interrupted my pity party of one as she came back out to the salon area, minus her shoulder bag.

"Both of our first appointments are late."

"Huh. Weird." She took four long strides across the floor to the desk and looked down at the appointment book. "Connie and Maria?"

"Both taking the day off."

"Double weird. What do you suppose is up with that?" She lathered coconut lotion on her hands and turned to look at me.

"No idea." I suspected it wasn't coincidental. But it was just as well. This gave me a better opportunity to call Maria's client since she didn't answer her phone yesterday and didn't have voicemail.

"I'm gonna walk next door and get a croissant for breakfast. Want one?" I looked up and saw her looking like she had when she saw the raw meat by the garbage cans this morning. "What?"

"Like that?"

"Like *what*?"

"Nothing." She looked back down at the appointment book.

I probably would have been reluctant to proceed too after someone snapped at me. "Sorry. I'm just in a funk today."

"Anything I can do?"

That's my Claire. Always the rescuer, wanting to be sure everyone was taken care of. I felt a rush of guilt. I knew I was often quick-tongued, and Claire was used to it and the most forgiving person I'd ever known, aside from my grandmother. In fact, that was exactly what I needed to cure my ailment. A good dose of Nana.

"Naw. Thanks anyway." I pulled my hair back in a quick pony and dusted some light pink blush across my cheekbones and some pink gloss on my lips. "Better?"

"Much. You look beautiful."

"Liar. Good thing I love you. Now, do you want anything?"

"Yes. The biggest caramel roll they have. Better yet, get me two." Her eyes took on a dreamy look, reminding me of chocolate pudding.

"Two? Did I hear you correctly?"

"Yeah. I'm stress eating." She pulled a face. "And I am not, by the way."

"Am not what?"

"Lying. You seriously have no idea how beautiful you are."

"Touché." I knew she was stretching the truth, even if it was her truth. I mean, I was confident I wasn't ugly by any stretch, but I could be the poster child for Plain Jane if she were an actual person.

"Don't forget you promised to call the police. Maybe you should stay here and do that while I run next door."

"I'll git 'er done as soon as I get back." I made a mock salute and turned to open the door, nearly knocking William over as I flung it open.

"Oh!" I gasped, feeling my cheeks turn from light pink to hot crimson. "I'm so sorry!" I could have sworn I saw a flash of irritation spark in his eyes but dismissed it due to my own funk.

"Where are you off to?"

"Just next door. Want anything from the bakery?"

"Okay if I walk with you?"

"Wouldn't you rather just wait? I promise I'll be right back." I noticed how nice he looks in his tan crisp linen jacket. I looked up to see him focused on something other than me. My gaze followed to what—or who—had captured his attention. Claire.

"I think it would be best if I came with you."

I rolled my eyes. "You two have got to learn to play nice."

"I will if she will."

I stopped walking and turned to face him, my hand on his arm, turning him toward me as gently as I could at the moment. "Did you seriously just say that?" My head tipped back in a short laugh. "Oh my gosh! You so did!" I could see he was less than impressed with my amusement. But seriously? "William, I'm not laughing at you...well, okay, I guess I kind of am. But we're all adults here. Why can't everyone just get along?"

"I don't know, Melanie. Why don't you ask Claire?"

The unfamiliar chill in his tone took me back and fractured my composure, something that was unnerving in and of itself.

"She may be insecure with us, wondering where she fits in. William, she lost her husband, and she doesn't want to lose me too. Which means I have to make sure she doesn't have reason to feel insecure."

I turned to see Claire's first appointment, now nearly twenty minutes late and running toward the door, and my second appointment for the day, almost twenty minutes early, strolling leisurely, nearing us. Two people on opposite sides of the spectrum. Which was exactly what William and I were at this moment.

"Isn't that a little childish?"

I wasn't sure what was going on here, but whatever it was, I wasn't comfortable with it. I met his eyes with my own and said in a voice that I hoped would clear up any possibility of further problems in this area, "William, don't make me choose between you and Claire, because it will be Claire every time."

"I see." His tone turned chilly again. Dang! Midsummer and record heat, but it had been sweater weather lately.

"I don't want to discount what we may be starting here, but Claire has been — "

"I should go," he interrupted, glancing at his watch.

I hadn't taken him for being the sensitive type, but I guessed I was wrong. "No pastry?"

"No time." He leaned in and gave me a quick peck on my cheek, turned on his heel, and strode toward his car, hands jammed in his pockets.

I stood still for a moment, trying to make sense of what just happened, quickly realizing there was no sense to be made of it. I finally shook my head and went back into the salon empty-handed.

"No caramel rolls?" Claire asked, clearly disappointed.

"No time," I echoed William's words.

28

It was two o'clock before I had time to scoot over to the bakery to get our sweet treats. The day was hopping with people coming and going. We had more cuts and updos than chemical treatments today, which caused more people in and out of the salon than on an average day. Especially when it was just the two of us. I even had enough time to attempt calling Maria's client once more from the day Velma died but again, no one answered. For all I know, it wasn't even her number anymore.

I scanned the parking lot on my way to the grocery store, unsure if I was looking for the vehicle that seemed to follow me or for William. I ducked in, got the goods, and walked back quickly to get out of the heat, not to mention the fact that I was practically salivating as I thought of the gooey caramel oozing from the rolls in the bag I clutched. My stomach growled its impatience.

"Hey, Mel," Claire said as I opened the door. "Your phone rang while you were out. Looks like you have a ton of missed calls, but the latest one is Jack."

"Why didn't you answer it?"

"I figured if he wanted to talk to me, he would

have called my phone." Simple in her mind.

I scanned my missed call log to see numerous calls from Jack. "That's odd," I mumbled as I tapped his name on my phone to call him back.

"What is?"

"He's called a bunch of times. If it's that important, why didn't he call you?"

Claire reached for her phone and stopped short. "Oh, man! He probably did. I forgot it in the car this morning after I hung up from Sydney."

Just as she began to say something else, Jack answered. Everything else around me blurred out of focus while I listened to him. I didn't even realize I had sat down until I hung up and realized where I was. Claire stood over me looking worried to death.

" — wrong?"

"Jack had a visitor this morning."

"Where?"

"My house."

"Who?"

"I don't know."

"Melanie, you're not making any sense."

Her eyes pleaded with me to put together a coherent sentence that let her know what was going on. The problem was I didn't know yet.

"He saw someone duck behind a tree by the lake

when he came back in from picking up the trash. He went to investigate, and someone knocked him out cold from behind. When he came to, he was alone."

"Oh man!" She gasped, eyes wide as saucers. "What did the police say when you called them?" I could only stare at her, and she narrowed her eyes at me. "Melanie Hogan, you *did* call them, right?"

"I need to go." I quickly got up and gathered my shoulder bag, kicking off my heels so I could move faster. I looped my finger through the heel straps. "Think you can reschedule the rest of my appointments?" As luck would have it, the remaining clients were chemicals, so there would only be two to reschedule.

"Where is he now?"

"Still at my house."

"You can't go alone. I'll come with you."

"Everyone else is gone, so one of us needs to stay here. I'll be fine."

"You can't know that. Did he call the police? Cause you never did." Her voice was ripe with accusation.

"No. He's been waiting to get a hold of me."

"Seriously?" Exasperation was more than evident.

"What was he going to tell them? He has no description whatsoever."

"I swear there isn't one complete brain cell between the both of you sometimes," she grumbled.

"Thanks." I grabbed my keys and headed for the door.

"You know I'm right," she called after me.

"I know no such thing," I volleyed back over my shoulder, hoping the door quickly closed so I wouldn't have to hear another word.

My mind was traveling faster than my car could carry me. This was getting way out of hand. And now the well-being of one of my dearest friends had been compromised because of his connection to me. Jack would have to leave today, that was all there was to it. My thoughts took twists and turns as if maneuvering a winding road but speeding much faster than was even remotely safe.

As I thought of a million different scenarios, one thing kept popping back up. Why hadn't the assailant harmed Jack more than he had? I mean, it was terrible enough knocking him out, leaving what Jack described as an egg on the back of his head, as well as one nasty lingering headache. But why leave him? Was it because Jack hadn't seen who it was? Was it some kind of a warning? And if so, for Jack, letting him know to stay away? Or for me to know that he — or she — was in full control of the situation and could make things get ugly if he or she chose? How far was this creep willing to take this? And why? That was the million-dollar question. I hadn't seen so much as a whisper of the creeper from the café. But it still niggled at me.

I remembered William's unexpected visit this morning. It couldn't have been him. He wasn't exactly dressed for an excursion in the country, and certainly not one that included assault. Just one more piece of proof that William wasn't involved in this mess.

As my mind raced, my foot pressed harder on the accelerator, getting me to my driveway in record time.

***

Jack and I were sitting in the kitchen brainstorming when Claire called to say her last appointment of the day had left, and she was on her way. I told her not to come but to go home instead. I wasn't at all confident this psycho wouldn't target her as well. But she wasn't having it and insisted on coming.

She pulled into the drive and had no sooner gotten out of the car when two squad cars pulled in right behind her.

Her expression was priceless, a combination of

confusion and guilt. "I swear I wasn't speeding!"

Had it not been for the gravity of the situation, I would have found some humor in it. But as it was, I was worried sick. Not so much for me, but my friends. And for my grandmother. This person meant business.

"They're not here for you." I hugged her tight, feeling like a parent hugging her towering child. "When you said you were coming, I realized I needed to call them and make a report. If something happened to you or Jack or, God forbid, my grandmother, because I didn't report it, I would never forgive myself."

"Too late. Something *did* happen to Jack. Had you called—"

"Not again. I promise."

"Yeah? How? You're all of five feet tall. A veritable giant."

"Never underestimate the amount of dynamite a small package can hold," I said, an attempt to ease her worry.

Officer Mahoney strode over to us, talking to me but stealing glances at Claire. If I didn't know better, I'd think he was smitten. My heart hurt for him if he thought for a second he had a chance. Claire wasn't the least bit interested in dating anyone at this point.

Her heart was still hopelessly loyal to her fallen husband and Syd.

"Can you run me through what happened?" he asked me, notepad and pen in hand.

"I'll have to fill out a statement anyway, right? Can I just save having to say it twice and fill out the statement now?"

"Melanie," Claire scolded in a whisper that sounded anything but threatening. "He has to follow protocol. Can you just do it and not make things difficult?"

Far be it from me to suggest a more efficient way.

I saw Officer Mahoney try to conceal a smile and look down at his notepad. But he wasn't quick enough. "Sure," I said, more to Claire than him. "But the bottom line is I'm not the one who knows what happened. You'll need to talk to Jack."

"Officer Wilson is speaking with Jack right now." He nodded his head in their direction. I looked over and saw Jack apply pressure to his temples as he spoke to who must be Officer Wilson. I needed to get Jack to the urgent care to have his head looked at. It appeared the throbbing wasn't letting up.

"Well, since I came on the scene significantly later, I have nothing to add."

"You may have more than you think," Officer

Mahoney countered. "Start with what Jack told you when he talked with you."

I explained as best as I could remember my conversation with Jack, realizing there was a lot that seemed hazy since I'd been in such a state of shock when he told me. You'd almost think I was the one who was hit over the head.

"Do you have any idea of who might target you?"

"Yeah, a disgruntled client who didn't like getting dissed. Or maybe her new boyfriend," Claire felt the need to broadcast.

I shot her a look that only served to make her straighten her back in defiance. "He's not my boyfriend, and William was at the salon this morning, remember?" I said, probably more harshly than I should have.

"Well, Buford wasn't," she argued. "And he's weird enough to do—this." She dramatically gestured toward Jack.

Officer Mahoney's eyebrows furrow. "You ladies aren't only business partners but friends, right?"

"Yeah," Claire and I said in unison. It seemed an odd time to realize we did that a lot.

"Just making sure." He looked at me and then at Claire, where he lingered a little too long.

"Things have just been stressful lately. At best." I

added.

He painfully tore his attention away from Claire. "Is there anyone else you can think of?"

"Officer, I have a question—how likely do you think it is that this—this—stalker and the person who killed Velma in our salon are one and the same? Could Buford be responsible for both?"

Claire's eyes got as wide as those giant gumballs from those quarter machines I got Syd whenever her mother wasn't around. And about as big as the large, bright circles on the scarf she had in her hair today. "That guy Buford is the reason I don't date."

I looked at Officer Mahoney to be sure he caught that last statement loud and clear, to save him heartache and embarrassment if nothing else. But all I saw as he was looking at Claire was admiration bright enough to light up the blackest night to high noon. And frankly, where before I might have thought it endearing, right now it only irritated me. I rolled my eyes. He'd better not think about coming between mine and Claire's friendship. That's when it hit me— that's why Claire didn't like William.

"Buford?" Officer Mahoney said, amused.

"Yes, Buford. Woods. But he wasn't inside the salon when Velma died," I said, remembering that pertinent fact. "That I know of anyway."

Jack must have finished up because I saw the officer closing his notepad. I wished I had superhuman powers and could pull a Stretch Armstrong move and crane my neck over there to see what Jack told him. As it was, I hadn't even had a chance to fully find out what happened because Jack couldn't remember everything. Jack met my eyes, and I nodded him over to where we stood. Instead, he sat down and began writing on the form the officer gave him. His statement, no doubt.

Officer Mahoney waited for me to inform him about Buford as he kept sneaking peeks at Claire. The thing was, I couldn't tell if she noticed him or not. She didn't seem totally oblivious like she usually did, but kind of — aware.

"Melanie?" The infatuated man spoke. "You were telling me about Buford."

There! That stupid amusement again! I glared at him until I saw the kindness in his eyes. Okay, so maybe I was just sensitive and misreading him. I felt like there was a string that ran down the very center of me, and it kept getting tighter, threatening to snap. *Breathe, Melanie.*

"Yeah — about Buford. He started coming into the salon about a year ago. After the first couple of months, he began asking me out and coming in more frequently."

"Like every three weeks frequently," Claire added. She looked at the smitten officer and wrinkled her nose. "The guy's ultra-creepy."

"As I was saying," I said, giving her *the* look. "I said no the first time, but it didn't stop him from asking again. And the time after that. Each time I said no, but then he started calling between haircuts, *in case you changed your mind*, he'd say. Like that was gonna happen any time soon."

"Or ever," Claire interjected.

"Does he still come in?"

"No, he doesn't. Not to see me, anyway. I told him I couldn't cut his hair anymore."

"Not to see you, but he still comes in?"

"Yeah. I guess he'd been in a time or two when I wasn't there. To see Gina, a manicurist who works at the salon."

"I would guess not to get a manicure."

"Unlikely, since his nails are always dirty no matter how dressed up he tries to be."

"What do you suppose is up with that?"

"With what, coming in to see Gina or his dirty nails?"

"Gina."

"I would have no way of knowing."

"Tell him what else you saw," Claire said. "About—"

"He was talking to Gina outside the salon right after Velma died." I interrupted Claire with lightning speed before she could mention the photos I found in Velma's house.

If there was one thing Officer Mahoney wasn't, it was hard to read. And right now I read disappointment. He obviously expected a tastier crumb than he got.

"You're not very good at hiding what you're thinking," I blurted. Claire looked like she had just swallowed a furball and was about to choke. "Sorry," I muttered. "That was rude."

"We already have the information about Buford being at the salon. What makes you think he would go to this extreme with you?"

"He called me a snob and threatened me by telling me to watch my back cause he'd have the last laugh."

Officer Mahoney's eyebrow raised. "Not too smart to make an outward threat."

"Right? With a name like Buford, you'd think he'd be a little smarter about the whole thing." I was only half joking. And maybe a little patronizing.

Jack finished writing what I assumed was his

statement and set it down beside him. When he stood up, he swayed slightly, but I saw it. He walked over to us, still intermittently rubbing his temples.

"Are we done here?" I asked the officer. "I need to get my friend here checked out by a doctor to see if he has a concussion." I placed a protective arm around Jack.

"Want me to call an ambulance?" he asked Jack.

"Not necessary. Melanie drives faster than any ambulance I know of."

"Jack! Were you struck so hard you forgot you're talking to a police officer? I can't help you if my butt gets thrown in jail."

"True that. I'm fine," he said to no one in particular. "I think I just need to get some rest."

"After someone I trust checks you out and tells me you're okay. That someone being a doctor. Come on, let's go," I ordered.

"You know she won't take no for an answer, Jack," Claire said. "Might as well just go."

"You won't be here alone, will you? It's probably not safe since we don't know who hit Mr. Dancy," Officer Mahoney asked Claire with obvious concern.

"No, I'll go with them. But thank you."

Was that an extra dose of color I saw in Claire's cheeks? And an extra batting of those mile-long coal-black eyelashes? Now I felt like someone had hit *me* on the head. What in God's name was going on? Could things get any weirder around here?

I shook my head and led Jack to my car, Claire right on our heels.

29

As it turned out, Jack had a concussion, complete with a few rush trips to the bathroom as nausea hit. Poor guy. I felt absolutely terrible. A fresh surge of anger pulsed through me. This had to end. Hopefully, the police could track down my buddy Buford.

As soon as we got back to my house, Claire headed home, and Jack settled into his bed, propped up on a few pillows with a good book. The doctor's orders were to keep him awake as long as I could and then wake him periodically throughout the night after he fell asleep. Guess I could sing. That would keep him awake. Or make his headache even worse. I spared us both the pain of listening to my off-tune vocals and let him rest in silence. I did, however, grab a book and prop myself up on the bed next to Jack in case he needed me before he dozed off to sleep. I stayed there all night. It wasn't like there was anything to worry about, and it was no different than if it was Claire. Jack was one of my best friends, like Claire.

Once Jack had fallen asleep, I took the phone and quietly tiptoed out of the room to give my grandmother a call to check in with her. After making plans to go over and have dinner with her after work the following day, panic seized me as we hung up, and I realized Claire hadn't called. I gave her direct orders right before she left to contact me as soon as she got home so I knew she arrived safely. I wondered if I would be able to not worry about any of them ever again. And what that would feel like when — and if — it happened.

Claire answered on the first ring. "Oh my gosh, Melanie! I'm so sorry! I called to say goodnight to Syd and completely spaced calling you!"

"Yeah, I noticed. I won't beat you too badly," I said with as much affection as my tired self could muster.

"Like I'm afraid of you. I really am sorry, though. I didn't mean to make you worry."

"I know." I gave her the latest on Jack before we hung up. But not before she said her usual.

"Melanie—"

"I know. Say my prayers." Every time we talked on the phone in the evening, she always said the same thing. As if I would forget. Though truth be told, as tired as I was tonight, I might have.

I made the rounds, checking all the doors and windows, and anger rose in me again that I even had to do that. I tiptoed back into Jack's room and lay down as slowly as possible so I didn't wake him.

I set the alarm on my cell phone for two hours from now and looked for any missed calls from William. Seeing none, I decided he was probably licking his wounds from this morning when I refused to take his side over Claire. I wondered when he was leaving town to go back home. I picked up my phone, debating whether I should send him a text, and realized I didn't even know if he texted or not. He didn't particularly seem like the texting type. And, again, I realized how little I knew about him. For only meeting him a week ago, it seemed like much longer than that.

I lay back, sinking into the comfort and security of several pillows. When I felt Jack stir, I looked at the clock and realized that I had drifted off. It was nearly time for the first two-hour patient check.

Check complete, but not without Jack's attitude about getting woken up, I smiled to myself, feeling oddly grateful at that very moment.

***

I was in the kitchen pouring a cup of coffee when Jack came in the room behind me, scaring me half to death.

"Geez!" I exhaled loudly, clutching my chest. "Give the girl a little warning, huh?"

"Sorry. Thought you heard me."

"How'd you sleep?"

"How do you think I slept? I didn't."

"That good, huh?"

"You kept waking me up," he complained.

"I did. Doctor's orders, remember?"

"I told him I was fine."

"I remember. But he seemed to think differently. And I don't know about you, but I believe a professional before someone who's just being stubborn. Coffee?"

"Yes, please." He reached for the cup I held out to him. He took a sip and focused on the contents of his cup so hard I thought maybe something had fallen in. "I'm going to head back today."

"I kind of figured you would. That was the plan, right?"

"I want you to stay at your grandma's until this whole thing is done and over."

"I can't do that, Jack." I looked at him, my eyes begging him to understand. "That could put her in danger. I would die if anything ever happened to her."

"You might if you don't stay somewhere safe."

"That's a little dramatic, don't you think?" I didn't want to admit that I was scared and that my brain was scrambling to find somewhere to stay that wouldn't jeopardize the people I loved. But I didn't have to admit it. He knew.

"Okay, fine. Then how about a hotel. I'll pay for it. You're not staying here a single night by yourself, Melanie. That's final."

His demeanor surprised me. I wasn't sure I'd ever seen Jack this worked up before.

"Sure. That's a good idea."

"Excuse me?" He looked at me over the rim of his cup without blinking.

"I will. Stay at a hotel."

"Halleluiah! She has a thread of sense!"

I made a face at him and took a drink of coffee. "I'll call today and make a reservation. I'm going to have dinner with my grandmother first, though. Before I check in, I mean."

"Fine. Gather your things this morning because I have to leave soon, and I'm not leaving you here alone."

"When did you get so bossy?"

"The day I was born."

We drained our coffee, each packed up our things,

and hugged our good-byes not even an hour later. I turned before I closed the door and gave the house a once-over, eager to get back and feel safe. But in the meantime, I had to think of something to tell my grandmother. I couldn't chance that she would make any surprise visits. Not that she ever did, but with the way things were going lately, this would probably be when she did just that.

Halfway to work, my cell phone began vibrating, and I glanced at the unfamiliar number on the caller ID and decided not to answer but let it go to voicemail. On second thought, maybe that wasn't such a good idea. With everything that'd been happening around me, I couldn't afford to let go of any opportunity that may give me a heads up.

I pulled over on the side of the road and listened to the voicemail. I was beyond surprised to learn it was Anne Sinclair, Maria's client from the day Velma died.

I punched the dial-back number and waited for her to answer. "Thank you so much for calling," I said. "But how did you know I called you? I wasn't able to leave a voicemail."

"I check my phone for any missed calls and saw your number on there. Except I didn't know it was you until I called."

"Of course." I felt like a moron.

"What do you need?"

"I was wondering if you knew Velma Johnson."

"Who?"

"The woman who died at the salon when you were there getting your hair done."

"Oh, her. No."

"How long have you lived here?"

"In Iowa?"

I quickly glanced at the prefix of her phone number. It wasn't Iowa. Suspicion awoke. "Birch Haven."

"All my life. Until a week ago, that is."

My suspicion grew. Anyone and everyone who had been around Birch Haven for any length of time knew Velma. "Why the move?"

"I told Maria why I was moving. My son needed my help. I moved into the mother-in-law's suite at his house to help with the kids."

"Yes, she mentioned that. But I thought she said it was your daughter."

A moment of silence. "She must have gotten it confused."

"Yes, she must have. Do you have a daughter?"

"No. Two boys."

How well do you know Maria?"

"Quite well."

And yet Maria didn't know Anne didn't have a daughter? "I see."

"Is there anything else?"

"Just one thing—do you know Buford Woods?"

"Maria's brother?"

"Yes, that one," I said, calmly despite my now-racing heart.

"Of course that one. How many Bufords could there be, right? It's actually her half-brother. Her dad was screwing around on her mom and, well, along came Buford. Listen, I have to go. I'm already late." I could hear someone calling her name in the background. A man's voice. Her son?

"Thank you for calling me back, Anne."

"Just a minute!" she shouted, making me jump. "Not you. Men—they can be so impatient. And Sam's among the most impatient of them all."

"Sam?" The familiar name didn't escape me. The line went dead.

30

I was thrilled when I pulled up to the salon and saw Claire's car in the parking lot. Knowing she was here safe made me feel a whole lot better. As soon as Anne hung up, I had called my grandmother to be sure we were still on for tonight, and having seen Jack off, a shred of the elusive contentment found its way back. All my peeps were safe and sound.

That contentment became shadowed, however, when I noticed that darn nuisance of a BMW on the far side of the parking lot. Something about it just— what was it? It was like those times when I knew the word I wanted to use in a sentence but couldn't for the life of me remember what it was at that moment. Other than seeing it every time I turned around, this car had such familiarity about it, but I couldn't remember why, no matter how hard I tried.

One of my migraines threatened its impending arrival like thunder on the horizon coming near too quickly. I headed for cover to the door of the salon, one of my three comfort zones, the others being my grandmother's and my home. Or at least it used to be. Not so much anymore, and I wanted that back.

I reached for the door handle and pulled hard, but

it didn't budge. Why was it locked? Claire must have run next door. Sometimes it seemed like we spent more time at the grocery store than at our own business. We'd probably purchased enough to own stock in them by now.

I unlocked the door and let myself in. "Claire?" I called out in case she was in the restroom or back in the office. Maybe she was here, and she just didn't want to leave the door unlocked. But only silence answered.

Setting my things down on the reception desk, I scanned the schedule. All four of us would be here today. Possibly five if Gina came in. I was so ready for a day off to do nothing but spend time with my grandmother. Maybe she could teach me a new recipe. Everyone knew I was a little challenged in the cooking department, but despite the old saying, I believed you could teach an old dog new tricks. I was proof, getting better despite what Claire said. And maybe we could even have the old comfort food she always served when her always spot-on intuition knew I was having a bad day. Wild rice hotdish, glazed carrots, and rye rolls with honey. Claire used to tease me about the hotdish scene. Apparently hotdish is only served in Minnesota. I was practically raised on them and was sure my grandmother knew at least a hundred different hotdish recipes. I even knew how to make some of them thanks to her.

Sunlight glistened off something shiny, and I looked up to see Claire approaching the door, her keys with all their bling attached hanging on one finger as she maneuvered two large bags, one in each arm. At the same time she came into the salon, the green BMW drove out of the parking lot. *Good riddance to you.*

"Melanie Hogan! Why is the door unlocked?"

"Ummm...cause I just got here?"

"You shouldn't leave it unlocked, and you know it. With everything that's been goin' on around here, even during business hours, if we don't have any appointments, it should stay locked."

"Well, first, my dear friend, that kind of defeats the purpose of our 'walk-ins welcome' policy. Second, when do we not have appointments? Besides," I added as I looked back at the appointment book, "maybe you should say thank you instead of jumping all over my stuff. Did you buy out the store or what?" I motioned to the two large paper bags carrying more than just breakfast.

She smiled at me, letting me know she'd forgiven me for leaving the door unlocked. "Got most of what I need for the week, plus a few housekeeping items for here."

"Housekeeping items?"

"Toilet paper and paper towels. How was Jack this morning?"

"Better. He left to go back home."

She stopped dead in her tracks. "He what? What about—"

"He made me promise I would stay at a hotel until things are under control."

"And he believed you? How gullible is he?" She sounded angry, something rare for Claire.

"Relax, Cinderella. I've already made the reservations. I'm going to do it."

I thought her eyes might pop right out of her head. "For real?"

"Yes, for real. I may be independent, but I'm not stupid. Well, not always, anyway."

"Which one are you staying at?"

"I can't answer that for purposes of anonymity. How can I be safe if everyone knows where I am?" I ducked the proverbial arrow she shot at me from across the room. "Country Inn."

"Tell me you had the sense to book something other than the first floor. And not under your own name."

"Like I said, not even a minute ago. I'm not a

complete idiot." I rolled my eyes at her. "Who are you, my mother?" A painful jolt ripped through me. "Forget I said that."

"You don't know her complete story. She might have—"

"Stop defending her. She doesn't deserve it," I warned. Claire turned and walked to the back room only to emerge a second later, minus the bags. She slid an arm around my shoulders and laid her cheek on the top of my head.

"Sorry."

"I know."

"Do you think I'll ever get the chance to meet her? I wanna make sure she knows how much she's lost out on."

"'He who has ears to hear, let him hear.' Matthew 11:15," I explained.

"I know what verse it is, but—"

"You can tell her anything you want, but if it's not what she wants to hear—like how wonderful she is— she won't hear you."

I was adamant I knew Violet better than I really did. My grandmother was always careful not to speak ill of her around me, but that my mother hurt my grandmother the way she had was enough to make me more than a little bitter toward her. But if Violet cared about me thinking anything other than the worst, she should have made a point of making an occasional appearance to prove me wrong. Her bad, as far as I was concerned. And yet it stung beyond belief sometimes. Especially the times I saw how Claire's mother would do anything to spend a mere moment with her. Or sometimes when I watched Claire with Sydney. How I wished I had had that with Violet. But somewhere in the last thirty-some years, I'd begun to believe it wasn't to be.

Maria came through the door with a barely audible hello before she began getting her things ready for the day.

"Maria, I talked with Anne this morning." She continued her busy work at her station, but I saw her back stiffen slightly. "What did you say her daughter's name is?"

"I didn't, because I don't know."

"Oh, I was under the impression that—"

"I don't know her very well."

Liar. "That's very odd. Because she said she knows you well."

"Is there something you want to say, Melanie?" She turned to look at me, meeting my eyes, hers hard. "Because if there is, just say it."

"Okay, I will. I find it interesting that Buford is

your half-brother. You've never mentioned that before."

"I don't talk about my personal life."

"No, I guess you don't." Claire watched the exchange with interest.

"Buford's not the villain you think he is, you know." Her eyes glinted steel.

"I didn't say that. Not exactly. Maria, what does he drive, by the way?"

"I don't know."

"I think you do. It wouldn't happen to be a green BMW, would it?"

"I said I don't know. But if it is, what's the big deal?"

Connie opened the door and called a cheery greeting, oblivious to the tension. When no one answered, she stopped, her smile fading. "Is everything okay?" she asked slowly.

"Fine," Maria answered, her voice like an over-tightened guitar string.

***

The day passed by blissfully uneventfully other than my gut telling me something was seriously up with Maria. It was obvious how protective she was of

Buford. Was that protective nature enough to make her want to hurt me? Would she have the strength to hurt Jack? Could she and Buford be in on this together? That would explain the suspicion that two people were involved as well as both incidents being connected. I remembered the mixed feelings of discontent with contentment I'd felt little more than a week ago. How much had changed in that time, external circumstances and internal battles? It felt like it had been a lifetime ago.

My last client of the day was running notoriously late, so I took advantage of the moment to sit in my chair to leaf through the latest issue of *People* magazine. Claire was entertaining her client with a funny story about Sydney making friends with the neighbor's pet ferret.

"I swear that girl would make friends with a polar bear!" Claire laughed.

Experiencing the joy of the moment, of some sort of normalcy, had me so captivated that I barely heard the bell above the door jingle. I looked up, expecting to see my late appointment, but saw William instead. I looked past him through the large glass wall behind him. I willed my heartbeat to slow down as it began reaching dangerous levels. That darn car was going to be the death of me! I took a deep breath.

"Driving the beamer again?" I asked.

"Belongs to a friend. I've already told you that."

"Which friend?" I challenged him with my eyes. *Come on, William. Be honest with me. Just once. Please.*

The challenge wasn't accepted but manipulated. "What are you doing tonight?"

"I have plans."

"Can we talk privately?" he asked, his voice little more than a whisper.

"I have an appointment that should be here any minute."

"Can you spare me the minute until she arrives?"

What was it that had me so on edge about the growing familiarity with this car? Other than seeing it everywhere I went. I begged my subconscious to remember something. Anything that would help make sense of my mood. I could chalk it up to paranoia, but under the circumstances, paranoia was warranted.

"Then what about after work?"

"I'm having dinner with my grandmother." The minute the words were out of my mouth, I wanted to kick myself into next week. The last thing I wanted anyone to know, other than Claire, was where I was going to be. Everyone had become a suspect in my eyes. "Whose car is that?" I asked, hoping for something a little more believable and less vague than "a friend's."

"I told you—"

"Yes, I know. A friend's. I'm just curious what friend it belongs to. I thought you don't know anyone around here."

"Melanie, why the twenty questions?" His voice was quiet, undoubtedly not to draw attention.

"No reason," I lied. I knew I was being unfair by assuming he was withholding information from me, but under the circumstances, I was a little on edge with anyone connected to a green BMW. Heck, at this point, *any* color BMW.

I was literally saved by the bell as my last client walked in. I laid down the magazine and stood to greet her with a warm hug. "Have a seat, Suzanne. I'll be right there." I turned to William. "Talk later?" I smiled at him, trying to act as normal as possible when normal was the furthest thing from what I was feeling.

"I'll call you." But I wasn't sure I was convinced. What I was convinced of more than ever, though, is that whatever this was between he and I, it wasn't the right time. It took too much energy. And I needed all of that I could get just to keep my friends and myself safe. But I also didn't know if I had the energy to do anything about it, either. I'd have to see how things played out.

31

After we closed up and locked the door, Claire and I finished the books and put the money in the drop box we just had installed.

"So what's Maria's deal?" she asked me as I covered the floor safe with the cut tile lid.

"I have no idea. Maybe she's finally revealing her true colors."

"Or she has something to hide."

"So your suspicion of William has disappeared?"

"Eh...I didn't say that. Not exactly anyway. I don't know who to trust at this point."

I tried to determine if the whole thing with William was jealousy. "You know no one will ever take your place, right? If I ever start seeing someone—"

"You *are* seeing someone."

"I will never leave you out, Claire. You have to know that."

"I do." She stood and picked her bag up from the floor. "Let's go."

I was eager to get to my grandmother's house and to the warmth and safety of her kitchen. I could almost smell the aroma of dinner and something special baking in the oven.

I glanced in my rearview mirror as I sped off after stopping for a red light, and there I saw a green car turn off in the opposite direction. As long as it kept going in the opposite direction, I was okay, I told myself. And yet — well, something was still niggling at me. Something uncomfortable. About as uncomfortable as the new migraine that was threatening. The one from earlier never came to pass, and for that I was grateful. I'd had more in the past couple of weeks than I'd had in a long while. As far as I was concerned, I was well over my quota. At least I hadn't had another dream for the past couple of nights. That talk with my grandmother must have helped keep them at bay for now.

I just wished I could remember more and see faces in my dream. I knew I needed to have at least one more if I was going to have any hope of that, and I couldn't say I wanted to know that badly.

In my mind I saw Buford Woods's face and the evilness that was just beneath the fake exterior he tried to project. I could even hear his sinister last words and the smell of his disgusting dragon breath that was right in front of my face. *We'll see who gets the last laugh, Melanie.*

At the time, I thought he was just full of hot air.

Should I have taken him more seriously? Did me not taking him more seriously cause him to take things to this level? I wondered what kind of car he drove. As soon as I got to the hotel, I planned to search the internet to find an address for him. Heck, if one knew anything about using the internet at all, you could find out everything about anyone. That thought made me shudder. Is that how this creep found out where I lived and how the guy from the café got my phone number? Where did he come from, and where had he been? Behind the steering wheel and tinted windows of a green BMW?

My thoughts traveled back to Buford. If I could find out where he lived, I could drive by his house and see the car that sat out front. But what if he lived in an apartment? I guess I could go around the parking lot of the apartment complex to see if I could spot a green BMW. But then again, it wasn't exactly an uncommon car and would prove absolutely nothing if I saw one. And that William showed up in one again today, did that have to do with anything at all? I wished I had looked at the license plate, but in my surprise, I hadn't even thought of it. Some detective I would make. I guessed Angela Lansbury could rest comfortably knowing I wouldn't be stealing her title as queen of mystery.

Before I knew it, I pulled into the circle drive in front of my grandmother's house. The sun was shifting slowly down the horizon, making the heat of the day more tolerable. I reached for my bag and stuffed my cell phone into a side pocket. I turned to open my door and jumped a mile, stifling a scream as Nana stood just outside my window.

"Good grief, dear! I didn't mean to scare you. I was just coming out to greet you as I often do." She placed a comforting hand on my back.

I saw the concern in her eyes and leaned in for a hug. "Sorry, Nana. Guess I'm a little jumpy."

"A little?" She took my hand in her own. "Come on. I have the perfect remedy for that."

I stole glances at her as we walked side by side, hand in hand. Her silver hair was pulled back in the braid I knew so well, wiry strands straying free. Her skin was so flawless from her years of careful protection from the sun that it almost looked translucent. The skin at the corners of her periwinkle eyes crinkled as she smiled. What did I ever do to deserve someone so wonderful to raise me? Me, who was so sarcastic and, at times, unforgiving. Despite what Nana taught by example, I was still a long yard behind her in being half the woman she was. I wondered if I would ever get there.

The minute she opened the door, the smell of chocolate wafted toward me. I could almost see the stream right beneath my nose as it showed in cartoons from my days of youth.

I closed my eyes and inhaled the heavenly aroma. "Mmm..." I murmured dreamily, the events of the last couple of weeks fading to nothing more than a distant memory. One that I couldn't recall right now as I only saw what was immediately surrounding me at this moment. Nana and the most delightful, gooey, double-chocolate brownies waiting just for me. "How about I sample one right now?" I asked, hopefully. "You know, just to be sure they're —"

"Don't you even think about it," she warned. "It will —"

"Spoil my dinner," I finished for her, pouting. "What are we having?"

"Good old-fashioned spaghetti."

"With the gigantic meatballs and homemade noodles?" I asked, knowing I sounded more like thirteen than nearly forty.

"Of course."

Glimpses of talking with Nana after an evening out with girlfriends or after a date journeyed through my memory. My friends envied me for the relationship I had with my grandmother. A relationship that was more solid than any of them had with their biological mothers.

"Hello?" she sang. "Where did you go just now?"

Nana's voice jarred me back to the present, and I hugged her. I had an absentee mother, a crazy psycho after me, and a killer in my salon, but all of that faded into the background right now.

"Right here, Nana. Right here," I whispered through tears that threatened to fall and the lump in my throat. Emotions rarely got the best of me, but they were working hard at it right now. "Do you miss Granddad a lot?"

"Every day," she said softly.

"Do you ever regret not remarrying?"

"That thought has never entered my mind."

"Don't you ever get lonely?" I looked deep into those bluer-than-blue eyes I loved so much.

"I have you," she answered gently. "Besides, I was married to my best friend for half my life. I would never want more than that."

"That's something I'll never be able to say." I couldn't decide if I felt pity for myself or anger at the situation. Or merely resignation that that was the way it was.

"You're still young."

"I don't feel so young sometimes. I feel like my

biological clock is ticking away. In fact, it's racing into Neverland. It's jack hammering its way right out of the childbearing years, even for adoption. I'm already too old as it is."

She squeezed me, walked over to peek in the oven, and stirred the spaghetti sauce with the old, stained wooden spoon she used for everything from soup to nuts. "What's the latest on the gentleman you're seeing? Walter?"

"Walter?" I chuckled despite the seriousness of the conversation. "You mean William?"

"Walter, William...I had it close." She grinned at me. "Is there romance blossoming?"

I sighed loudly and plopped down on the stool at the counter, watching her from the back as she tasted the sauce. "Nah. It's—complicated."

"Try me. I think I'll be able to understand," she teased gently, sounding like Claire a couple of short, long days ago.

"It's just—I'm not sure I understand what it is. I don't know if it's there."

"If what is there?"

"It."

"For you or for him?"

"For both of us, I think. I mean, he's drop-dead gorgeous, but..."

"But what?" She turned to look at me and leaned against the counter.

How could I tell her I had too much going on right now to get involved with anyone? Especially when I didn't want her to know what I had going on. "Well, for starters, I think he's the most private person I've ever known in my life."

"I can see where that would be a problem," she said matter-of-factly.

"It just doesn't feel—Oh, I don't even know. I want what you and Granddad had."

"And I want that for you. But it doesn't just happen. It takes hard work. And sacrifice."

"I'm not sure I'm willing to sacrifice anything right now. I don't know, Nana. I can't put my finger on it."

"What does Claire think?"

I half grunted, half laughed. "She doesn't like him very much." I didn't tell her why. "But I think she was coming around."

"Well? I think that says a whole lot right there. That girl likes everybody." She looked at me and turned to take the brownies out of the oven.

"Yes, she does. And Syd is exactly like her."

"Any news on Velma?"

"Nope. Not from the police anyway."

"What does that mean, child? Have you been up to no good?" She turned and narrowed her eyes at me.

"Of course not." My head dropped as I pretended to pick at the pale pink polish on my pinky.

"Melanie Hogan, you're a terrible liar."

"But I love you, Nana. Does that count?" I looked up at her sheepishly.

"You're impossible."

"But impossibly happy you're my grandmother." I heard her chuckle and knew everything was okay.

Suddenly famished, my stomach grumbled its agreement.

32

When I woke up the following morning, the first thought that came to mind was that I needed to call William. As flattered as I was that someone that good-looking wanted to spend his time with me, the timing just wasn't right. I needed to focus on finding out who was after me and who killed my client. Because by the looks of things, the police weren't going to find out, and I would forever remain under a cloud of suspicion. I couldn't afford to be distracted by a relationship until this whole thing was over. It may be too late for William by then, but that was a chance I was willing to take. This relationship stuff was too hard.

I was stuck, however, on exactly how to break something off that really never began. Would it be lame to use the whole *it's not you, it's me*? I couldn't help but wonder why I was worried about telling him. So I didn't want to see him anymore. What was the big deal? I didn't have a problem telling Buford no. But then again, look where that got me—nearly killed. And my gut was telling me it was far from over with that man. Worrying about hurting William's feelings was assuming he was that into me.

How presumptuous was that?

As I lay in bed, the sun streaming across the unfamiliar room illuminating what looked like millions of little dust particles in the air, my mind traveled to the latest events that had been consuming my life. The reason I was waking up where I was instead of in my own bed.

Could Buford be capable of such behavior? I didn't know him well enough to believe one way or another, but his last words certainly sounded like a threat.

And how well did I know Cain? I mean, *really* know him. Obviously not as well as I thought I did, or I wouldn't have married him. Did he want me out of the way permanently? If so, what purpose would that serve? It wasn't like anything tied us together. Like a kid. And if that were the case and he wanted me literally deleted, he would have had ample opportunity to kill me off rather than just scare me to death. And what did he have to gain by hurting Jack?

I began replaying the years of our short-lived marriage, all the way back to the robbery and assault I had witnessed in a convenience store when we were on our last vacation in California. Was I some kind of a threat to the assailants? They were wearing ski masks, and I hadn't seen their faces. But maybe they thought I had. But there again, why go through all the trouble of scaring me and interfering with my life instead of just eliminating me?

I shuddered at how easily it could happen if that was someone's intent. I lived alone in the country, coming and going without so much as a glance over my shoulder, day or night. There had been many times I hadn't even locked my door. If nothing else, this whole thing had taught me that one should never be too complacent.

I remembered the conversation I had with a friend from my church and the story she'd told me of someone trying to get back at her for inheriting a resort that he believed belonged to him. But I didn't inherit this house, and it wasn't a family gift. When Cain left, I bought him out, so it was mine free and clear.

I lay looking up at the ceiling, stretching my memory to remember anything and everything I could. I thought about my dreams again and tried to remember the one I had last night. It wasn't nearly as vivid as some of them have been, but there was something about it that was unsettling. What *was* it?

And then it hit me like a brick crashing through the glassy surface of a pool of water, and I bolted upright, clutching the sheet to my chest, my breath coming short. The puzzle pieces were finally beginning to fit together and lock in place. At least the beginning of the puzzle, getting it started which is usually the most challenging part.

I reached for the phone to call Claire but hung up before punching her number. I needed to talk to her in person.

I swung my legs over the side of the bed, my feet touching the carpet, yet one more reminder that I wasn't in my own home where the first thing my feet touched was the refreshing coolness of the hardwood floor. The same hardwood floor that felt like ice in the winter months. I peeled off my T-shirt and started the water in the shower, letting it run while I crossed the room to be sure I'd locked the door and slid the chain in place. A little late, I know. If it wasn't secured last night, it meant someone would have had all night to come in. And who was to say someone working there that had access to a master key couldn't have come in anytime anyway. Like the puny little chain would keep someone out. I always got a kick out of those. I, in all of my five-foot-two power, could break in through one of those had I really wanted. And yet here I was, hearing the clink as I slid the chain in place.

I called my grandmother to let her know I was

okay. I had told her only the bare minimum the night before over dinner, and just as I thought she would be, she was worried to death. She made me promise to check in with her first thing when I woke up and several times throughout the day. I thought it was overkill, but it was the least I could do given the circumstances.

I allowed the hot water to pulsate some of the tension out of my shoulders before finishing up and dressing in my standard jeans and heels, paired with a loose, flowing ruffled floral silk tank top. I dried my hair and pulled it back into a braid, loose tendrils falling around my face. I quickly applied my makeup staples, mascara and tinted lip gloss, gave myself a quick once over in the full-length mirror, grabbed my shoulder bag, and began unlocking the three locks on the door.

The lobby was already hopping with activity. As I stepped outside, the brilliant sunshine nearly blinded me, and I narrowly missed walking into someone coming in the door. In fact it wasn't a complete miss. "Sorry," I muttered, rubbing my arm where a briefcase scratched it. I turned to look at the person I'd nearly run over, looking at the back of a tall, well-dressed man—was that *him*? It looked eerily similar to the creeper from the café, though I'd never seen him from the back. My breathing became faster until I forced a slow, deep breath, reasoning with myself—if that indeed was him, it would explain why I'd seen him in area eateries a couple of times. And how could I know for sure that it was him who texted me? It could have been Buford, or even Maria, if they were working as a team.

I raced across the parking lot to my car. I couldn't wait to talk to Claire about my discovery from earlier.

I pulled through the drive-through of the Caribou Coffee that was directly across from the hotel and, being the creature of habit that I was, ordered my usual, the Northern Lite Latte. Sometimes I wondered if that was why I got so bored with my life occasionally. Because I so rarely stepped out of my comfort zone and tried something new. I fall into the comfortable rut of day-to-day living without a second thought. I felt comfort in that revelation. At least if I recognized it for what it was, I could do something about it. But if it was because I was like Violet, which was the furthest thing from what I would wish on anybody, then it would be a curse. Something I could easily change versus a curse. Easy choice.

I was disappointed when I pulled up to the salon and didn't see Claire's vehicle. Other than of late, it was a rare day that she arrived before me. When

Sydney was home, she wasn't at the salon any more than she had to be, which I completely understood. But when Syd was at her parents' or at Tyler's parents' for visits, it wasn't unusual for her to get in early. As luck would have it, today wasn't one of those days.

I attempted to keep myself busy by doing paperwork, something Claire hates and something I find comfort in. It took a few minutes to rein in my mind to the task at hand, and once I realized it was a futile effort, I closed the books, stood, and stretched. I was too wound up to focus on anything other than one thing.

As if on cue, and just as I walked into the main salon area, Claire breezed through the door, her happy, jovial self a breath of fresh air as always, proof that things staying the same on a day-to-day basis wasn't such a bad thing.

I hugged her, squeezing tighter than usual.

"Geez!" she laughed. "I just saw you yesterday."

I slid her bag off her shoulder and put it on the front desk. "We need to talk."

"Can I get a cup of coffee first?"

"Oh man! I forgot to make it. I stopped at Caribou on my way in."

"You forgot to make coffee? That's a first, even

when you get Caribou." Her eyebrows raised in question. "You okay there, my friend?"

"I just thought you'd never get here."

"I was in the parking lot for a little bit. That stupid green car is parked across the lot again, so I called Officer Mahoney to see if he can check it out. Just in—"

I jumped up from the chair I had just sat in and strode across the floor to the window.

"Melanie, tell me what's going on." I could hear the concern in her voice.

"I don't see the car. Where is it?"

"It's parked in the back parking lot, behind the buildings. It may be nothing, but I wanted to have him check. Just in case. After what happened to Jack, and with you seeing the same car everywhere you go, including out by your house, well..."

"Claire, I figured something out this morning." I sat back down in the small waiting area tucked into the corner of the salon, and Claire took the chair opposite me. "Okay, listen. You know those migraines I've been having? And the dreams? I think they're connected to what's been going on."

"How?" Her eyebrows knit together. She took my cup from my hand, took a drink of my coffee, and kept the cup.

"When I was in my car accident, I had a head injury, and—"

"This isn't one of those times like in the movies where everything turns out to be a dream, is it? Cause let me tell you, it's not a dream."

I couldn't help but let out an adrenaline-induced chortle. "No, you sweet thing. Just listen. Anyway, I finally remembered the car that's in my dream. The one that's chasing me." I grabbed her arm. "Claire, it's a green BMW. Exactly like the one that has been haunting me for real these last couple of weeks. I woke up this morning trying to remember; it seemed fuzzier than it usually does, but all of a sudden, *wham!* It hit me full on!"

"Well, maybe it's in your dream because you've been seeing it a lot."

"No, it's been in my dreams before I saw it around here. Way before. I've just realized it now is all." I was sitting on the edge of my chair, my hands now rubbing the knees of my jeans, the friction making my legs feel like they were on fire. "I've been recalling clips of my accident, and this morning I remembered something huge. There is a green BMW, exactly like the one that's been around here, that ran me off the road and into that cement pillar of the underpass."

"You mean someone was after you way back

then?" I could have gone for a swim in the depths of Claire's eyes, wide as the ocean as she stared at me. "But—but why?"

"That part I don't know," I answered, sitting back in my chair, biting my lower lip. I was feeling defeated again. "That's where the trail ends." I had tried fruitlessly to remember more while I drove to the salon and couldn't. "Everyone just assumed I had fallen asleep at the wheel because it was at night, and there were no witnesses. Heck, I even believed that. Until now."

Claire leaned forward, set the coffee cup on the floor beside her chair, and took my hands in her own. "Mel," she said calmly, her big, brown eyes looking deep into mine, "maybe you fell asleep at the wheel, and the dream is just a dream. This car might be a mere coincidence. Completely unrelated."

"I don't think so. I can feel it. Besides, you know how I feel about coincidence."

"The same as me. People chalk things up to coincidence too easily when it's often the hand of God. But sometimes—well, don't you think it's a possibility here?"

I looked into her eyes, not really seeing them but trying to make sense of all of this in my own mind.

"Claire, I know I remember the car running me off

the road. It's all so clear now." I was pleading with her to believe me. I could tell she didn't know what to think.

"Did you see the driver?"

"I don't think I've ever seen the driver's face. But the last time, it kind of morphed into Buford's face. I know it sounds weird," I added quickly, seeing the skepticism in her eyes.

"You know I don't like him any more than you do, but this is —"

"Not only strange but confusing. I know. The other confusing part is that somewhere in there, I'm injured. But I saw you emerge from the driver's seat of the car uninjured."

"What do you think it means?" I could almost see the wheels churning beneath her orange-and-yellow plaid headscarf as she tried to make sense of what I was telling her.

"That even though part of it is very real, it's still a dream?" I was losing my enthusiasm that I'd had a breakthrough. Maybe I was having nothing but a break*down*.

"Tell ya what. Why don't we stop by your grandmother's house after work today and talk to her about it. Maybe she knows something that —"

But I was already shaking my head. "No."

"Why not?"

"Because if she doesn't know anything except what everyone has maintained as the truth, that I simply fell asleep at the wheel, then it would only cause her to worry."

"And she would have every right to."

"I don't want to put her through that unless it's inevitable. Claire," I warned, "you have got to promise me you will not mention a word of this to her."

She sighed loudly, sat back in her chair again, picked up the coffee cup, and took another drink. "Fine."

"You're welcome, by the way."

"For what?"

"For finishing my coffee."

"Yeah. That." She grinned. "Thanks."

We heard a loud knock on the door, and we both startled. Claire spilled coffee down the front of her bright orange sundress. I peeked around the corner and saw Officer Mahoney standing there.

"It's Officer Ma—"

"I'll get it." Claire jumped up, forgetting all about the coffee on her dress.

"Ms. Hogan?" he said to me, looking at me for the briefest moment before turning his sights back on

Claire. "Buford Woods won't be bothering you anymore."

"What are you talking about?" I wanted to stand on the chair and jump up and down, shouting, *Yoo-hoo! Over here!* He finally looked back at me as if reading my mind.

"The car Claire called about, the one you've seen around here, belongs to Buford Woods. I called for backup, and they've taken him in for questioning. As it is, they've got nothing to hold him on though, nothing that ties him to the events that have happened here or at your house. He's denying that he had anything to do with any of it."

"I'm sure he is," I muttered with more than a little sarcasm. And I certainly didn't miss the fact that he insisted on calling me Ms. Hogan or ma'am but called Claire by her first name. "Why is he stalking me? Because I wouldn't go out with him?"

"He said someone bought him the car as a gift."

"Who?"

"He doesn't know who. He received a phone call from someone who told him the car is his. All he had to do was promise to drive it around here. Since he works nights in the stockroom of the grocery store, it wasn't a problem for him to agree to that."

Humiliation seeped in that I had assumed it was

all about me. That Buford would harbor a grudge just because I wouldn't go out with him. Yet I was relieved that it could be something so simple, that the car had nothing to do with me at all. But even if it was that simple, that didn't negate the fact that someone attacked Jack at my home, and I didn't for a second believe it was a coincidence that all of it was happening at the same time. Coincidence, my butt. Something wasn't adding up, and I had to find out what it was.

"Officer, doesn't the fact that a stranger bought him the car—and not just any car, but a luxury car— seem a little odd? When he doesn't know who or why, just that he was to drive it around here?"

"I don't buy his story, Ms. Hogan. I think we've got our man, and we'll know that after they finish questioning him."

"And what about Velma? Do you think it was Buford who killed Velma, too? She's rela—" I bit my tongue to stop talking. I had just come within a fraction of getting myself in trouble for breaking into Velma's house. His eyes waited expectantly for me to finish my sentence. "It's nothing," I mumbled, looking away for fear he'd know I was lying. He began to leave after nodding at Claire. "Just a quick question before you leave," I said. I needed to know.

"Is Buford being questioned for Velma's murder too?"

"Detective Wescott is handling the death. But what makes you think he's involved in the murder?"

"Other than appearing outside the salon shortly after, he has connections to two of our staff members. Maria, who's been less than civil since the murder, and Gina."

"Speaking of Gina," Claire said, "does she even still work here? I haven't seen hide nor hair of her."

"You might want to pass that information along to Detective Wescott," I said to Officer Mahoney.

33

Mrs. Tilbury had left the salon an hour ago. She'd wanted more blond weaved through her already too-blond hair. The last couple of times she'd been in, I suggested putting in some lowlights to add some depth and color, but she insisted on blond. Pretty soon she'd be sporting a wig. This time though, she not only didn't have anything good to say about her son-in-law, she didn't have anything to say about him at all. I wondered what was up with that.

Since my stalker had was caught and no longer a threat, I'd decided to enjoy some after-hours quiet time, tucked away in the office finishing up some last-minute paperwork. Music piped through the speakers in the ceiling. I turned out all the lights in the salon, save for the tiny security light left on in the corner by the product shelves. I left only the desk lamp on in the office. Even with Claire having the day off, it had been hectic today, and I was reveling in the silence. Gina even had back-to-back appointments all day. My feet were killing me tonight. I kicked off my heels, hitting my shin on the underside of the desk as I thrust one leg too hard and too high. I cursed under my breath and gently rubbed what was sure to be a bruise come morning.

I heard a sound by the door at the end of the short hallway that ran alongside the office, separating it from the restrooms. The door that led to the back parking lot. My curiosity piqued and then waned as I listened carefully and heard nothing further. I wondered if Buford was released but thought it unlikely that someone wouldn't have let me know if he had.

I pulled my hair back in a haphazard ponytail and just got refocused on the paperwork that lay on the desk in front of me when I heard it again. I stood and walked barefoot to the office door and peered around the corner, down the dark hallway toward the door that faced the back of the building. Nothing but silence and stillness. I swore I must be losing my mind. I grabbed the remote control for the radio and turned it up, a niggling suspicion leading me to turn it off instead. Just in case. In case of what, I didn't know, but just in case anyway. My nerves were still a little raw after everything I'd been through the past couple of weeks. I was sure the police would find some connection between Buford and Velma's murder while they questioned him about stalking me. He'd said it wasn't about me, but if Officer Mahoney didn't believe him, then I didn't either. At the very least, I was certain that Buford would have information to give them to aid in an arrest. Sitting back down again, I picked up my pencil and prepared to add some numbers.

There! It did it again. I bolted upright in the chair, the hair on the back of my neck prickling in fear. I stayed completely still, afraid to move for fear the noise would hear me, as stupid and irrational as that was. I heard the door handle jiggle with force, and now the hair on my arms stood on goosebumps. I knew it wasn't Jack or Claire because they would both use the front door, and no one else had any reason to want to be inside, much less by way of the back door. Not unless they had no business being here and were up to no good. So much for my moment of peace and relaxation after a busy day. I had a hunch things were about to be anything but quiet and a whole lot more crazy.

A flash of anger seared through me, first that Buford would have the guts to come back, and second that they released him and no one told me about it. It was time to reclaim what this jerk was trying to take from me — my sense of independence and well-being. But in the flash of a moment, that feeling of self-empowerment threatened to melt into a puddle of fear. Of all times, I was turning into a wimp *now*?

I reached for my cell phone to call 911 when a loud bang on the door scared me senseless. I stifled a scream and jumped, sending my phone clattering behind the metal cabinet in the corner of the office. Darn! I reached to turn off the light just as I heard the door creak open. My heart fluttered wildly, and I quickly wedged myself between the wall and the cabinet, a space so small I was sure it would take the jaws of life to get me out. I wasn't even sure how I got in there to begin with. All I knew was that I could scarcely breathe from fear and lack of space for my lungs to expand enough to take in adequate air. I looked down and saw my cell phone at my feet, grateful the back light dimmed, and then went off. I didn't want him to see the light and find me back here. As it was, there was no way he could possibly think anyone would fit here. I began praying to hear a voice, wondering if it was possible Buford hadn't been released and it was Connie, Maria, or Gina. It occurred to me it was strange Gina chose today to show up after being gone for days.

Footsteps came toward the office, the sound of the *click click click* on the tile floor getting closer until they stopped in the doorway. Gina wore only tennis shoes, so the sound ruled her out. Maria getting revenge for Buford's arrest? I held my breath, what little I could get in, not daring to move a muscle or even exercise a brain cell until the footsteps began retreating from the office door and into the salon area.

"Melanie?" A voice called out eerily. "I know you're here. Don't play hard to get."

My blood froze when it wasn't Maria's voice, but another I knew all too well. William! Why hadn't I listened to my instincts to begin with? Or Claire, for that matter!

"Come on, Melanie," he called evilly, now sounding anything like the William I knew. Did my taste in men ever stink! "It's just harmless, little ol' me."

Harmless, my butt!

"Melanie!" he called, enjoying himself far too much. "I've always liked a game of cat and mouse, but you know the mouse rarely gets away unharmed. Cats are very crafty." I could hear him making his way through the salon, now over by the product shelves as he swiped the contents of an entire display onto the floor, bottles rolling in every direction.

I willed my beating heart to stop for fear he would hear it. I swore it was pounding against the metal cabinet. Heaven help me if I should have to sneeze from the dust back here. If I got out of here alive, I was going to clean this little nook.

"Melanie!" He sounded out, his voice sharp, impatience penetrating his enjoyment. "You don't like green BMWs so much, do you? Your friend Buford was all too happy to play along for a free car."

He'd been telling the truth after all!

"I have to say it was a fun little game, Melanie. Not one, not two, but three of them. Everywhere you went. A reminder of what you took from me."

What was he talking about? I willed my brain to think despite the lack of oxygen. I heard his steps come back to the office and the sound of a gun cock. Crap! I was so dead! I was just about to spring out to catch him off guard when there was a noise out in the salon. It must have caught his attention as well because I heard his feet shuffle as he turned directions.

"Well, well, well..." he muttered. "Two for the price of one. How did I get so lucky?"

I wanted to see who was out there. Two for the price of one? What did that mean? I wished I could sneak a peek but knew it wasn't possible without him hearing me move against the metal cabinet. Besides that, I wasn't entirely sure he was out of eyesight from the office.

Everything was deathly quiet for a moment, and I wondered if he'd given up and left. And then there was a scuffle followed by cursing. I guessed he'd tripped over one of the bottles on the floor.

"Melanie!" he barked. "You know what you did. Now it's time to pay the price. There are consequences. Pay up!"

My mind raced to figure out what he was talking about. Figuring that out could very well mean the difference between getting out of here alive or in a body bag. Consequences of what? Not sleeping with him? But he hadn't even shown an interest. And he had been with me when I got the text message from my stalker. That was what convinced me it wasn't William. Did he hire Buford to help with more than just haunting me with the BMW?

"Melanie," he hissed again, sounding nothing like William at all, but something so sinister. So evil. "You ran me off the road. You cut me off. Nobody does that and not pay for it. Come on now. It's time to take your medicine like a big girl."

My mind whirled as I tried desperately to make sense of what he was saying. Maybe there was no sense to be made. That would assume he was rational, and I was quickly finding out he was anything but rational. And what happened to the noise I heard just a moment ago that gave me hope? I began feeling slightly dizzy and lightheaded from lack of oxygen, and fear rippled through me as I tried to determine if I was going to die from lack of oxygen or at the hands of this maniac.

"Come on, Melanie," I could hear him talking, but he was standing completely still. "Your carelessness may have cost you inconvenient little headaches, but it cost my sister her life. A life for a life, Melanie, isn't that what they say?"

And like a crack of thunder opening the skies of heaven, memories rained down. I vividly remembered changing lanes on the interstate as if it were yesterday, seeing blinding lights behind me, realizing too late how close the car behind me was, feeling terrible for cutting someone off. And then the lights had vanished. I remembered looking into my rearview mirror again in confusion, seeing what looked like a single headlight off a distance from the road at an odd angle. I remembered thinking it all very bizarre. And then, out of nowhere, a dark BMW was right on my bumper, and that was the last I saw before everything went black. I cringed when I heard myself gasp. William chuckled, an evil sound from the devil himself.

His footsteps came back toward the office door again, his voice all too close. "Well, well, well..." He came closer, slowly, every step painfully closer. There was another noise out by the front door, and I could see just enough to know that he had turned his head away from me. I seized the moment to quickly slide one leg out from the small space that seemed to get smaller the longer I was hostage there. I bent the knee of my free leg and picked up my heel that had been tossed there accidentally. Coincidence? I thought not. I grasped the sole of my shoe in my hand, and as William spun around, I brought it down hard on his head. *Crack!* One, two, three times in rapid succession, making him fall off-balance, allowing me to escape past him. Almost. Until I went tumbling down face first as he grabbed hold of my ankle.

"You brat!" he spat.

I stretched my fingers, reaching my other shoe and hitting his hand that held onto my ankle until he let go. I ran out into the salon, tripping over a bottle, hitting my head on the tile floor. Pain seared through my skull as I went in and out of consciousness. And somewhere between the darkness of unconsciousness and the hope of consciousness, I remembered something huge. I remembered William being in the salon the day Velma died. In fact, right before she died, he was at my station leaving me a surprise. His phone number. It would appear he left Velma a surprise as well.

There was nothing but silence, and I wondered if I'd crossed over to the other side. Were it not for the splitting headache, I might have believed it.

"Mel?" Claire! Oh no! I had to warn her! I tried to yell her name, but my throat was so parched that I couldn't get anything to come out but a squeak. It was like one of those nightmares where someone was after you, and try as you might, you couldn't make a sound or move a muscle to get away.

"Claire!" I finally squeaked louder. And suddenly she materialized, kneeling by my side, her face hovering over me, concern etched in the worry lines around her mouth.

"Melanie, are you okay?"

"William—"

"Is out cold." She reached for my hand and pulled me into a hug, my head feeling like it was going to split right open.

"As in dead?"

"Unfortunately, no. He's alive."

"Man, my head hurts," I complained. I thought it would split right open as the wail of sirens got closer and finally screeched to a halt in front of the shop.

"It should. You cracked it pretty hard. And the tile is harder than your head." I attempted to laugh but winced when pain shot through my head like a spear through ice.

"Did he hurt you?" I whispered, my voice now hoarse.

"No. But I hurt him." She grinned at me, proud of herself. "I saved your scrawny butt."

"No, sir."

"Yes, sir," she argued.

"How?" A medic kneeled by my side as Claire backed up to give him space.

"I coldcocked him."

"With what?" I gasped.

She held up her hand. "With this, dummy."

"What—"

"We'll talk later," she interrupted me.

As the paramedic was inspecting my head and taking my vitals, I watched the officers permeating the place, all in different directions. The one charged with taking care of us winked at Claire.

"Ms. Hogan, we need to stop meeting like this."

"Indeed, we do, Officer Mahoney."

He looked at Claire. "She can't be too bad. She remembered my name."

"Only cause I've been seeing way too much of you," I croaked.

I saw the smile he and Claire exchanged, an exchange that as polite as it would look to strangers, looked to me to be almost intimate. I must have hit my head harder than I even thought. The look he and Claire shared, however brief, made me wonder if Claire had something to tell me. As many offers as she'd had since her husband died, she'd never taken a single one. And now I wished I could have been more like that. Look where it got me with the one offer I took.

"You're always the officer to the rescue here, aren't you?" I asked when I could finally stand.

"Yes, ma'am, I guess I am."

"Melanie," I corrected him. Again. He smiled gently, his eyes kind, before glancing back at Claire to ask for her account of what happened. And probably for a date by the time he was through.

Corporal Matthews appeared before me, pad in hand, asking for my statement. "We have to stop meeting like this, Corporal. People are gonna talk," I commented dryly. Though I could care less what people would say now or ever. I was just glad I was alive for people to talk about.

Two EMTs worked on William, who was regaining consciousness.

Done with my part for now, I walked with purpose to where he was now on a stretcher. I bent over, leaning in close to his ear. "If you ever try to hurt my friends again, it'll be the last thing you ever do," I hissed.

"Officer," he attempted to call out, but his voice was weak and thready. "This woman is threatening me." He looked up at the medic. "You heard it."

"I didn't hear nothin'," the medic said and winked at me.

I looked at William, trying to suppress a small victory smile. Unsuccessfully, I had to admit.

"You can bet I'll be back," he whispered.

"I dare you," I challenged. "But if you do, next time you won't be so lucky."

34

I hitched a ride home with Claire—actually, she insisted on it—and left my car at the salon. She also insisted that I stay with her for the night or until they caught the second party who was involved, to be sure I was okay. Like she thought I was weak, or what? And since when had she become the strong one? Officer Mahoney said they believed there was another person involved besides Buford. Since the third BMW registered to Samuel Wilson, they were going to look into that.

"What are you thinking?" she asked.

I cast her a sideways glance. "What makes you think I'm thinking anything at all?"

"Because you're always thinking. Your mind never shuts down. Besides," she added with a smirk, "you're looking all perplexed."

I shook my head slightly, wincing as the movement caused pain to slice clean through my head. "Here I've always thought you couldn't hurt a fly."

"That man is below a fly. He's a snake."

"But you coldcocked him?"

"Self-defense classes. Black belt, to be exact."

I was baffled, and perhaps a little miffed, she'd never confided something so huge to me. "When? How?"

"I had a husband in the military, remember? He insisted I be fully capable of protecting myself and our little girl when he was away." I could feel her look at me briefly before focusing on the road before she continued, answering the question I hadn't asked but the one that was burning in me. "I didn't tell you because it was part of Tyler that I wanted to keep private. It was *us*, you know? I needed to keep something as just *us*. He taught me how to protect myself and our baby girl, and he wasn't able to protect himself." Her voice shook, and I saw a tear streak down her cheek.

I remembered the off-handed comment she made the other day about knowing taekwondo but I had assumed she was joking. We both fell into reflective silence, me wondering who this woman was that I was riding with, and I assumed Claire was thinking about what had transpired tonight. I looked at her staring straight ahead out the windshield, the lights from an oncoming car reflecting in her eyes that were far away from where she was at that moment.

"You okay?" I asked, my whispered words sounding loud in the car's silence.

"Yeah."

"A quarter for your thoughts."

She looked at me and then back at the road. For a moment I thought she wouldn't answer me. And then she spoke, her voice trembling, another oncoming car showing new tears glistening in her eyes. "I'm thinking how close I came to losing you tonight."

"Claire—"

"And for the record, my thoughts are worth more than a quarter."

I smiled and leaned my still-throbbing head back against the headrest. I reached over and placed a hand on her arm, feeling it shiver slightly. "I'm right here. And I'm fine."

"But what if—"

"Don't entertain the 'what ifs.' The reality is you saved my butt. My *scrawny* butt, as you so rudely said. Tyler would be so proud of you. I can just see him smiling down on you."

"Sometimes it feels like he's so close. And other times…" She trailed off.

"What else is bothering you?" I asked gently.

"You mean there has to be something else?" she asked to divert my focus.

"Don't make me offer you fifty cents this time." I saw her smile. "I know you. Or at least I thought I did until I found out things tonight I'd never have guessed in a million years."

"Officer Mahoney asked if he could call me."

"Well, I would certainly hope he would. Both of us, for that matter." I was confused why that would bother her. "You've been through a horrific event tonight. And I'm sure he will have follow-up questions. Not to mention a criminal case that's sure to develop from this—this nightmare."

"I mean he asked if he could *call* me. At home. As in a personal call."

"And, again, I don't know why that should surprise you. You get offers about every day of the week."

"I said yes," she blurted so quickly I was sure I must have misheard. "Did you hear me?"

I heard all right, but I needed a moment to recover.

"I said yes."

"I heard you."

"Then why didn't you—"

"Claire—wow! I—I got nothin'."

"You speechless? Now I got nothin'."

We rode the rest of the way in silence until we reached Claire's house. She haphazardly parked by the curb. I opened my door and looked down at the curb and then at her. "It looks like you've had a few too many drinks by the way you're parked."

"This is how I always park, and I've never gotten a ticket, so it can't be that bad."

I looked down again, at the front tire tight against the curb, the rear of her car sticking out. "Oh, yeah, it can. And it is."

Epilogue
Two Weeks Later

Jack, Claire, and I were chilling out on the deck overlooking the lake, each of us quietly drinking in the beauty of the brilliant ball of orange that was slowly, yet too quickly, sliding down below the line of trees across the lake. Claire and I were each sipping a glass of red wine, and Jack was nursing a Bud Lime longneck.

Officer Mahoney had called me two days after the incident to let me know William had confessed to everything, including giving the name of the person he was essentially working for—his brother-in-law, who had been married to his sister. His brother-in-law's name was Samuel Wilson, owner of the third BMW, and Maria and Buford's uncle. It sure was a small world. Because Samuel was the mastermind behind the entire scheme and paid all the parties involved, he was charged with contract killing.

And Tillie Tilbury? Well, turned out William was her son-in-law, so her instincts weren't far off. If anything, it was much worse than even she suspected. Velma found out the truth about William and was setting to tell Mrs. Tilbury. William wasn't going to allow that to happen.

"So I was thinking…"

Claire and Jack let out a groan in unison, and I smiled knowingly.

"Do you ever *not* think, Hogan?" Jack asked.

"Sometimes. As I was saying." I shot him a look, daring him to say something. "The next time something like this happens—"

"The *next* time?" They both chimed, looking at me as though I'd lost my mind. I laughed. Maybe I had lost it.

"I'm just sayin'—*if* there's a next time…" I paused and looked at each of them. "Is that better? *If?*" Claire smiled and leaned her head against the back of her chair, and Jack shook his head slowly. "*If* there's a next time, I can't think of two better friends to share the experience with."

"Seriously, Hogan?" Jack grumbled. "Sharing is way overrated if this is how you think of sharing. People share a good time. They share a drink or a meal. Heck, they even share a good cry. But only you would think of wanting to share something like what happened to you. Girlfriend…" His voice trailed off.

Claire and I busted out laughing at the look of disgust that contorted Jack's face. He looked at us cautiously until he, too, joined in. We raised our glasses, and Jack lifted his bottle as we toasted our friendship. We may have been an odd group, but we were a tight group. And we would always have each other's backs no matter what. I had never been so sure of anything in my life.

Nana's Wild Rice Hotdish

1 cup wild rice (Bring to boil 3-4 times, pouring off water and adding new each time.)

1 pound browned hamburger, drained

1/8–1/4 cup soy sauce

1/8 cup white rice

1/2–1 cup chopped celery

1 can cream of chicken soup

1 can water or milk

1/2 package onion soup mix

Combine all in a small roaster and bake at 325 degrees for about 1 hour and 30 minutes. Add water or milk if it's too dry when baking.

Nana's Gooey Double Chocolate Brownies

1 stick of margarine

1 cup sugar

4 eggs, beaten

1 can (16 oz.) Hershey's chocolate syrup

1 cup flour

1/2 cup chopped walnuts

Mix well and bake at 350 degrees for 30–35 minutes in a greased 9x13 pan. Remove and cover with miniature marshmallows. Return to the oven for 3 minutes or until marshmallows are soft. Let cool slightly and frost. (Recipe below.)

Frosting:

1 cup sugar

1/4 cup milk

1/4 cup butter

Bring to a boil and add 1/2 cup dark chocolate chips. Remove from heat and beat about 3 minutes. Spread on slightly warm brownies. Frosting will be thin but thickens as it's beaten.

Dear Reader,

Word of mouth is the best promotion for an author. Please consider leaving a review on Amazon and Goodreads. A sentence or two is all that is needed. By doing this, it helps me, as the author, as well as other readers.

I would love for you to connect with me at:

Website: www.rhondablackhurst.com
Email: rhondablackhurst@gmail.com
Facebook: www.facebook.com/rjblackhurst
Rhonda's Rockin' Readers Facebook Group
Instagram: rhonda.blackhurst
Newsletter Sign-Up

Best,
   Rhonda

Acknowledgments

Special thanks and blessings go to:

My husband, Clint, for your support, encouragement, and loving guidance. I'm so blessed to have you in my corner and to share my life with you. Thank you, also, for always being so willing to share your expertise regarding my questions on police procedure. In my eyes you are, and always will be, the world's top cop.

To my boys, Ben and Alex. During the busiest and best days of my life, those of raising you, my love of writing was kept alive by keeping journals for each of you. My heart and soul poured onto the pages of those journals that now await the perfect time to give them to you. And to Yvette, the perfect wife to my son and mama to five precious gifts from God. You are so loved.

Thank you to my granddaughters, Zoey, Olivia, Emilia, and Annabelle, and grandson Benny, for the unequaled gift of being your Grammy. Being a grandmother brings more joy than I ever could have expected.

Thank you to Jennifer for allowing me into the precious world that is your life.

Thank you to my dad, who taught me the art of storytelling by telling me endless stories of his own in a way that only he could do, and to my mom, who gives me ideas when she doesn't even realize it.

Thank you to my "Brighton Group" (you know who you are) for accepting me just as I am, broken and flawed. I truly am one lucky lady.

Thank you to Sarah and Jade. Your time, insight, and suggestions were priceless.

And most of all, thank you to my Heavenly Father, my Lord and Savior, who has blessed me more than this girl could ever deserve. Thank You for strategically placing every person in my life exactly when and where I needed them most. May I always strive to honor You in all things.

About the Author

Rhonda lives in Colorado but frequently escapes to her Arizona home. She is an avid reader, writer, lover of words, and coffee and dark chocolate connoisseur. Her writing career began at the tender age of four when she began writing with crayons on the knotty pine walls of the family home. She has 10 published novels: The Inheritance, a contemporary fiction novel; Shear Madness, Shear Deception, Shear Malice, Shear Murder, Shear Holiday Mayhem, Shear Fear, Shear Misfortune, and Shear Camping Caper--A Short Story, in the Melanie Hogan Mysteries; and Finding Abby and Abby's Redemption in the Whispering Pines Romantic Suspense duology. She has a non-fiction book, Finding Peace Through Gratitude, under the pen name Alexandra Benn. She is also an indie author consultant, certified life coach, and was awarded the 2022 Master of Literary Arts Award from the Brighton Chamber. She can be found at her online home at www.rhondablackhurst.com.